Destiny

By

Bud Fussell

Deep Indigo Books
Published by Indigo Sea Press
Winston-Salem

Deep Indigo Books
Indigo Sea Press
PO Box 26701
Winston-Salem, NC 27114
This book is a work of fiction. Names, characters,
locations and events are either a product of the author's
imagination, fictitious or used fictitiously. Any resemblance
to any event, locale or person, living or dead, is purely
coincidental.

For information regarding bulk purchases of this book,
digital purchase and special discounts, please contact the publisher
at indigoseapress@gmail.com

Cover Concept by Bud Fussell
Cover design by Pan Morelli
Manufactured in the United States of America
ISBN 978-1-63066-468-8

Chapter One

Tuesday was going to be a big day for Jerry and Martin Builders, and he was so keyed up he didn't sleep very well Monday night. He went to bed around eleven and woke up at one o'clock, then at two-thirty; he got up at three and went to the bathroom and then dozed back off and slept until around five at which time he got up and put on a pot of coffee. Tracy had left Sunday on a flight to London in her job as Flight Attendant and was scheduled to return to Atlanta late Tuesday afternoon, and Jerry thought, *I wish Tracy was here. I could sure use her calming presence right now.*

Normally, due to his *hands-on* way of working he wore jeans and golf shirts, but that day he put on a nice pair of khakis with a pretty blue polo, and instead of boots, he wore a nice pair of penny-loafers. He knew John, the fellow at the bank who he had been talking to, but John indicated that due to the size of the project he wanted to get financed, he would have to talk to someone with more authority, so Jerry thought it wouldn't hurt to try and make an impression on the fellow. John would go with him to see the guy and would put in a good word for him, but it was going to be up to him to get the approval.

His appointment was at eleven o'clock, and that gave him plenty of time to check on some of the jobs he had going. He arrived at the first one around seven o'clock and stayed for thirty to forty-five minutes and then went to the second one. He had named that job *the Jewel* because of its location on a beautiful ten-acre lake and the very tasteful appointments that made it look to him like a piece of fine jewelry.

As he was getting out of his pickup a car drove up and let Reed Thomas and Stony Gray out. In a minute another car drove up and Tammy Mills got out. As Tammy opened the door, he could hear her and her mother arguing about something, but it was none of his business, so he didn't say anything.

Those were the three kids who had seriously damaged one of the houses earlier and who he was able to convince the judge to let work out their sentences by working for him. He was impressed

1

with the large Mercedes that delivered the two boys. It belonged to Reed's dad who obviously wasn't doing too badly.

He went over to where they were and spoke. "Hi Guys. How're you doing?"

Reed, as their leader, answered, "Fine, Mr. Martin. How are you?"

"I'm doing well. Stony, how are you doing?"

"Fine."

"Tammy, how about you. Are you okay?"

"Yes sir, I'm good."

"How are you liking this kind of work? It's not too bad, is it?"

"It's better than we thought it would be," Reed answered.

"What do you think, Tammy? Would you like to do this all the time?"

"No sir, but it's not too bad."

"How's your mother?"

"She's okay."

"Good; tell her I said hello."

Tammy mumbled something and Jerry took that to mean "Okay."

"Okay, I'll see you guys later. Have a great day."

He walked around the nearly completed house while Bobby Kunkle, his foreman, got the three teenagers started with their respective jobs. Soon, Bobby joined him and they finished up their morning meeting.

As he was getting ready to get into his truck, Stony saw him and ran over to him. He shouted, "Mr. Martin, can I see you for a minute, please."

Jerry stopped where he was and waited on Stony to get to him and then asked, "What do you need, Padna?"

"Mr. Martin, when we're through working off the debt to you, do you think there's a chance that you would hire me? I think I would like to do this kind of work after I get out of school."

"Wow! That's great that you would want to get into this. Where do you plan to go to college after graduation?"

"I probably won't go to college. I don't think my folks can afford it, so I'll more than likely just go to work. I thought if you would hire me while I'm still in school, then maybe I'd have a head start on a job when I get out."

"Tell you what, Stony. I can probably find something for you, but I'll have to talk to you more about it a little later. I have a very important meeting this morning, and I've got to go. Maybe we can talk again sometime later this week, okay?"

"Yes sir. Thank you, sir."

Jerry made a quick stop at one more job and then drove to his office where he gathered what seemed like a mountain of maps, plats, blueprints, ledger sheets and other things he thought he might need for his meeting at the bank. He told Beverly, his Secretary, to wish him luck as he walked out the door.

The drive from his office to the bank was only ten minutes, and when he pulled into the bank's parking lot, he sat in the pickup and said a prayer before getting out and going inside. He prayed, *"Father, thank you for allowing me to be in a position to possibly work out a project like this. I realize, Lord, that I can't do it without your help, so I'm asking, in Jesus' name, that You stand beside me as I present my plans to these bankers, and I thank you in advance for your help. Amen."*

He gathered everything from the back seat and headed toward the front door of the bank. Before he opened the door he paused and took a deep breath and then went in. He told the receptionist that he wanted to see John Smitherman and she sent him right on back to John's office. John invited him to have a seat and it seemed to Jerry that John was more interested in making small-talk than getting to the heart of why he had come to the bank. Finally, Jerry turned the subject to the project he was wanting financing for, and John said, "Jerry, remember me telling you that this is larger than I have the authority to handle, and it will be necessary for us to talk to someone *up-the-ladder* from me? Come on and I'll introduce you to the gentleman."

John led him past all the offices where Jerry was sure one of them held the person he was to talk to, but instead, they stopped at the elevator and he was taken up to the second floor. On the second floor, John led him down a long hall, past several offices, and finally, they came to a lady seated in front of an office on which the name, *R. Frank Thomas, Chairman,* was printed on the door.

As soon as John told the receptionist that they wanted to see Mr. Thomas, Jerry said, in a very low voice, "Man, John, I didn't know we were coming all the way to the top."

3

John replied, "Mr. Thomas wants to see you."

"Does he know me?"

Before John could answer, the receptionist told them to go on into Mr. Thomas's office.

As soon as Jerry saw him, he was speechless at first, and then he said, "Wow, I'm not believing this. Hello, Sir."

"Hi Jerry. Surprised?"

"You two already know each other?" John asked.

"Yeah, Jerry and I worked on something else a while back," Frank said. "How are you, Jerry?"

"I'm fine," Jerry said. "And I'll be on top of the world if you accept and finance the program I want to show you."

"Well, let's see what you're so excited about. It looks as if you've got some sizeable papers there. Why don't you lay them out on the conference table?"

Jerry moved a couple of chairs out of the way and began laying out his materials, talking as he went. When he had finished, and they met his approval, he looked at Mr. Thomas and said, "Mr. Thomas, I want to preface my presentation by saying that if you agree to finance this program, you will be a part of creating one of the top residential sections in all of greater Atlanta that will be known as White Rock Estates. "Now this is the plat of the land where I hope to build the homes. It consists of one hundred and seventy-five acres, including a nine-acre lake, and this map is an enlargement of the plat showing the proposed locations of the streets. The dotted lines are home sites with each lot being a minimum of three acres. Based on current material costs, each home will run between seven-hundred and fifty thousand to a million dollars, depending of course on the home, and there will be forty-five homes. And oh yeah, I want to put a three-rail vinyl fence along both sides of the road for the complete length of the streets."

Frank said, "This is very impressive. Do you already have the land?"

"No sir, but I have a signed agreement with the owner committing the land to my company."

"Well, what are you wanting us to do, Jerry?"

"I'm hoping you'll finance the whole program."

"Have you come up with any figures as to how much you're looking at?"

"Yes sir, I have." Dreading to mention the amount he said, "Counting everything, as near as I can tell, it will cost between twenty-two and thirty million dollars."

Frank whistled and asked, "Do you really think it will cost that much?"

"Yes sir, I do, and with the type houses I plan to build we can conservatively plan on recouping between six and three quarter and nine million dollars net profit."

Whistling again, he said, "I just don't see nine million profit on a thirty million dollar investment. How are you figuring that?"

"I'm figuring it based on one-hundred-fifty to two-hundred thousand profit per house. There should be no problem making two-hundred thousand on a three quarter million dollar home, and as the price goes up, the profit increases without much substantial cost increase. Most of the homes will cost in the neighborhood of five-hundred and fifty thousand to build; some more and some less."

Jerry then showed Frank some photographs of some of the homes he had built and told him what they cost and what he sold them for; all in line with what he was presenting to him. When he finished his presentation he said, "I'm sure you can see the possibilities here and since I know how to build a quality home that is cost-effective, I really think you would be wise to consider this project."

When their meeting was over, Frank said, "John, thank you for bringing this guy to see me. You can go on back to your office if you want to. I want to talk to Jerry about something else if he has time."

After John had left, Frank told Jerry, "Jerry, I'm impressed with your project, and I think we'll be able to work out something with you, but we'll have to follow the red tape trail as with everything. Don't worry; I'll push it."

"Thank you, Mr. Thomas. You've made my day."

"Now here's what I really wanted to talk to you about; have you ever built an apartment complex?"

"Yes sir, I built one nice sized one down in the Cowart Lake area. Do you know where that is?"

"I certainly do."

"Well, it's on County Line Road on the Douglas side."

"I know exactly where that is. Those are nice apartments. I

5

didn't know you built them. Would you be interested in building an eight building, sixty-four-unit complex for me and some friends of mine?"

"I sure would."

"If we approve the financing for your neighborhood project, do you think you will be able to take on another large project like the one I'm talking about?"

"Oh yes sir. That shouldn't be a problem."

"Great. It looks as if you and I are going to become business partners, and I think that's wonderful. Why don't we meet again on Thursday, and I'll have some plans and other things to show you."

"Thursday will be fine. Thank you very much, Mr. Thomas."

"Since we're going to be business partners, do you think you can call me Frank?"

"I sure can—Frank."

"Oh, one final thing; how is Reed working out for you?"

"Fine. He's a good worker, and he's doing a good job."

"Well, I just want you to know how much I appreciate what you're doing for him and what you're doing for his mother and me."

"You're quite welcome. I'm glad to have him; he's a good boy."

"How is Stony working out? He's kinda like another son; he spends so much time at our house."

"Stony's doing good, too. He told me he wants to come work for me when he gets out of school. He said he didn't think he would be able to go to college. I told him we'd talk about it later this week."

"How's that little girl doing? What's her name, Tammy?"

"Yeah, Tammy; she's doing okay, but she doesn't have as much on the ball as the boys do. I just hope she hangs in there until she finishes her sentence. How did she get hooked up with Reed and Stony, anyway?"

"I'm not really sure. They know her from school. Reed said she just showed up where they were one day and started hanging around with them. He said she didn't do anything to cause any problem and seemed to be comfortable with them, so they just let her hang with them. On the other hand, they're the ones who caused her a problem, weren't they?"

"Yeah, I guess so. Well Frank, I need to go and thank you very, very much. What time do you want me to be here Thursday?"

"How does ten o'clock sound?"

"Sounds good. I'll see you then."

They shook hands and Jerry left. He was so excited he wanted to tell somebody what just happened at the bank, and since Tracy wasn't back from London yet, he thought he would go out to Richards Building Supply and talk to Jack. After all, Jack was his father-in-law, and he would be buying all his materials from him, so that seemed like the appropriate place to go. On the way, he thought he would take Jack out to lunch, but when he arrived at the store Jack had already eaten, so he just went in and spent some time with him and Charley.

He told Jack about his visit at the bank that morning, and when he came to the part about building the apartments for Frank and what that might lead to, he jokingly said, "Jack, I may give you so much business that you'll have to expand," not thinking Jack would take him seriously.

Charley was really the one to take him seriously because he said, "We will probably have to buy another truck. We need one anyway, and if we have to start delivering that much stuff, we'll definitely have to have another one."

After about thirty minutes Jack and Charley were almost as excited as he was.

He was about to starve, so on the way to the first job he was going to visit, he stopped at a fast food restaurant and got a spicy chicken sandwich with fries and a chocolate milkshake.

There wasn't much that he had to do at any of the three jobs he had going except to check and make sure everything was running okay, so he didn't spend much time at any of them. Tracy was supposed to come home that afternoon, and he wanted to get home before she did in order to make sure the house was clean and *standing tall*.

Tracy's flight landed on-time and after her post-flight duties and the drive home, she arrived home a little before five o'clock. They were so glad to see each other that they embraced for a really long time. She was tired and certainly didn't feel like cooking, and Jerry was still excited over the events of the day, so they decided to go up to the 129 Café and grab a bite. They called to see if Jack would like to go with them, but he had stopped on the way home and picked up some barbeque.

Having eaten at the 129 so many times, they knew pretty much what they wanted before they got there, so reading the menu was an unnecessary formality, but they read it anyway. While waiting for their food Tracy shared some of the highlights of her London trip, and before she could finish, their food came. Both of them were really hungry, so they began eating immediately, and Jerry waited on a better time to tell her about his good news.

In a little bit Tracy asked, "Have you had a good three days since I left?"

"Yeah, I have. In fact; I think I might have hit the jackpot today."

"How did you do that?"

And then he told her about the financing for his White Rock project, and then he asked, "Do you remember the three kids that I got the judge to let work for me to work out their sentences for damaging one of my jobs?"

"Yeah, I remember; why?"

"Well, Frank Thomas, the head man at the bank, is the father of Reed, one of the kids."

"Really? You've got to be kidding."

"Really, and guess what else?"

"What?"

"Frank might want me to build a large apartment complex for him, and you know what, honey? If he likes our work and we make money, there's no telling where this might lead. This guy is a sure-enough heavy-hitter. Of course we don't have it yet. It still has to go before the Board for approval, and sometimes those people are real tough customers, but we have Frank on our side, and he packs a lot of weight, so I think we'll get it."

"That's wonderful, Darling. I'm so happy for you."

"Not me; us. We're partners in this aren't we?"

"Yeah, I guess we are. Let me re-phrase what I said. I'm so happy for us."

"That's better. Are you ready to go?"

"Yeah. I'm ready to get out of this uniform and these shoes."

"When do you have to leave again?"

"I don't know. I have to call Barbara Lawrence tomorrow. She didn't have the schedule set before I left."

On the way home Jerry said, "Do you know which house I call the *Jewel*?"

"No, I'm not sure. Why?"

"It's the one on that pretty little lake out in Green Hills. Anyway, it's almost finished, and I'm about ready to list it. I thought you might like to come see it tomorrow. I'm going to be there in the morning doing some final *tweaking* on it, and I'll probably be there most of the morning. It's truly a jewel."

"I may just take you up on that."

"Good."

When they got to their house, they went in and crashed in the den for a few minutes before they got ready for bed. It was still fairly early and a little too early to go to bed, but Tracy had had a long day, and she was tired. After all; she had traveled over four thousand miles since breakfast.

In a few minutes Jerry asked, "How about a glass of wine?"

"I think that would be good. Let's have one."

They both got up and went into the kitchen where Jerry gave her a couple of choices, and then after she selected one he poured each of them a glass, and they went back into the den and sat close on the loveseat. Neither of them wanted a second glass, and the one that they had apparently did the trick, so when they finished, they locked lips and in just a very few minutes they were lying on the bed in a passionate embrace where they remained until finally going to the bathroom before getting under the covers and going to sleep.

Chapter Two

The next morning Jerry got up, had a couple of cups of coffee, then dressed and left for work, leaving Tracy in bed. On the way to the first job he stopped and picked up a couple of steak biscuits and was full by the time he got to work.

He went to two jobs and then left for the job that he called the *jewel*. When he got there he saw that Bobby had had all three of the teenagers come there to put the final touches on the beautiful place. Reed and Stony were outside; each with a leaf-rake and a trash bag. Tammy was inside with a bottle of glass cleaner and a roll of paper towels.

Jerry walked through and caught up with Bobby Kunkle, and in a few minutes they went back to where Tammy was, and before Jerry could say anything, Bobby said in a loud voice, "Tammy! Hang up that phone."

When she saw them she immediately hung up, even as Bobby was telling her to. Bobby told Jerry, "Excuse me a minute, Jerry," and then walked over to her.

Jerry could hear him say to her, "Tammy, this is about the third time I've told you about talking on the phone, and you need to make yourself a mental note; this is the last time. If I see you talking again on work-time, I'm going to tell Mr. Martin that I had to let you go. Is that clear?"

"That's clear." The whole time Bobby was talking to her, she was looking at Jerry. She knew she couldn't afford to get fired. If she did, the judge would make her finish her sentence in jail, and she sure didn't want that.

When Bobby returned to Jerry, Jerry asked, "Has she been giving you trouble?"

"She didn't until just a few days ago, and then, one morning, she showed up with that cell phone, and I'm afraid it's going to become a problem if we don't nip it in the bud."

Jerry said, "I'll talk to her. Maybe she'll listen to what I tell her."

"Well, good luck. It wouldn't be so bad if she didn't have such an attitude."

"Yeah, I've experienced that before."

He excused himself from Bobby and walked over to Tammy. "Are you having a problem, Tammy?"

"No, why?"

"Well, I thought something might be wrong since you were talking on the phone instead of working. Are you sure everything is all right?"

"Yeah; nothing's wrong. I won't do it again."

"Good. I sure would hate for your sentence to be changed just because you couldn't stay off the phone."

While he was still with Tammy, Tracy walked up and said, "Good morning."

"Good morning, Sweetheart."

"Tammy, this is my wife, Tracy. Tracy, this is Tammy."

"Hi Tammy, how are you?"

"I'm okay."

Tracy could tell she didn't want to talk, so she didn't say anything else to her and devoted her attention to Jerry and Bobby.

"Come on; let me show you around. When they had finished touring the house Jerry asked, "Now, can you see why I call this place the jewel?"

"I certainly can. It's beautiful. I'll bet you won't have any trouble selling it,"

"I hope not. I've got a lot of money tied up in it."

Smiling, Tracy said, "Well, speaking as an expert I can assure you it will sell fast."

"That makes me feel much better, Ms. Expert."

"I thought it would. Listen, I talked to Wendy, and we're going to go shopping. Is there anything that you need?"

"Can't think of anything. Why don't you see if she and Tommy would like to eat out tonight?"

"Okay; I'll ask. I'll call you this afternoon."

She told Bobby goodbye and gave Jerry a light kiss. As she was leaving she passed Tammy and told her that it was nice to have met her. Tammy just grunted and mumbled something inaudible without ever looking in her direction.

Pretty soon after she left, Jerry checked out with Bobby, and he left. He went straight to his Realtor's office and told them the *jewel* would be ready to show the following week. There were still a few things that had to be done by the landscaper, and that shouldn't take more than a couple more days.

Shortly after lunch Reed and Stony finished their projects and went into the house to see what Bobby wanted them to do for the rest of the day. Tammy still had some things to do before she finished and was upset when Bobby let the two boys take off the rest of the afternoon and made her stay and work. Before he let them leave he gathered all three around him and told them to go to the job over on Peakland Drive the next morning. Reed called someone to come get him and Stony, and they went outside to wait for their ride.

Tammy had a big frown on her face as she went back to work, and Bobby started to say something, but decided not to. To make matters worse, he had her cleaning windows, and when he checked on what she had already done, he found several panes that were only half-way done, and he told her she would have to go back over them. With what she still had to clean plus the ones she had to redo, it looked as if she would be there most of the afternoon, and she was fit to be tied.

At one point, a sales representative went by and Bobby had to spend some time with him, and that meant to Tammy that she could use her cell phone. She called somebody and while she talked she kept a watchful eye on Bobby. She hung up a couple of minutes before the salesman left, and when Bobby checked on her she was busy at work.

In about a half-hour a cruddy-looking character showed up on a Kawasaki crotch-rocket, and he looked like something a dog wouldn't even drag in. Apparently, that was who Tammy called. He looked to be around five seven and he had long, dirty, disheveled hair. Earrings were hanging on places that didn't even have names. There were multiple rings in both ears; one in his nose like a bull and one in each side of his lower lip. Each eyebrow had one also, and a Swastika was tattooed on his left shoulder.

He was wearing a pair of jeans with holes in both legs, a tee shirt with a vulgar word printed on it and the only thing he had on that was presentable was a pair of Nike shoes that must have cost at least a hundred and fifty dollars. His name was Randy Price.

He got off his bike and walked slowly around the house, and in a few minutes he spotted Tammy through the window and walked inside to where she was.

"Hi Tam; 'sup?"

"Whatta ya say, Randy? I'm surprised you came. What are you up to?"

"After you called, I decided to come pick you up. A bunch of us are meetin' at the Papermoon later this afternoon, and I didn't think you would have a ride."

"You're right; I don't, but I can't leave 'til five o'clock."

"Sure you can. Tell somebody else to clean the damn windows. We're goin' up to Rome to meet some people and do some serious partying tonight."

"I can't Randy. You just don't understand."

In about two minutes, Bobby walked by and spotted the two. He called for Tammy, and while she was walking to him he moved out into the hall. When she reached him he asked, "Who and what is that you're talking to?"

When he asked what she was talking to, anger showed up in her face, and she answered, "He is not a what. He's my friend. He came by to give me a ride."

"Does he not know that you have to work?"

"I don't know what he knows."

"Well tell him you're working, and he'll have to leave."

"Can't he just stay for a little while and talk to me while I work?"

"No ma'am. Now go get rid of him or I will."

"Okay. But I think you're mean."

She walked back into the room where Randy was and told him what Bobby said, and he acted as if he wanted to challenge Bobby until Bobby stepped into the room. He was well over six feet tall with a great build. His arms looked like the Arm and Hammer baking soda box, and Randy decided he didn't want any part of that.

He mumbled something to Tammy and walked out, being sure not to touch Bobby as he passed by.

Everyone finished their respective jobs at the *jewel* around four o'clock and Bobby let them all go. He offered Tammy a ride, but she said she would just call her mother to come get her. It was beginning to rain, and Bobby didn't want to leave her outside to get wet, so he told her he would give her a ride to Speedy's, a convenience store about a mile away, and her mother could pick her up there, and she agreed. On their way to the convenience store

13

Bobby reminded her where she should report for work the next morning, and when they reached Speedy's, she got out. Immediately, she tried to dial Randy's number, but she had forgotten to charge her phone, and the battery was dead. Then, she went to a pay phone and tried to call him, but got his voice mail. She thought, *I guess he's on his way to Rome and can't hear the phone on his bike. Darn it; I guess I'll have to call Mom to come get me.*

She dialed her mother's number, but got her voice mail, also. A nice looking young fellow, who looked to be in his mid to late thirties had come into the store while she was trying to reach her mother and stood behind her as if he were waiting to use the phone when she finished. When she got her mother's voice mail, she said, "Darn it" and mumbled something else that was inaudible.

The young man asked, "Are they not there?"

She answered, "No, and now I've got to wait here until my Mom gets off to come get me."

He said, "I'll give you a ride if you want me to. Where are you going?"

"I guess I'll go home. There's no place else to go."

"Come on. I'll take you home. Let me make a quick phone call first, and then we'll take off." He looked clean-cut enough and had a good personality, so she agreed to go with him.

She watched him carefully while he was on the phone and decided he might be fun to be with. In a minute he got through with his call and asked, "Are you ready?"

"Yeah."

"By the way, what's your name?"

"Tammy."

"Tammy what?"

"Tammy Mills. What's yours?"

"They call me Tink."

"Tink what?"

"Just Tink."

"You've got to have a last name. What is it"

"It's not important." As soon as he said that, they came to his van; a brownish color Ford with no windows except for the ones next to the driver's and passenger seats, two little *teardrop* windows; one on each side in the back, and the ones in the two rear doors. He said, "Here are our wheels," and he opened the passenger side door for her, and she got in.

She looked around the van after she got in and noticed that the floor behind the seat was partially covered with what she considered to be an ugly, orange carpet. There was a large box about six feet long and maybe two feet wide that reminded her of a casket, and it was covered with the same ugly orange carpet and held a variety of strange-looking tools. Some small rugs were rolled up and laid crossways behind the seats. She also saw some boxes of what looked like tile lying on the other side toward the back.

When he had walked around the front of the van and got in the driver's seat, he asked, "Where do you live, Tammy?"

"Do you know where Lovell Street is?"

"No, I don't believe I do. Can you show me?"

"Yeah, I can show you. Do you know where Lebanon Street is"

"Yeah, I know where Lebanon is."

"Well, Lovell turns off of Lebanon."

"Okay. I got you."

He put the van in gear and started out in the opposite direction to Lovell Street.

Tammy looked at him and said, "I thought you said you knew where Lovell Street was. You're going the wrong way."

"I know, but you don't mind taking a little ride with me, do you?"

"Yeah I do. Now if you are not going to take me home, take me back to the store." Her heart was starting to beat faster, and fear was creeping in.

"Relax. You'll like where we're going."

Tammy continued to protest, but Tink kept driving until they were out in the country; in the middle of nowhere.

"Where are we? I want to go back to the store," she told him.

"We'll go back when we get through," he said.

"Through with what? I want to go back now." She tried to open the door to get out, but he stopped her.

After he stopped the van, Tink moved to the back and unrolled a rug that he had back there and laid it out on the floor. Then he reached up front and grabbed Tammy and pulled her back to where he was. She resisted, but he was much stronger and as soon as he had her subdued, he started kissing her and began taking her clothes

15

off. She fought him as best as she could, but she was not nearly as strong as he was, and he overpowered her. She soon realized that she was no match for him, physically, so she just relaxed as much as she could while he raped her. She tried to be strong, but couldn't stop the tears.

When he was through, he tried to talk to her and convince her that she enjoyed the whole thing, but the more he talked the more she cried. After about an hour, he got her down again and raped her for the second time.

After he finished, he opened the lid on the large box. It was completely upholstered on the inside with carpet that cushioned the strange looking tools that it held. He removed everything inside the box and picked Tammy up to put her inside. She fought and screamed to no avail, and while she was fighting with him she said she had to use the bathroom. He didn't want her to use the bathroom in his nice, upholstered box, so he let her put her clothes on and the two of them got out of the van. He tied a rope around her neck and held on to the end of it. She used the bathroom, and as soon as she was through he untied the rope and grabbed her and forced her back into the van. He was determined to keep her in the box, and no matter how hard she fought, she couldn't do anything. When he finally got her inside the box he closed the lid and put a lock on the hasp outside and dummy locked it. She continued to scream, but the box was so well insulated with the carpet she could hardly be heard. It would be impossible to be heard outside the van.

Tink had partially dressed when he got out with Tammy when she used the bathroom, and after she was securely in the box he got out of the van again, used the bathroom himself, and finished putting his clothes on. There was no one around, so he didn't have to worry about anyone seeing him. When he had made himself presentable, he got into the van and started driving. Tammy could feel the movement of the van, but of course had no way of knowing where they were going. He drove for what seemed like forever to Tammy, but in reality it was only about forty-five minutes.

When they stopped, Tammy could hear and sort of feel the slamming of the door as he got out. She was panicking because she felt that she might be left in the box to die. She tried screaming, but it was useless. She finally cried herself to sleep.

Surprisingly, Tink had driven home and parked in his own

16

driveway. He went into the house and kissed his wife and two children.

He said, "I want to take a shower before we go eat."

His wife said, "That's fine; we don't have to be in any hurry." She could hear him whistling in the shower and thought to herself, *it sounds like he's in a good mood. He must have had a good day.* He finished showering and got dressed in some clean clothes and in a few minutes, he and his family went out to a restaurant and after a nice meal, they returned home and spent the rest of the evening the way they always did, and in the meantime, Tammy was still locked inside the box in the van.

Chapter Three

Barbara was frantically trying to think where her daughter could be. That afternoon, she had gone to the job-site the way she always did, and of course Tammy wasn't there. She tried to call her cell phone, but it wouldn't ring on Tammy's end because of the battery being down.

She had had problems with her before; going places without telling her, and she just thought that was one of those times, but at the same time, she had an uneasy feeling. She had heard Tammy mention the name of Bobby Kunkle, but she didn't have his number. She did have Jerry Martin's number, so she called him. "Hello."

"Hello Mr. Martin, this is Barbara Mills. How are you?"

"Hi Barbara. I'm fine. How're you doing?"

"Mr. Martin, I'm fine, but I'm a little worried about Tammy. I'm at the house where she's been working, and there's nobody here. I tried her cell phone, but there's no answer. Do you have any idea where she is?"

"Barbara, I don't know where she could be. Is Bobby Kunkle not there?"

"No sir; there's nobody here."

"Just stay there, and I'll try to get in touch Bobby, okay? He'll probably know where she is."

"Okay, thank you."

Jerry called Bobby and Bobby told him about them finishing up early, and how he took her up to Speedy's where she said she was going to call her mother."

"Okay; thanks Bobby. I'll call her and tell her. She's getting worried. It's been so long now; she must have called one of her friends to get her. Maybe they'll know at the store. Talk to you later. Bye."

As soon as he hung up from talking to Bobby, he called Barbara and told her what Bobby said. "Okay, thank you, Mr. Martin. I'll go to Speedy's right now. I hope she's there."

"I do too. Let me know when you find her, will you?"

"I will; thanks."

She knew where Speedy's was, and she went straight there when she hung up from Jerry. She went inside and looked around, but there was no Tammy. She went up to the counter and asked the man who worked there if he had seen her, and he said he had seen her earlier that afternoon. He told Barbara that she left with some guy, but he didn't know who he was. He said they left in a Brown van. As soon as he told her that she called Jerry. "Hello."

"Mr. Martin, this is Barbara. I'm at Speedy's and the man here said he saw who he thought was Tammy, and that she left with a man in a van. What should I do now?"

"I'm not sure, Barbara. Do you know any of her friends that she might have called? If you do, I would suggest you call them."

"Do you think I should call the police?"

"I don't think they would act on this since it hasn't been but a couple of hours. They'll probably tell you what I just told you; to call her friends."

"Okay, but I'll have to go home and try to find their numbers. I don't know any of them, but maybe Tammy has some of them written down in her room. Thank you, Mr. Martin. I'll talk to you later."

"Barbara, if there is anything that I can do, let me know, okay? And Barbara, I'm sure she'll show up. You know, these young folks don't think about how we old-timers worry."

"I know. I'll call you when she gets home. Bye."

"Bye Barbara."

Barbara went home and scoured Tammy's room trying to find the names and numbers of any of her friends, but only came up with two. She called them and neither one had seen or heard from Tammy in several days. Then, she remembered the boys she had gotten into trouble with and knew their names, so she called them. They hadn't seen her since earlier that afternoon when they finished work and were let off early. Reed gave her the name of a boy who he knew had been talking to her, and she called him, but no luck; he hadn't seen her in about a week.

She was beside herself with worry. Her ex-husband had moved to Savannah, and she didn't think Tammy would have gone down there, but she called anyway, and just as she figured, she wasn't there. By then it was almost nine o'clock, and all she knew to do was to sit and wait. It got later and later, and she wasn't about to go to bed, so she sat in her living room all night, worrying.

Tammy didn't come home at all that night, and when it got to six-thirty the next morning, she called Jerry.

When he answered, she said, Mr. Martin, I hate to call you this early, but Tammy didn't come home last night. What should I do?"

"Barbara, I think maybe it's time to get the police involved. Do you know where the Douglasville Police station is?"

"Yes sir; I know where it is."

"When could you meet me down there?"

"All I have to do is change clothes and freshen up a little. I didn't go to bed last night. I think I can be ready in about fifteen minutes. How about we meet at seven fifteen? Is that alright?"

"Let's make it seven-thirty. I live farther away than you do."

"Okay, I'll see you at seven-thirty."

"Oh Barbara, if you have any recent pictures of Tammy, bring one with you. In case they want to make a poster, a picture will help."

"I'll bring her latest school picture. It's a real good one, and believe it or not, she's smiling in it."

"Sounds good. I'll see you in a little bit."

The phone and Jerry's talking woke Tracy up, and she wanted to know what was going on. Jerry explained the situation as he shaved and got dressed. He kissed her goodbye and rushed out the door to go meet Barbara.

When they arrived at the police station, Barbara asked Jerry if he would do most of the talking, which he did. Of course, there was much that he couldn't tell them, so Barbara had to furnish most of the information. In a little while, Grey Yokley, the Detective that seemed to be in charge asked Jerry what his connection was to Tammy, and he explained about the trouble she and Reed, and Stony got into, and how he was trying to help them out.

Due to Tammy's young age, the Detective explained that they would put out an Amber Alert for her, and he very much appreciated Barbara bringing her picture to use. He said he wished there was something he could tell her to do, but actually, the best thing she could do would be to go home and wait on Tammy to either call or come home. In the meantime, if they got any leads they would keep her informed. He tried to reassure her as he walked them to the door, and they left.

Jerry asked, "How about some breakfast?"

She replied, "I'm really not hungry, but I sure could use some coffee."

"Great! There's a Waffle House not too far. Do you know where it is?"

"Yeah, I know where it is."

"Is that alright with you?"

"That's fine."

"Come on. You can ride with me and I'll bring you back."

They got into his pickup and headed to the Waffle House. When they got inside and smelled the coffee and other good things, Barbara decided she was hungry after all, so they both ate a hearty breakfast before he took her back to her car.

As she was getting out of the pickup Jerry told her, "Barbara, I'm interested in you and Tammy and in your welfare, so I hope you'll keep me informed on what's going on. Will you do that?"

"I certainly will, and thank you for your concern."

"I'll have my cell with me all day, so if you need me for anything, just give me a call, okay?"

"Okay, and thanks for the breakfast. I guess I was hungrier than I thought."

They parted ways, and Barbara went home to wait on Tammy or at least a call saying where she was. Jerry had a meeting with Frank Thomas at ten o'clock, so he went to his office to pick up some papers and to wait until time to go.

****

Tink got up around six and as usual, had coffee and a bagel with his wife. He told her he had a busy day; that he had two jobs to do, and he was going to have to leave a little early. He finished his bagel and got ready to leave, and before he left, he kissed his wife goodbye. The kids weren't up yet, so he told his wife to kiss them goodbye for him, and she assured him that she would.

He went to the van and started it up and sat there as if trying to decide what to do. In a minute he pulled out of the driveway and then went through the drive through at McDonalds where he ordered two egg McMuffins and two small coffees.

After he got the food, he put the sack in the passenger seat and began another ride to the out-of-the-way place where he took Tammy the afternoon before. When he got there, he took the lock out of the hasp that was keeping her in the box and opened the lid. The sudden shock of the light hitting her eyes, after she had been in total darkness for so long, made her squint until she became used to the light.

Tink said, "Good morning. I brought you something." He then opened the McDonalds bag and handed her one of the egg McMuffins and one of the cups of coffee. She said, "I have to go to the bathroom," so the two of them got out of the van, and like the day before, he tied a rope around her, and she used the bathroom. When she finished they got back into the van and sat down. He figured she would still be so upset that she wouldn't want anything to eat, but to his surprise, she took the muffin and just gobbled it down. Normally, she didn't like coffee, but she drank that, too.

While they ate and drank their coffee, Tink tried to be nice to her by the way he talked to her, but it didn't seem to work very well. When they finished their coffee, he put his arms around her and tried to give her a hug and kiss, but she pushed him away. She said, "Take me home. My Mama's probably worried sick about me. Will you please take me home?"

"I can't do that just yet, Sweet Thing. We're not through with what we came out here for."

Naively she asked, "What did we come out here for?"

"You know the answer to that. Come here," and with that, he grabbed her. She was already naked except for her bra and panties, and she learned the day before that she couldn't win in a scuffle with him, so she just let him do what he was going to do. When he had her completely naked he raped her again, and that time she didn't cry.

They stayed where they were for about another hour, and he raped her one more time.

When they left, they left in kind of a hurry. Tink probably would have stayed longer, but a truck came out there with some men, that according to the sign on their truck were surveyors, and they stopped just a few yards from them. Tink picked up a huge pair of scissors and told Tammy not to make a sound. He threatened to do something bad to her if she did.

While they were riding, Tink gave her permission to get

22

dressed, and he didn't make her get back into the box. Instead, he drove to an area of town where there were dozens of railroads track and not very many buildings. All at once he stopped and told her to get out. He said, "I hope you enjoyed our time together as much as I did," and then he stomped the gas and sped away.

She didn't know which way to turn; there was nothing but railroad tracks for about as far as she could see, so she just started walking. In a few minutes she came to a section where there was what looked like apartment buildings, and when she passed three or four buildings, she saw a group of boys playing basketball. She walked over to where they were and said to no one in particular, "I've been raped."

They stopped playing when she said that and stared at her, but said nothing. In a minute, they began to play again, but one boy, a white boy, left the group and came over to her and said, "What did you say?"

She said, "I've been raped."

"Come with me. I'll get you some help," and he led her to a small store just around the corner from where they were. When they went into the store, the boy told the lady in the store what Tammy had said, and after the lady talked to Tammy for a minute, she called the police and said, "Hello Police Department. This is Sonalben Patel at West End Grocery. I have a girl here who says she was kidnapped and raped. Can you send someone over here to talk to her? That's right; West End Grocery and my name is Sonalben Patel. Alright, I'll look for you."

She looked at Tammy and asked, "What is your name?"

"Tammy Mills."

"Okay Tammy Mills, the police said they would be right over. They will help you.

The boy who took her to the store started to leave, and Tammy asked him his name. "I'm Bobby Huffman."

"Thank you, Bobby."

"No problem; did you say your name is Tammy?"

"Yeah, Tammy; Tammy Mills."

"Cool; see ya Tammy. I'm glad you're alright."

It wasn't but a few minutes until a police car drove up, and an officer got out and came into the store. He had a piece of paper in his hand which was a picture of Tammy, and when he looked at her

23

he said, "Young lady, I sure am glad to see you. We've been looking for you, and I'm sure Sergeant Yokley will be happy to see you, too."

Who is Sergeant Yokley?"

"He's the officer that listed you as missing after he talked with your Mother. Why don't we call your Mother right now?"

"That would be super."

"Ms. Patel, would it be alright if we used your phone?"

"Of course. Go ahead."

"What is your Mother's number, Tammy?"

He dialed as Tammy gave him the number, and Barbara answered on the second ring. "Hello."

"Hello Mrs. Mills. This is Officer Dan Hartman with the Douglasville Police Department. I have someone here who wants to talk to you," and he gave Tammy the phone.

"Hey Mama."

Tammy!! It's really you. Where have you been, Darling?"

"I don't know, Mama, but I want to come home."

"Is the officer going to bring you?"

"I don't know." She held the phone down and asked Officer Hartman, "Are you going to take me home?"

He shook his head and said, "Not just yet," and Tammy said, "Here, I'm gonna let you talk to him."

Officer Hartman took the phone and said, "Mrs. Mills I guess you're happy now, aren't you?"

"You can't imagine how happy. Are you going to bring Tammy home?"

"No Ma'am, not just yet. Tammy says she was kidnapped and raped, and I will have to take her to our office so we can, hopefully, find out what happened and who did it. And then, we'll more than likely take her to the Fulton Medical Center so she can be evaluated. You can meet us at the Police Department if you'd like. We'll be leaving here after I talk to a couple of people and we should be there shortly."

"Wonderful; I'll see you there and thank you."

Officer Hartman then asked Ms. Patel a few questions, but she couldn't answer any of them. All she could say was that a young man brought Tammy in and said she had been raped. She did hear him tell Tammy that his name was Bobby Huffman.

And then, he asked Tammy, "Tammy, Honey, do you know where you were when you met Bobby Huffman?"

"Yeah; him and some other guys were playing basketball not too far from here."

"Do you think you could show me?"

"Yeah, but he didn't have anything to do with anything. I just happened up on them after Tink let me out of the van."

"Did you say Tink? Who's Tink?"

"Yeah; he's the one who kidnapped me."

"Okay then. Let's go see if we can find Bobby, and then we'll go down to the Police Department.

I'm sure Sergeant Yokley will want to find out more about this Tink fellow when he talks to you." He thanked Ms. Patel and then he and Tammy went out and got into his car.

"Okay, Tammy. Show me where you found Bobby."

She gave him directions which were just right around the corner from Ms. Patel's store. A group of boys was still playing ball, and Bobby was easy to pick out because he was one of only two white boys in the group. He and Tammy got out of the car and, Tammy pointed Bobby out to him. Officer Hartman asked Bobby if he would come over and talk to him for a minute.

"Bobby, my name is Officer Dan Hartman. Tammy tells me that you are the one who took her to the store when you first saw her."

"Yes sir. She just appeared and said she had been raped. I didn't know what to do other than find someone to help her, and that's why I took her to the store."

"You did the right thing, Bobby. Did you see anybody with her before you saw her?"

"No sir, I didn't see nobody."

"Did you see a car or a van or any kind of vehicle?"

"No sir. She was walking when she got to us."

"Okay; I guess that's all I need. Just in case someone in the department needs to ask you anything else, would you please give me your address and phone number if you have one?" He gave Bobby a pad and asked him to write the information on it, which he did.

Thank you, Bobby, and he and Tammy returned to his car and got in. Dan had laid the pad with Bobby's information on the seat between them, and she made a mental note of the address. She thought she might want to get in touch with him sometime.

Soon they reached the Police Department, and Officer Hartman parked out front. He and Tammy walked in and went straight back to Sergeant Yokley's desk. Officer Hartman said, "Sergeant Yokley, this is Tammy Mills. Tammy, this is Sergeant Yokley."

"Hi Tammy, I'm sure glad to see you. Have a seat in that chair right there."

Tammy obeyed and sat down in one of the chairs across from his desk.

"Now Tammy, I understand you said you were kidnapped and raped. Why don't you tell me what happened?"

Tammy told him what happened beginning when Bobby Kunkle dropped her off at Speedy's, and when she finished, Sergeant Yokley looked her straight in the eye and said, "Tammy, that's a good story, but you don't act like someone who has been kidnapped and raped. Are you sure you didn't just go somewhere with this Tink fellow and claim he raped you because you couldn't explain being out all night to your mother?"

His statement infuriated her, and in almost a yell, she stood up, looked him in the eye and said, "I'm not lying. What I told you happened, and I don't care whether you believe me or not. I'm leaving. Come on Mama. Take me home. Let's get out of this stupid place."

Chapter Four

She started toward the door and Sergeant Yokley said, "Whoa, hold on there. I believe you Tammy. I just had to be sure you were shooting straight with me. How about sitting back down and let's talk, okay?"

She hesitated, and reluctantly sat back down.

Before he asked his first question, he stood up and walked over to her, put his arms around her and squeezed. He asked, "Are you mad at me?"

With a half-smile, she said, "I was, but I don't guess I am now."

"Good, now let's talk, okay?"

"Okay."

"Tammy, can you tell me how you got those bruises on your arms?"

"No; not really. I guess they got there when Tink grabbed me so tight. He grabbed me so tight it hurt."

"Can you tell me Tink's last name?"

"No. I asked him what it was, but he wouldn't tell me."

"Okay. Let's concentrate on his vehicle for a minute; did you say it was a van?"

"Yeah, what I think you call a work van."

"Why do you call it that?"

"Because it don't have any windows except for the driver and passenger sides. It does have one little bubble window on each side toward the back."

"What color is it, Tammy?"

"Brown; a Brown ford.

"Does it have any distinguishing characteristics such as a dented fender or any kind of damage anywhere?"

"No, it was in pretty good shape."

"Did you happen to notice if it had Georgia tags or not?"

"No, I didn't notice."

"Okay, Tammy, that's all for now. We need to send you over to the Fulton Medical Center so they can check you out, and then when you come back here after they've finished evaluating you we'll get into more detailed questioning about your experience. In the meantime, we'll see if we can come up with this Tink guy.

"If you don't mind, you will have to change out of your clothes into one of our snappy-looking gowns and robes, so we can see if there might be any clues on your clothes.

When he had told her that, he called Detective Laura Bean from about five desks down and said, "Laura, we're going to keep Tammy's clothes here. Will you please get her one of our fashionable gowns and robes and take her to where she can change, and oh yeah, get her some of those cute slippers."

Smiling, she said, "I'll do it. Come on Tammy."

When she got back to Sergeant Yokley's desk, he said, "I'll have Officer Hartman take you, and the only time you will be outside will be between Officer Hartman's car and the door to the hospital, so you will hardly be seen by anybody in your gown and robe."

Officer Hartman had stayed there after he brought Tammy in, and Sergeant Yokley said, "Dan, how about taking Tammy over to the Fulton MC. You might want to drive around back to pick her up so she won't have to get out on the street."

"You bet; ready to go Tammy?"

"I guess. What are they going to do to me?"

"They're just going to give you a good physical check-up. It won't be bad."

He drove around and pulled up right at the door, and Tammy hardly had to even get outside. When they arrived at the hospital, he pulled up close to the building, and once again, she hardly had to get outside.

As soon as Tammy and Officer Hartman left, Grey said, "Fred, she'll be gone for a pretty good while. Why don't we make a quick run out to Speedy's to see if we can find out anything?"

"Good idea. I'm ready when you are."

"Okay, let's roll."

They both knew where Speedy's was, and it didn't take long to get there. They pulled into a parking space out front and walked into the store. Behind the counter was a large man who looked to be in his mid-fifties, and Grey asked him, "Are you Speedy?"

"Yeah, that's me. What can I do for you?"

Showing his badge and talking at the same time, he asked,

"What's your name, Speedy?"

"My Name is Robert Treadwell. What can I do for you?"

"Speedy, I'm Sergeant Grey Yokley and this is my partner, Detective Fred Melwiki with the Douglasville Police Department. We have a young lady who says she was kidnapped from here yesterday afternoon. Were you here yesterday afternoon?"

"Yes sir; I was here all afternoon."

"Did you happen to see any kind of disturbance or anything that looked like any kind of abduction?"

"No sir, I didn't see anything like that."

"This young lady says she was offered and accepted a ride from a man who she identifies as someone who goes by the name of Tink. Do you know anyone by that name?"

"No sir; I don't."

"She says he drives a brown Ford van and might be a carpet layer. Does that ring any kind of bell?"

"No sir, but I do remember seeing a brown van in here yesterday afternoon."

"Did you recognize the driver?"

"Yeah, but I don't know who he is. He comes in here every once in a while to use the phone and to get something to drink. He's always by himself and never talks to anybody as far as I know."

"Have you ever heard anyone in here use the word, Tink?"

"I don't think so. Is that his name?"

"We think so. Speedy, here's my card. If you happen to see this guy come in here again, please call me anytime; day or night. We need to get this guy. Will you do that?"

Opening the cash register and putting the card under the cash drawer he said, "I sure will."

"Thanks, Speedy." He looked at his partner and asked, "Before we go, do you want something to drink, Fred?"

"Yeah, I think I'll get a Dr. Pepper."

Grey got a Coke and handed Speedy a five. Speedy gave him three dollars back.

"Okay Speedy; thanks."

They walked out to their car and returned to their office.

****

Tammy waited inside the patrol car until Officer Hartman came around and opened the door for her, and then he led her inside to a desk where there were several doctors and nurses.

He introduced her to a nurse who offered to help them, and after the initial greeting, the nurse took her back to an examining room where a Doctor performed what they called a Rape Kit Exam, which was necessary to preserve possible DNA evidence. She was examined from top to bottom. She was poked, prodded, and swabbed. The Doctor ran instruments up inside her to get fluid samples and did other things necessary for the forensic examination. While he was taking fluid samples, a nurse was feeling around on her trying to find signs of bruising and made notes on everything she found. After an exhaustive examination, which took nearly five hours, she was told that everything looked relatively good, and she could leave.

Barbara had waited in a waiting room outside the ER while the Doctor did his exam, and she remembered that she had told Jerry that she would call him when they found Tammy or had heard something, so she took that opportunity to call him.

When he answered she said, "Mr. Martin, this is Barbara. We found Tammy."

"Great!! Where was she?"

"She said she was kidnapped and raped, but the kidnapper let her go, and she's here at the hospital being examined right now."

"Is she okay?"

"She seems to be. I don't know very much yet. I just wanted to let you know that we found her."

"Well, I really appreciate that. When you know more, will you call and let me know?"

"I sure will."

"Good! I'll be anxious to hear. Thanks for calling, Barbara."

"You're welcome. Bye."

Officer Hartman had waited with Barbara while she was being examined, and when she was told she could leave, he took her back to the Police station in his car and Barbara followed them in hers. When they arrived at the station, Officer Hartman again drove around back for privacy reasons and when they got out, he took her back to Detective Yokley's desk for an extensive question and answer session; the main topic being Tink.

They had given Barbara permission to be present during the questioning, and she was shocked at some of the things she heard.

They wanted to know everything that happened the afternoon of the abduction, and she told them everything she could remember except the part about Randy, and she didn't want to bring him up. In her story about the happenings of the afternoon, she mentioned Bobby Kunkle, Reed Thomas, and Stony Gray. She didn't mention Jerry or Tracy since she saw them that morning.

As she was talking, Grey Yokley was writing the names of the people she mentioned in order that he could contact them later for questioning, if necessary.

When he finished taking the names he said, "Now Tammy, I need to know exactly what happened from the time you first came into contact with Tink. Mrs. Mills, you might not want to listen to this. If you would rather leave, I'm sure Tammy will understand."

"No. no; I want to know everything that happened to my baby."

"Alright, but it might not be pleasant."

"That's alright; I want to know everything."

Chapter Four

"Tammy, before we get into the events of what happened I want you to tell me everything you can about Tink. I know we talked about this before you went to the hospital, but it's important that we know everything we can about him. How old is he? How tall is he? The color of his hair and eyes, and anything you can think of that might help us track him down; okay?"

"Okay. He looked to be in his late twenties or early thirties, and he was fairly good-looking. His hair was brown and short and his eyes were brown. He had one dimple on his left cheek and a scar just above it. I would say he was about as tall as you are and was slender, but well built.

"I think he used his van in his work because he had a lot of tools in it. He might be in the carpet business or tile or something because he had a rug rolled up behind the front seat. That was what he rolled out when he laid me down. The big box he put me in was covered inside with carpet and carpet was on the outside, and some of his tools looked like something he might use when he works with the carpet. I know two of the tools were funny-looking and had something on them that looked like what you would hit with your knee. They had thick padding on them. It seems like I remember seeing those kinds of tools when they put carpet in our house."

"Was the thick padding on the whole tool?"

She looked at him as if he were so dumb. "No; the part that looked like where they hit it with their knee." Under her breath she said, "Man, what a dumb question."

"Can you identify any of the other tools?"

"There were some big scissors and a curved knife of some sort."

"Anything else?"

"Oh yeah; there was a real long ruler made out of some kind of metal."

"Anything else?"

"There were a lot of things, but I don't know what they were. In one spot there were some tools, and several pieces of tile, like your bathroom tile, were in a box next to the tools. What I remember most was the big box he had. It was about as big as a casket, and it had that ugly orange carpet on it both inside and outside. That's where he kept me when he wasn't raping me."

"Okay, Tammy, this may be hard for you, but we need to know everything that happened from the time you first met Tink until you left him. Can you tell us that?"

"I don't want to, but I'll try."

"Atta girl. You said you first saw him when you were at Speedy's. How about starting at that point?"

"Okay. I got off work early, and my boss gave me a ride to Speedy's so I could call my Mom to come get me there, but when I tried to call her, my phone was dead. There was a pay phone there, so I tried to call her on that, but I got her voice mail. Tink was standing behind me while I tried to call Mom because he later told me that he needed to use the phone. When I couldn't reach Mom, he asked me something; I don't remember what it was, and when I told him I couldn't get hold of her, he told me he would take me home. I looked him over real careful, and he looked to be okay, so I let him take me.

"When we got in his van he asked me where I lived and when I told him he said he knew where that was, but when we started up he headed in the wrong direction. When I told him we were going the wrong way, he said, "You don't mind taking a ride with me, do you, and I said I did, but he kept driving."

"Do you know where he took you?"

"No, but it was way out in the country where there weren't any houses or anything around."

"What did he do when you all got out there?"

"The first thing he did was try to kiss me."

"Did you let him kiss you?"

"Are you kidding? Heck no. I wasn't going to let somebody like that kiss me."

"What did he do next?"

"He had a rug rolled up behind the driver's seat, and he unrolled it and took my clothes off."

"Did you resist?"

"I fought him with everything I had, but he was too strong for me."

"What then?"

33

"Then he got on me and raped me."

"What did you all do when he finished raping you?"

"We stayed in the van, and after a while he raped me again."

"When you all were in the van, and during the times when Tink wasn't busy, did he talk to you?"

"Yeah, some."

"What did he talk about?"

"He tried to convince me that I liked being with him, and that I liked doing it."

"You said he raped you twice. Were those the only two times he raped you?"

"Yeah; yesterday."

"Do you mean he raped you again, later?"

"Yeah; this morning."

"What did he do with you last night?"

"After he got through raping me, I told him I had to go to the bathroom, and he let me out of the van so I could go, but he had a rope, and he tied one end around my neck, and he held onto the other end so I couldn't escape while I peed. When I finished peeing, he made me get back in the van. He let me put on my panties and bra, and then he put me in that big box, and drove somewhere. It took a long time before we stopped, and he left me in the box all night."

"And you don't know where you were?"

Again, looking at him as if she thought he was stupid for asking such a dumb question she said, "How would I know that? I was locked up in a box for crying out loud. Man; what a question."

"Okay; then what happened?"

"This morning he came back to the van and we rode for a long time again. He stopped one time during the ride and when he opened the box, we were back at the same place we were at yesterday afternoon. He must have stopped at McDonalds because he gave me an Egg McMuffin and a cup of coffee when I got out of the box."

"What did he do then?"

"He tried to put his arms around me, but I pushed him away. We fought and I told him I had to go to the bathroom, and he let me out of the van to go, but he tied the rope to me while I went the way he did yesterday. He said he didn't want me to mess up his van. Then, he forced me back into the van, and when we got back in, he grabbed me and fondled me and raped me again."

"That was this morning?"

"Yeah."

"Then what?"

"A little while later he raped me again, and right after he finished, a truck drove up with some men in it, and that's when he let me get dressed and we left there."

"Were you naked all night?"

"Yeah, except for my bra and panties."

"What kind of truck was it? Do you know?"

"It was a yellow four-door pickup with something painted on the door."

"Do you know what the painting on the door said?"

"It was parked at an angle, but I could make out the word *Surveyor*. I couldn't see the rest.*"

"Where did you go when you left there?"

"He brought me close to where I saw those boys playing basketball and let me out. He left me out there by myself, and that's when I walked to where they were playing."

"Do you know what time that was?"

"No, but you can ask the lady at the store that called you. She might know."

Just then, Barbara spoke up and said, "You should know that. Don't you record the times on your calls?"

"Yes ma'am, we have it. I just wanted to see how aware Tammy was about the whole situation."

Then looking at Tammy, he asked, "Tammy is there anything else you want to tell us?"

"No, I think I've told you everything. Now, when can I go? I want to go home and take a bath."

"You can leave right now, and I'm real sorry for what happened to you, but don't worry; we're going to catch this guy."

Barbara and Tammy left the Police station and walked to Barbara's car. Barbara had her arm around Tammy's shoulder, and Tammy didn't offer to pull away the way she would normally do. She seemed happy to be in the security of her mother. The experience that she had had over the last two days had definitely made a mark on her; for just how long only time would tell.

When they got home the first thing she did was start the water running in the bathtub while she got undressed. She could hardly wait to get into the tub to try and wash the Tink off of her. They had cleaned her up at the hospital, but she still felt dirty. After a long time the water began to cool off, so she washed and got out of the tub.

While she was taking a bath, Barbara called Jerry and told him that they were home, and he wanted to know if he could come by and see them. Of course she said he could, so he told her he would be over around eight o'clock and assured her he wouldn't stay; he just wanted to be sure that they were alright.

When Tammy got out of the tub, she put on a pair of jeans and a large, baggy sweat-shirt, even though it was warm outside. She just wanted to cover up every inch of her body.

Barbara went to her room and while she brushed her hair she said, "Tam, since we've been gone all day, I haven't had time to fix any dinner. Do you want to go out or would you like for me to just fix you a sandwich or something?"

"Let's just have something here."

"Okay; any idea what you'd like to have?"

"Yeah; why don't we have breakfast for dinner?"

"That sounds good; good idea. I'll get started on it. How do you want your eggs?"

"Scrambled sounds good."

"Okay; scrambled it is," and she began to fix bacon, scrambled eggs, and since they lived in Georgia, grits were required. She heated up the oven and baked some frozen biscuits that she had bought and when it all was done, they sat down and had a veritable feast. Tammy made the comment that it was better than steak, and Barbara agreed.

Tracy had met Jerry at the 129 Café and while they were there, Jerry told her about Tammy being found safe, and he said he told Barbara that he would like to stop by. "Do you want to go with me? I'm not going to stay; I just want to make sure they are both okay, and I want to see if they need anything since they don't have a man around."

"Yeah, I'll go with you. Do you know where they live?"

"No, but I have the address, and the GPS should be able to take us there. Why don't you leave your car here, and we can go from here when we finish eating?"

Tracy said, "Honey, can I ask you something?"

36

"You know you can; what is it?"

"I'm just wondering what there is about Tammy that kindles your interest so. I feel like she's nothing more than just a little juvenile delinquent."

"I don't know; there's something about her that tells me she's not all bad. Ever since she and her friends did all that damage to my house and got caught, there was something that sparked an interest; despicable attitude and all. Maybe she's a challenge; I don't know, but I feel like I have to try and help her. Do you mind?"

"No, I don't mind. I've only seen her that one time; yesterday, and she didn't show me much, but if you feel you need to help her, knock yourself out, and Honey, if you need my help you can count me in. Maybe she'll grow on me."

"She just may. What did I ever do before I met you?"

"You did just fine."

"I love you."

"Love you, too, Big Boy."

In a few minutes they finished their dinner and when Jerry paid the bill he asked, "Ready to roll?"

"I'm ready."

They went to his car, and he set the GPS while he looked at the note he had with the address on it. The GPS directed them right to where they wanted to go, and Jerry was surprised that it only took about fifteen minutes to get there.

"Okay, let's go in and see what kind of shape Miss Tammy is in."

"Didn't her Mother say she was in pretty good shape?"

"Yeah, that's what she said, but I can't imagine a young girl being in good shape after what she went through."

"Well, let's go in and see."

Barbara must have been close to the door because when Jerry rang the bell it only took a couple of seconds for her to open the door. She said, "Mr. Martin, hi, come in."

Before they entered Jerry said, "Hi Barbara; I'd like for you to meet my wife. Honey, this is Barbara Mills. Barbara, this is Tracy."

"Hi Barbara; it's nice to meet you."

"It's nice to meet you, too. Come in."

They walked into the living room where Tammy was sitting, and Tracy was the first to speak. "Hi Tammy."

"Hi."

Jerry followed by saying, "Hi Tammy; how're you doing?"

"I'm okay."

"Well, you look like you're doing okay, and I'm very thankful for that. I'm just sorry that you had to go through what you did."

He looked over at Barbara and said, "Mama, do you agree that your little girl is doing okay?"

"I think she is. She says she is, anyway."

"Well, what's next? Have they told you anything that you have to do?"

"The Police seem to think they'll be able to catch the guy who took her, and both the Police and the hospital think she needs to have some counseling, and they're supposed be setting it up."

"That's good. You're going to do what they tell you, aren't you Tammy?"

"Yeah, I guess, but I don't know how I'm going to do everything. I have to go to school and then I have to work every day after school. There's just not enough time for any counseling."

Jerry asked, "Would it help if you didn't have to go to work every day?"

"Yeah, that would help, but what about my sentence?"

"Tammy, your sentence is a part of your growing up. It's designed to teach you that for every bad act there's a consequence, and you committed a very bad act, but I happen to know your boss, and I think I can guarantee that you can get off on the days when you have counseling. You'll still have to work the required number of hours to take care of your sentence, but that should be no problem if you're willing to cooperate. What do you think?"

Tammy said, "I'll cooperate; thank you."

Barbara spoke up and said, "Thank you, Mr. Martin. You've been awfully good to us, and we appreciate it."

"Barbara, I'd appreciate it if you would call me Jerry. Mr. Martin is my Dad, besides; you and I are pretty close to the same age."

"Okay, Jerry, thank you."

Then Jerry said to whoever wanted to answer, "I know you were kidnapped and raped, but I don't know any of the details. Am I out of line if I ask what happened?"

Barbara began to tell what happened, and Tammy broke in and

said, "Let me tell it Mama," and she began talking and told everything that happened and didn't leave out a single detail."

When she finished, Tracy said, "Wow," and went over to her and put her arms around her and gave her a huge hug.

"I'm so sorry, Tammy, but you're a very strong young lady, and I'm sure you're going to come out of this and be even stronger. If you need for me to do anything for you, I hope you'll call me; will you do that?"

"I won't need anything."

"I'm sure you won't, but if you do, promise that you'll call me."

"Okay, I promise."

Jerry was true to his word; they didn't stay very long. After he saw that she was okay, he told them that he had to go, and he and Tracy left.

Chapter Five

Detective Yokley and his partner, Fred Melwiki got their heads together first thing Thursday morning and began mapping out plans for how they would investigate the case.

Tammy stayed right under her Mother and went everywhere she did. She had two or three calls from some of her friends, who didn't know about her bad experience, asking her to get together and hang out, but she declined all of them, and that was a big change for her. Barbara noticed the change in her behavior and was glad to see it, although she didn't want her to be permanently handicapped by the unspeakable experience she had had.

The hospital had scheduled her for her first session of counseling for Monday morning, and even though Tammy didn't feel she needed any counseling, Barbara could easily see that she did. Her behavior had made a full one hundred and eighty degree turn since she was kidnapped. Tammy fell asleep while sitting on the sofa listening to music, and Barbara had time to think about the things she had been through within the last few months.

The first thing she thought of was the time Tammy and the two boys damaged Jerry Martin's house and how Jerry had been so nice to them. She remembered how her terrible attitude had almost caused Jerry to let her go to jail instead of working to get her released. She just hoped some of these things would be brought out during counseling, and Tammy would realize that a good attitude would go a long way toward building relationships with other people.

She didn't actually know what transpired between her and the guy named Tink before the abduction, but she wondered if her attitude might have played some part in Tink's coming on to her the way he did.

On Thursday morning Barbara told Tammy the hospital called and said they had changed her first counseling session from Monday to tomorrow, Friday.

"I wonder why they changed it," Tammy said.

"Because they think you need to get started as soon as possible."

****

Thursday at ten o'clock was when Jerry was to meet with Frank Thomas to hopefully, find out about the financing he had asked for, for his White Rock Estates neighborhood and also to discuss building the large apartment complex that Frank had talked about. This was going to be a big day in his life, and he had butterflies the way he used to before a big ball game that he would be playing in.

Tracy left earlier that morning for Paris, and she got up at five o'clock so she could get ready and be at the airport by seven. She and Jerry had not been married that long, but Jerry felt insecure about certain things, and he depended on her to be his security blanket in times like that. He was as nervous as a cat, and he really wished she was there with him, but she wasn't, and he told himself, "I'm a big boy now, and everything is going to be great. I'll have unbelievable news for her when she gets back.

He arrived at the bank a little early and instead of going to see John, the way he had always done, he went straight upstairs to Frank's office. He went into the outer office and told the lady that he had an appointment with Frank at ten o'clock, and she asked him to be seated because Mr. Thomas had someone with him. Jerry was a little aggravated at that until he looked at his watch and saw that it was only ten 'til ten, so he sat down and waited.

About five 'til, an unbelievably pretty woman came out and introduced herself. "Are you Jerry?"

"Yes I am."

"Hi Jerry; I'm Melissa. I'm Mr. Thomas' assistant. He'll be with you in just a minute. He's finishing up with someone now. He tells me you're quite a builder, and you all might be on the verge of doing some business together."

"I hope so."

There were three chairs in the outer office, and Jerry was sitting in one on the end. When Melissa said they might be doing business together, she sat down in the one in the middle. She crossed her legs and turned toward him and said, "Jerry, Frank's excited about your building his apartment complex," and with that, she put her hand on his arm and asked, "Would you like to have something to drink; coffee or a Coke or something?"

"No, thank you."

He had worn a long-sleeve shirt that morning and had rolled the sleeves up two cuffs to where they rested just a little above his wrists. When she put her hand on his arm, she at first put it on his wristwatch and then slid it above the watch to touch his arm. It didn't take a genius to know that the way the move took place was clearly a come-on, and even though Jerry had had quite a bit of experience with women before he met Tracy, he was uncomfortable with that situation. He knew exactly what she had in mind, but with so much at stake, he wasn't sure just how to handle it.

Melissa was starting to ask him something when Frank came to the door and said, "Good morning, Jerry; come in."

When Melissa saw him, she jerked her hand back and stood up.

He got up and followed Frank into his office, glad to escape Melissa's advances when out of the corner of his eye, he saw that she had followed them into the office. When they were inside Frank said, "I see you two have already met. Jerry, Melissa is my assistant, and if you and I are able to come to an agreement on doing various projects together, you two will be working quite a lot together.

"Now, Jerry, the reason you came to see me in the first place was to get me to okay the financing for the White Rock Estates neighborhood you want to build. I've got to say you did a masterful job of convincing me that I would be a fool not to get in it with you, therefore, I was able, in turn, to convince our board that we would be fools not to approve it, so you'll get what you asked for. Melissa will get all the paperwork drawn up and you can sign it when it's ready. When will that be, Melissa?"

"I have most of it done now, but tomorrow will be better if Jerry can come back,"

Jerry smiled and interjected, "I'll come back at midnight if that's what I need to do. Tomorrow will be fine. Thank you so much."

"Good; just come back when Melissa tells you to. You won't have to come up here; you can go straight to her office and she'll take care of you. Now that we've got that out of the way, let's look at some blueprints, okay?"

"That sounds great."

"Jerry, how about a cup of coffee?"

"Are you going to have one?"

"Yeah, I'm going to have one. I didn't sleep too well last night, and I need a little pick-me-up."

"Then I'd like some, too."

"How do you take it?"

"Black with a little sweetener if that's okay."

"Melissa, would you do the honors?"

"I will. I'll be back in a jiffy."

"Thanks,"

"Jerry, have you thought any more about the apartment complex I mentioned to you when you were here before?"

"Yes sir; I've thought a whole lot about it, and I hope we're going to be able to get together on it. I know I can build you a complex that you will be proud of."

"I'm confident you can; in fact, I have so much confidence in you that I'm going to give you this job without shopping it around to other contractors."

"Wow!"

"Do you know why I'm doing that?"

"No sir, but I'd like to."

"Well, you told me that you built that complex down in the Cowart Lake area, and after you left here the other day, I called John Shelton, the owner of that complex; you know John, and I asked if I could go through one of the units. John is a long-time friend of mine, and he said he would be happy to show me one, so I went down there that same day, and I liked what I saw, so wallah, you're my contractor."

"Frank, I really appreciate that, and I'll call John and thank him. I can't wait to get started."

"Well, we're ready when you are. Now, let's go over these blueprints."

The complex was going to comprise of eight buildings containing eight apartments in each building; four two bedroom and four three bedroom units. Instead of each building sitting right next to another, they would be spread out and built at different angles, depending on the direction of the road. The whole complex would sit on twenty-eight acres of land and in addition to the eight buildings, there would be a very nice size swimming pool and two lighted tennis courts. It was going to be state-of-the-art in every way.

"Jerry, after looking over the plans, do you have any suggestions?"

"No sir, but I do have one question."

"What is that?"

"Are you wanting the entire complex finished at one time or do you want to stagger it?"

"I don't know what you mean, exactly. What do you mean, stagger it?"

"Well, sometimes with multi-building complexes, the owners will not want to have them all built at one time, but have only one or two concentrated on and finished before the others. That way, if we finish one or two buildings while we work on the others, you can rent eight or sixteen units and begin getting income from them. Then we can finish one or two more, and you can rent them and so forth. By doing it that way, by the time the entire complex is finished, you could conceivably have a large percentage, if not all the units rented without having to wait"

"That's a great idea; let's do it that way."

They talked at length about building the complex, and finally, a little before noon, their meeting broke up, and Jerry decided to go to his office before going to any of his jobs. He was dying to tell somebody what happened. Even before he left the bank, he wanted to tell somebody about his good news, and since Tracy was gone, he thought he would call Tom Sharpe and tell him.

He had not wanted to take his cell phone into his meeting, so he left it in the truck, and rather than wait until he got outside, he thought he would call Tom from inside the bank. He ducked into Melissa's office and asked her if he could use her phone, and naturally, she said he could.

"Melissa, can I see your phone book, too?"

She didn't say anything; she just handed him the book.

He looked up the number and dialed it. When someone answered on the other end, he asked to speak to Tom Sharpe and in a few minutes Tom picked up. "Hello, this is Tom."

"Hey Tom, what's up?"

"Jerry, what's cooking?"

"Tom, I just consummated two huge deals, and I needed to tell somebody. Since Tracy is gone, and you're my best friend, I wanted to share my news with you."

"That's great, and I appreciate you thinking enough of me to want to share your good news with me. What is this good news?"

Jerry told him some of what had happened and then said, "Look, since both our wives are out of town, why don't we get together after work, and I'll buy you a drink; or two, or three."

Tom said, "That would be nice. Where do you want to go?"

"How about the Oak Grove?"

"That's good. Want me to pick you up?"

"No thanks, I live too far. Why don't we just meet at say, eight o'clock?"

"Great; I'm anxious to hear about your deals. See you at eight."

Melissa was listening to every word and making mental notes of everything that Jerry said. She thought, *Oak Grove huh? I guess I need to see what's at Oak Grove. I'll see if Kim would like to go out there.*

When Jerry hung up, she said, "I heard you say your wife is out of town; where is she?"

"She's in Paris, France. She's a Flight Attendant and flies all over the world. This week it's Paris. There's no telling where she'll be next week."

"Don't you get lonesome?"

"Yeah, but it's not too bad. She's usually only gone for two or three days at a time, then she's home for a few days before she has to leave again. She loves what she's doing, and I'm not going to try to stop her."

"Just the same, I bet you get lonesome. When will she be back?"

"She'll be back Saturday night. He could see where the conversation was going, so he said, "I've got to go, Melissa. What time tomorrow do you want me to come sign the papers?"

"They should be ready late morning. You can come by any time after eleven o'clock. Maybe if you come around noon we can go somewhere and grab a sandwich."

"I'll see; it looks as if tomorrow is going to be a crusher, but I'll see."

"Okay. It was sure a pleasure meeting you, Jerry, and I look forward to working with you."

"So long, Melissa. See ya tomorrow."

He intended to go straight from the bank to his office, but he was so excited he felt like he needed to talk to somebody, so he detoured to Richards' Building Supply to talk to Jack. When he walked in Jack looked at him and said, "Boy, it must be good. You're grinning like a Cheshire cat."

"It is good, Jack. I just got the financing for my White Rock Estates neighborhood, and I also consummated a deal to build a sixty-four unit high-end apartment complex. I hope you've got the credit line to buy all the lumber and everything else we're going to need to build all these things."

"Fantastic! Don't you worry about my credit line; I can buy anything and everything you need. When are you going to start?"

"Almost immediately. I'll have to start the apartments first because before I can start on White Rock, I will have to finalize the sale on the land and then have streets and curbs put in, and unless I can get the County to put water lines in, I'll have to build a water system."

"Do you think they'll put one in?"

"I don't know. I've had several meetings with this one guy, and every time I meet with him, his attitude is different, but now that I've got the financing, I should be able to pin him down; one way or the other."

"Does Tracy know about this?"

"No, she's in Paris until Saturday."

"Well, I bet she'll be tickled when she finds out."

"I'm sure she will be. I've got to go, Jack. I've got to go to my office and try to get my mind on making some plans."

"Okay, Padna. I'm happy for you, and if you want us to be one of your suppliers, we'll be happy to do it."

"Don't worry about that. You'll be our main supplier. Gotta go. See ya Jack."

Chapter Six

That night, Jerry arrived at Oak Grove right at eight o'clock and Tom was already there; in fact, he had already found a table and had ordered drinks for them both and didn't wait to start working on his. Jerry sat down and was all smiles.

Tom said, "Boy, Jer, this must have been a heck of a day. You told me a little over the phone, so tell me the rest of it."

Jerry told him pretty much everything that happened that morning and how it was not only a huge deal for his White Rock Estates thing, but what it could lead to if Frank and his partners liked his work on the apartments. During the telling, they finished their drinks, and Jerry ordered another, and they continued to talk, with Jerry doing most of it.

About half way through their second drink, Tom looked over Jerry's right shoulder with a smile on his face, and at the same time, Jerry felt a hand on his shoulder and a squeeze. He looked up and it was Melissa Morris, Frank Thomas's assistant.

"Hi Melissa; what are you doing out here?"

"Well, it's been a long time since I've been out here, and when I heard you say Oak Grove this morning, I thought this would be a good chance for me and my friend, Kim, to come see if it had changed any since we were last here. Are you having a good time?"

Jerry introduced her to Tom, and she kept standing there, obviously hoping for an invitation to sit down, but the invitation never came, so she finally went back to her table and sat down with her friend. Every time Jerry would look in her direction, she would be looking at him. Once, when he looked over there, and she saw him looking, she raised her glass as if making a toast.

Tom said, after she left their table, "Hey old Buddy, have you been holding out on me? That's a good-looking woman coming on to you. What's the deal here?"

"No deal; I just met her this morning. She's the assistant to the man I'm working with at the bank."

"Well, assistant or not, she looks and acts like she's sitting on ready."

"I know, and it worries me a little. This relationship I'm building with her boss is something that can affect me financially in a good way for the rest of my life, and I'd hate for something like her to ruin it for me, besides, I'm not going to be disloyal to Tracy."

In a few minutes, Melissa and Kim, got up to go to the ladies' room, and on their way back to their table they detoured around to Jerry and Tom's table. She stood up close to Jerry and put her hand on his shoulder and asked, "Jerry, why don't you and your friend come over to our table and have a drink with us?" The whole time she was talking, Kim was giving Tom a very inviting look.

Jerry said, "That sounds nice, Melissa, but we're gonna cut out when we finish these. Tom has an early morning, and when I get home I have to work on some materials lists so I can get some things ordered tomorrow. I'm getting ready to start on a huge project, thanks to Frank' approving my loan, and between that and the job I'll be doing for him, I'm going to be a busy boy. Thanks anyway. I'll see you in the morning, when I come sign the papers."

She smiled and said, "I'll be looking forward to it."

"Me too; see ya then."

As they were walking back to their table, Tom said, "Unbelievable; you might want to change your position. That's what you call a good-looking woman, and it looks as if she's yours for the asking."

"What about you, Mister Naïve? Were you paying any attention to the way Kim was looking at you? All you had to do was say the word, and she would eat you up." Smiling, he asked, "Want me to get you her number?"

Red faced, he said, "No, thank you."

"I think we need to get out of here before we both get into trouble."

"I think you're right. Let's go."

****

Barbara told Tammy she would go to work at the regular time and would take off in time to take her to counseling. Due to the circumstances, Tammy wasn't going to school the next day, so she could sleep late. She told her to set her alarm so she could get up and be ready when she got home to pick her up.

Trying to think ahead, in her mind she just knew Tammy wouldn't be ready to go to counseling when she got there, so just to be safe, she would get there early, in case they had to get her ready after she got home. Surprise, surprise!! When she arrived home Tammy was up and ready to go. Barbara thought, *life is full of surprises isn't it?*

"Mama, did you call Mr. Martin and tell him I wouldn't be at work today?"

"No, I completely forgot to. I'll call him right now."

She called Jerry and told him about Tammy having to go to counseling, and he told her that was fine. She could come on the days when she didn't have to go.

Barbara thanked him and they left.

Detectives Yokley and Melwiki got to their office a little before eight, Friday morning, and immediately began mapping out their day when they would be looking for Tink.

Overnight, the Forensics Lab had found fibers in Tammy's clothes and had determined that they were orange Acrylic fibers. They were found, not only on her clothes, but in her hair as well at the hospital, so the detectives felt pretty comfortable that Tink had something to do with carpet the way Tammy had suggested.

She had told them that she thought he might be a carpet layer or something to do with carpet and maybe something to do with tile, also. They figured the easiest way to get a list of the people they wanted to contact would be from the yellow pages first, so they made copies from the phone book. Unless they found Tink with one of their first contacts, it would take more than just Friday to complete the list because there were many listings under Carpet Installation plus related headings such Carpet Layers' Equipment and Supplies. That didn't count all the people that worked for the companies that sold carpet and had their own carpet layers; furniture stores even sold carpet, so their work was cut out for them unless they found him early on in their calls.

Then again, they didn't know for sure that he was a carpet layer; that was just what Tammy said she thought he was, and she was just guessing based on what she saw in his van, but that was all they had to go on, except for the forensics report, so that's where they started.

Grey said, "Fred, you start on the list, and I'm going to call the big boys; Home Depot and Lowes. If he's working for one of them, then our job might be a lot easier."

"Good idea. I'll start with A-1 Carpet Installation."

Gray dialed the number for Home Depot and after two rings a very pleasant voice said, "Good morning. Home Depot; how may direct your call?"

"Good morning. This is Detective Grey Yokley with the Douglasville Police Department. May I please speak to the person in charge of carpet installation?"

"Certainly; one moment please."

He could hear the phone ringing, and after several rings a voice on the other end said, "This is Brian. Can I help you?"

"Yes sir; I hope so. This is Detective Grey Yokley with the Douglasville Police Department, and we're looking for a person of interest who may or may not be a carpet layer. There's a possibility that he may also lay tile. He goes by the name of Tink. Do you have anyone by that name working for you?"

"No sir we don't; I'm sorry."

"Okay; thanks anyway."

Next, he called Lowes Home Improvement Company and had the same result. "Well Fred, it looks as if we're going to have a long day on the telephone, doesn't it?"

"Yeah, it looks that way, but who knows; maybe we'll get lucky."

All morning was spent calling businesses in hopes of finding Tink, but they struck out. About noon, they were sick of calling, and Fred said, "Grey, I'm ready for something to eat. Wanna go grab something?"

"Might as well. We're not doing much good here. Where do you want to go?"

"It doesn't matter; just take me somewhere."

They got into the car and Grey drove straight to Sonny's BBQ. When they got there, he told Fred, "I hope you're in the mood for barbeque. You wouldn't tell me where you wanted to go, and this sounded good to me."

"This is fine."

****

Jerry was so keyed up that he could hardly wait to get to the bank to finalize the loan he was getting for his huge neighborhood project. He had completed one house and listed it with a Realtor and only had two under construction at the time, and since they were both nearly finished, he didn't have to spend too much time with them, and that let his mind go to the financing.

Melissa had told him to come by her office sometime after eleven to sign the papers and suggested he come around lunchtime, and maybe they could go get some lunch together. He remembered what she said and thought he would get there around noon even though he didn't want to go out with her. He was no dummy; he knew exactly what she was up to, but at the same time he knew how important building a relationship with Frank Thomas was, and judging from the way Frank treated her when they met the day before, he thought he should just sort of go with the flow and not make any waves.

He arrived at the bank a little before twelve and went straight to her office where she was waiting for him. She invited him in and once he was seated she opened a folder and began removing official-looking papers. She organized them in the way she wanted them and instead of pointing out the places where he was to sign from across her desk, she got up and walked around to where he was seated and pointed out each place while leaning over his shoulder and touching him. He noticed it, but was careful not to make any obvious moves away from her.

When he had finished signing what seemed to him to be like a book of papers, Melissa said, "Okay, Mr. M; how do you plan to handle the withdrawal of these funds?

"Well, I already have an account here where I keep my construction money, and I just draw it out as I need it. Why can't I do the same thing with this money?"

"You can; I just needed to find out. Do you need any today?"

"No, not today, but I probably will need to draw out a substantial amount next week to pay for the land."

"Okay; just call me when you get ready, and I'll have it deposited into your account."

"That's great. Thank you."

"Okay. Now that we've got that done, would you like to get some lunch?"

"Yeah, if you would."

"Great, I was hoping you weren't going to be so standoffish the way you were last night at Oak Grove. What are you in the mood for?"

"I can get by with something light; maybe just a sandwich or a salad. What would you like?"

"You know what? The Olive Garden sounds good. You can get a good salad there and their Pasta Faggioli soup is to die for. Why don't we go there?"

"That sounds just fine. Do you want to drive two cars or just meet there?"

"Come on Big Boy. You can ride with me, okay?"

"Sounds like a winner; are you ready to go?"

"Ready." They walked out of the bank into the parking lot, and she led him to a slick, Dark Gray BMW Z4 Roadster. She pushed the buttons to unlock the doors, and in a minute they were on their way to the Olive Garden.

Jerry loved the car, and as they were driving to the restaurant, he asked Melissa, "What color do you call this?"

"She said, "The book says it's Spacegrau. I guess that's a fancy word for gray."

"Well whatever it is, I like it."

When they had been seated in the restaurant and the waiter was waiting on them, Melissa ordered soup, and Jerry ordered the all-you-can eat salad and then he decided he would like to have some soup, so he ordered the Pasta Faggioli in addition.

While they waited on their food Melissa began the conversation by asking, "Jerry, how long have you been married?"

"Not very long; less than a year."

"Oh wow! You're a newlywed, hunh?"

"Yep; that's me."

He said, "I don't see any rings, so I'm assuming you're single. Am I right?"

"You're right; the right guy hasn't showed up yet."

"Do you think you'll know the right guy when he comes?"

"I think so."

"What kind of guy will he be?"

"He'll be a lot like you."

"What makes you think you you'd like someone like me?"

"I just know I would." Grabbing his hand, smiling, she said,

"Why don't you leave your wife and you and I can run away to the Bahamas or somewhere?"

Trying to keep the conversation light, Jerry said, "Well, let's finish lunch first."

About that time their food came and they both did what they had to do to get ready to eat. During lunch, Jerry managed to steer the conversation to the building projects that he had coming up, and it turned out to be a nice lunch with pleasant company.

When they returned to the bank, Jerry thanked her for a nice lunch and told her he would see her later. She said she enjoyed it, too, and left him to go into the bank.

On the way back to his office, Jerry thought, *that was nice. Maybe I jumped to the wrong conclusion about her.* Then he thought back to their initial contact and to last night at Oak Grove, and then he decided, *no, I've got her pegged right. I'll just have to be careful.*

****

The two Detectives were so tired of talking on the telephone all morning that they said very little over lunch. When they were about through, Grey said, "Boy that was good. It really hit my spot. Did you enjoy yours?"

"Yeah, it was good. Ready to get back to those ever-loving phones?"

"Yeah. I'm going to think positive this afternoon and find Tink in the first hour after we get back."

"I hope you're right."

When they got back to the station, they talked briefly to some of the people in the office and went to the rest room before sitting back down at their desks. Then, they immediately picked up their phones and began calling carpet businesses again. True to Grey's prediction, when Fred called the Morton Flooring Company and asked if they had someone named Tink working for them, the man said, "Yes."

Fred then asked, "Who am I speaking with?" The man told him he was Henry Morton. Fred asked several questions, including the make and color of his vehicle, and his last name. He asked when Tink would be in, and Henry told him that he didn't necessarily come in every day; it depended on the particular job that he had at the time. Sometimes if he didn't finish a job in the afternoon he would have already taken the carpet to the job, and he would go back to it the next morning. He checked the job that he was doing that day and told Fred that it looked as if he would be coming in that afternoon.

Fred asked, "Do you have any idea what time he'll be there?"

"Not really, but if I have to guess, I'll say about five-thirty or six."

Fred told him, "Look, my partner and I are going to come out to your place this afternoon to see if we can talk to him. Please don't mention this call, okay?"

"Okay. I'll see you fellows when you get here."

"Thanks a lot."

After Fred's call to Morton Flooring, the two detectives spent some time reviewing their notes before going out to the business. Since it was still early afternoon, they just sort of hung out at the station for a couple of hours. Finally it was time to head out to Morton's, and they arrived out there around five o'clock.

They went inside and one man and one woman were working with customers, and another man was doing something behind a counter on the other side of the store. Grey walked up to him and said, "Excuse me; I'm looking for Henry."

"I'm Henry. You must be Detective Melwiki."

"No, I'm Detective Yokley. That's Detective Melwiki over there. Fred had stopped to look at a panel of carpet swatches. When he heard Grey mention his name, he put the samples down and walked over to where the two men were standing. Fred introduced himself and shook hands with Henry, and then Henry invited the two into his office.

"Can I get you all anything; coffee, coke, water?"

They both said, "No, thank you."

"Can you tell me why you are going to talk to Tink?"

Grey said, "No sir, we can't talk about it right now, but we can say that something happened, and we have reason to believe Tink was involved in it."

"Did he kill somebody?"

"Oh no; nothing like that. This is not a homicide investigation."

"Well, this guy works for me, and I don't want a criminal working for me. I guess I'll fire him when he comes in."

Grey said, "Mr. Morton, we would rather you not do that. You know, in this country, everybody is innocent until proven guilty, and we don't know for sure if he was involved in anything. If we find that he was involved in something, then there will be plenty of time for that. Besides, he must be a good worker or you wouldn't have him as an employee. Am I right?"

"I guess you're right, but how will I know?"

"You'll know."

In a minute Mr. Morton said, "Speak of the devil. There's Tink now. Excuse me, and I'll get him for you."

He led him into the office, and when Tink saw them he turned white. He knew immediately that they were the police.

Mr. Morton introduced him to the detectives and both detectives showed their badges. Mr. Morton said, "You all can talk in here. I've got some things to do in the back."

Grey said, "Thank you sir" and then told Tink to sit down.

He said, "Tink, before we get started, I'm interested in where you got the name Tink. Can you tell me?"

"Yes sir. My name is Thomas Nelson Key, and my initials are TNK. When I was in school somebody saw my initials and called me Tink, and it has stuck ever since. Now, what are you gentlemen wanting to talk to me about?"

"Normally, we would want to take you down to our office to talk to you, but since Mr. Morton has offered the use of his office, I think we can do it here. Tink, can you tell us where you were this past Tuesday afternoon, beginning around three o'clock through noon on Wednesday?"

He thought for a minute and then said, "Yes sir, I was at work until around five-thirty or six o'clock, and then I went home. Me and my wife and our children went out to eat Tuesday night, and then I came back to work on Wednesday morning. Why are you asking?"

Ignoring Tink's question, he asked, "What kind of vehicle do you drive in your work?"

"I drive a Ford Van."

"What color is it?"

"It's sort of a brownish color. Why are you asking me these questions?"

Again. Ignoring Tink's question he asked, "Do you have your van here?"

"Yes sir. It's parked out back."

"Would you mind showing it to us?"

"I wouldn't mind. Let's go out back."

On the way out back, Tink asked once more why they were asking the questions, and Grey told him they would talk about it when they got back inside, and that seemed to satisfy him. He was pretty sure he knew why, but at the same time, he wasn't positive.

Tink opened the van door for them, and they got in and went over the entire van very carefully. Tammy had tried to describe what kind of tool one of them was, and when they asked him he said it was called a carpet stretcher or kicker.

In a few minutes, Grey said, "Okay, let's go back inside."

They returned to the office where they were before and sat down. Tink said, "You said you would tell me why all the questions when we came in. Are you ready to tell me now?"

"Tink, this past Tuesday afternoon, a young girl was kidnapped from a convenience store named Speedy's. According to her, she was taken out in the country and raped by a guy named Tink, and all this took place in a brown Ford Van. She even described some of the tools in the van and they were very similar to the tools in your van.

"Can anyone verify the times that you were working Tuesday?"

"I doubt it. I was laying carpet in a new house and there wasn't anybody there except me, but you can check to make sure I laid it because it wasn't there on Monday."

"Fred, do have anything you want to ask Tink?"

"Yeah; Tink, you said you and your family went out to eat Tuesday night. Can you tell us a little more about that?"

"Well, I got home from work around six or six-thirty, and after I cleaned up and changed clothes, me and my wife and our two children went down to Coxes Restaurant and ate dinner."

"Can anybody verify that?"

"Yeah. My Wife and kids, of course, and also Arthur Cox at the restaurant."

"Anything else Fred?"

"I've got one more question; Tink do you know a young lady named Tammy Mills?"

"No. Who is Tammy Mills?"

Grey said, "She's someone who says she knows a fellow named

Tink. She's an attractive girl and here, the key word is girl. Tink, this girl is only sixteen years old, but we'll talk about that later. I will tell you this; whoever did this is going to be in a peck of trouble when we catch them."

When he said that, Tink had a very uncomfortable look on his face. He looked at Fred and asked, "Anything else Fred?"

"No; not right now. But Tink, don't leave town until we tell you that you can. We may want to ask you more questions."

"Okay; can I go now?"

"Yeah, you can go."

When he left, the two detectives went over to Henry Morton, and Grey asked, "Mr. Morton, do you by any chance have a picture of Tink? We'll get it back to you."

"As a matter of fact I do have one, but it's a group picture. We just had one made last week for a new ad campaign that we're starting. Will that work?"

"Yes sir; it sure will. Our people can isolate his picture from the rest, and that should work just fine."

"Come back in the office, and I'll get it for you."

They followed him to the office and after looking in one of the file cabinets, he retrieved a picture and handed it to Grey.

"Thank you very much, Mr. Morton."

"You're welcome. How about keeping me posted on what's going on with Tink. He's a good carpet layer, and I would hate to lose him, but I don't want him going into people's houses representing Morton Flooring if he's not one of the good guys."

"We can do that. Thanks again," and they went out to their car and headed back to the station.

On the way back, Fred said, "Grey, it's too early for the supper crowd, so why don't we swing by Coxes to see if Arthur Cox is there? We might be able to save a trip later on."

"Good idea. Let's do it."

The restaurant wasn't too far out of the way, and when they got there most of the patrons were older people who liked to eat early, but overall they weren't too busy. A man stood behind the cash register, and they recognized him as Arthur Cox, so they went up to him.

Grey said, "Good evening, Arthur."

"Good evening. What can I do for you fellows?"

They only knew him slightly from eating there a few times, so Grey and Fred both showed him their badges as they introduced themselves and then asked, "Do you happen to know a Tink Key?"

"Yeah, I know Tink."

"Was he in here this past Tuesday night?"

Arthur thought for a minute and then said, "Yes, he and his family were here. I remember because we were real busy Tuesday night, and his daughter spilled a glass of water on the floor, and we had to mop it up."

"Okay. Thank you very much," and after that they left for the station.

On the way back Grey asked, "What do you think?"

"I'm not sure. Tink was pretty believable especially the part about eating out with his family and the restaurant owner verifying it. What do you think?"

"I'm like you, but there's something that's not right. Did you see the expression on his face when you asked him if he knew Tammy? Tammy is believable, too. I think we should still talk to Tink's wife and get her side of the story. Why don't we go out there in the morning?"

Chapter Seven

They had gotten Tink's address and Saturday morning they went to his house to talk to his wife, but no one was at home. The garage door was open, so they went in and looked around. Almost immediately, Grey said, "Fred, look over there."

Next to the back wall of the garage was a large box covered with orange carpet. "Know what Fred? This box is big enough to put somebody inside. Whatta ya think?"

"It looks big enough to me. I think we need to get a search warrant and look inside, and we also need to get some carpet fibers from inside the van, too, don't you think?"

"Absolutely; let's do it."

On the way back in to the office Grey said, "While we're at the office, let's give the picture of Tink that we got from Mr. Morton, to Jeanette and have her put together a photo lineup and call Tammy in to look at it."

"Are you going to have her come in before we get the search warrant for Tink's place?"

"No, but I want to have the lineup ready the minute we get through searching his things."

****

Tracy's flight arrived at six-thirty-five Saturday evening, and not only was Jerry there to meet it, but Tom had gone too. Wendy's car had been in the shop, and she didn't have a way home, so Tom had to pick her up. By the time they got their special needs passengers off the plane and disarmed all the doors, it was nearly seven before they got off.

Tracy still didn't know about the big news Jerry had to tell her, and Jerry thought it would be really neat if he and Tracy and Wendy and Tom all went out to celebrate, so when the girls got off the plane Jerry told everybody what he would like to do. Wendy and Tracy looked at each other for a few seconds, and Tracy said, "That sounds like fun, but I need to go home and change first."

Wendy said, "No you don't. You look better than I do, and I'm going like I am. Tell her she looks good, Tom."

"You look good Tracy," Tom said.

Then Jerry said, "Well, that settles it. Let's go."

"Where are we going?" Tracy asked.

"Somewhere good and expensive. This will be my treat. We've got some celebrating to do. Tell you what; has anybody been to the King and Duke? I hear their food is great."

Nobody said they had been there, so Jerry asked, "Is that okay with everybody?" Everybody said that was fine with them, so after Jerry and Tom got their directions straight they got into their two cars and headed downtown.

As soon as they started their car Tracy asked Jerry, "Honey, you said we have some celebrating to do; what are we celebrating?"

"I'll tell you when we get to the restaurant. I've already told Tom, but I want Wendy to hear it too."

Curiosity was about to get the best of her and she asked, "Is it about White Rock?"

"I'll tell you when we get to the restaurant."

"Did you get your financing?"

"I'll tell you when we get to the restaurant, now stop asking questions, Nosey. By the way, Sweetie, I'm glad you're home; I missed you."

"I missed you too."

In about twenty minutes they arrived at the King and Duke. When they pulled into the parking lot a Valet opened the door for them and gave them a ticket to identify their car when they were ready to leave. He then disappeared with their cars.

After they were seated at their table inside the restaurant they were given huge menus to look at. There were surprisingly few items on such large menus, but Jerry guessed that at a place like that, outside of the food, appearances meant everything.

While they perused the menu, a waiter brought each of them a Margarita to sip on while they decided what they were going to eat. Wendy and Tracy decided to have Mahi, Mahi with bacon wrapped scallops and Tom and Jerry both chose the Prime Rib Eye as their main courses. Jerry and Wendy ordered Crab Dip appetizers and Tom and Tracy ordered Calamari.

Jerry was by no means a penny-pincher, but doing some quick

calculations in his head, he figured he had already spent over seventy-five dollars, and they hadn't even gotten to the main course. It looked as if it was going to be at least a three hundred dollar meal, or maybe more. Then he thought, *who cares? It's worth any price to celebrate with my wife and friends after what's happened this week. It would be worth a thousand dollars if I had another week like this one.* He took a final sip of his Margarita and asked, "Is everybody ready for another one?"

Tom and Wendy said they were, but Tracy said she was still good. After Jerry ordered more drinks Tracy said, "I thought we were coming out here to celebrate something, but you still haven't told us what it is."

"Oh right. Honey; remember me telling you who Frank Thomas is, and that I thought he might help me on my projects. Well, I met with him, Thursday, and he gave me the final go-ahead on the financing for the White Rock Estates neighborhood plus I got a job to build the sixty-four unit, high-end apartment complex I told you about with the likelihood of building more if they like the first ones. What's happened this week can set us up for life, and to me it's worth celebrating."

"Wow. I can see why. I'm very proud of you, Big Boy."

"Thanks. I'm kinda proud of me, too."

Wendy offered her congratulations as well and made a suggestion. "You know, tonight's celebration is wonderful, but how would you fellows like to extend it to somewhere like Paris or Lisbon or Rome? Tracy and I can get all of us tickets and it shouldn't cost so much with the plane fare paid for. How about it?"

Tom said, "What do you think, Jerry?"

"I think that would be wonderful, but it looks like I'm going to be tied down for quite a while. I don't see how I can get away."

Wendy said, "We're not talking about a long, extended vacation. We're only talking about three or four days at the most. You could work that, couldn't you? We could more than likely schedule it to coincide with a weekend so you really wouldn't lose more than a couple of days."

"When are you talking about?"

"I don't know; soon."

"Let me check and see what all I have to do." He looked at Tracy and asked, "Sweetie, is this something you'd like?"

"I'd love it. See what you can do, okay?"

"Okay."

During the lull after that conversation, their food was brought, and everybody got serious about eating. Tracy reached over to Jerry with a scallop on her fork and said, "Try this."

He ate it and said, "Wow, that's really good. That's what I'm going to order the next time I come here. Man, that's good. How's your steak, Tom?"

"Great. You can cut it with a fork."

They finished their meal while enjoying each other's company, and finally the evening ended and they went home with Jerry promising to try to work out a trip to Europe soon.

****

The search warrant was ready a little before noon Monday morning, and as soon as they got it they headed toward Tink's house. That time, Tink's wife was home, and they talked at length with her before presenting the warrant. When they showed her the search warrant, they immediately went out to the garage to look in the big box, but when they got out there the box was gone.

Going back to the front door, Grey rang the bell, and when Mrs. Key answered the bell he asked her, "Mrs. Key, Saturday, when we were here there was a large box in the garage that was covered with orange carpet, but it's not there this morning. Do you know where it could be?"

"No, I don't know anything about it. I think Tink uses it in his work. He must have taken it with him this morning."

"Do you know where he's working today?"

"No, he didn't say, but you can ask Henry Morton; he can tell you."

"May I use your phone?"

"I suppose, but I feel like I'm betraying my husband by cooperating with you."

"No. Mrs. Key. What you're doing is helping us find out who kidnapped and raped a little sixteen-year-old girl."

She had a terrified look on her face and didn't say anything, and Grey looked up the phone number in the directory. He dialed the number and when someone answered on the other end; he asked to speak to Henry.

Mr. Morton answered by saying, "Henry Morton, can I help you?"

"Good morning, Mr. Morton. Grey Yokley."

"Good morning, Sergeant."

"Mr. Morton, can you please tell me where Tink Key is working this morning?"

"Yeah, he's out at Pine Ridge doing a job."

"Would you mind giving me the address?"

"Hold on a minute; I'll have to look it up." He put the phone down and looked through the work orders and then picked it up and said, "Sergeant, he's at 1232 Pine Ridge Road, and I'd say he'll be there most of the day. Anything else I can help you with?"

"No, that's all; thank you very much."

They looked at a county map until they found Pine Ridge Road and then got in the car and headed that way. When they found 1232, they pulled in the driveway next to Tink's van. There was a clear view through the side-glass on the front door, and looking through it they saw Tink. Opening the door, they walked in and went back to where he was and Grey told him, "Hi Tink. We want to look through your van again, and we have brought a search warrant with us. Is it unlocked?"

Yeah, it's unlocked. What do you think you're going to find? It's just like it was the last time you looked through it."

Ignoring his question, the two detectives turned and went out the front door to the van. Fred opened the rear door and said, "Grey, look what I found."

There was the big box. They took samples of the yarn from the carpet that covered the inside and outside of the box and bagged it. Then they took samples of yarn from other parts of the van and bagged them as well.

While looking through tools and other things in the van, Fred happened upon a length of rope. "Hey Grey, do you think they can get DNA off a rope? You know, Tammy said that Tink tied a rope around her neck when she got out to use the bathroom. Well, here's a piece of rope that could be the one he used. Want me to bag it?"

"Yeah, it might be important."

Thinking that the yarn was really all they were looking for, they kept discovering additional pieces of what they thought was evidence. Grey happened to see a small to medium sized box that

Tink must have used as a trash can. He went through it and among other things, he found a couple of McDonald's coffee cups as well as wrappers from two Egg McMuffins. He yelled, "Fantastic!!"

Fred looked up and asked, "Why did you say that? Did you find something?"

"Remember Tammy saying that the morning after he kidnapped her he stopped on the way to the rape scene and bought them breakfast? Remember she said he gave her an Egg McMuffin and a cup of coffee? Well look what I just found." He held up the cups and wrappers and asked, "Do you have any bags with you that will hold these?"

"No, but I'll get one out of the car. This is unbelievable. Wanna bet that Tammy's DNA is all over them?"

And finally, down deep in the box that held the cups and wrappers, Grey saw something wadded up that looked almost like a credit card. He pulled it out of the box, straightened it out and looked at it. When he turned it over, it was a Lake Vista High School identification card with the name Tammy Mills on the front.

Grey said, "Let's get these back to Headquarters. We can talk to Tink's wife and go through his garage later."

After finding all those things Fred asked, "Grey, why don't we just arrest him now; while we're out here?"

"No; not yet. I want to have Tammy identify him out of a lineup before we arrest him."

Before they left they went back into the house and told Tink they were through and Grey asked him, "Tink is there anything you want to tell us before we go?"

"No; I have no idea what you're trying to find out from me. No; I don't have anything to say."

Grey and Fred left and started back to the Police station, and they were both as excited as a kid who had just got a new pony for Christmas. They could hardly wait to get there.

After they turned in the things they found in Tink's van, it was almost lunchtime, so before going to Tink's house, it was decided that a burger and shake would be in order.

While they were at the Steak and Shake, they talked about all the stuff they found in Tink's van and how *cut and dried* the case should be. Grey said, "We should have the results from the DNA tests by this time tomorrow. I'm going to call Tammy's mother and tell her we want her to bring Tammy down in the morning to look at a photo lineup. If she identifies him and the DNA on the things we found in the van matches hers, we'll arrest him tomorrow afternoon."

"Do you want to do that before we talk to Tink's wife?"

"I think so; don't you? If Tammy identifies him and her DNA is in his van, do you think we really need to talk to her?"

"I guess not."

By the time they got back to the station it was mid-afternoon. Since they had turned in all the evidence they had for DNA testing, and since they had to wait until the next day to see Tammy's reaction to the photo lineup they spent a little while reviewing what they had and what they were going to do and then went home.

Eight o'clock was considered starting time every morning, and both detectives were at their desks a little early, anxious to see the results of their hard work on the Tammy Mills rape case. Finally at nine-fifteen Grey's phone rang and it was the Forensics Lab.

"Hi Grey. This is David."

"Good morning David. Have you got some results for me?"

"I do, and you're going to like what I found."

"Great; lay it on me."

"This was really easy, Grey. The fibers that were found on the victim's clothes and in her hair all matched one or more of the fibers that you and Fred brought to us, so it looks as if without a doubt she was in that van."

"That's great. Thank you, David."

"You're welcome. I hope you nail that guy. You know, I've got a sixteen-year-old girl, and I don't know what I'd do if something like this happened to her."

"Don't worry; we're going to get him; maybe today."

"Good. See ya Grey."

"See ya."

A little after ten the DNA Lab called. "Hello, this is Detective Yokley. May I help you?"

"Good morning Grey; this is Casey. How ya doin?"

"I'm great Casey. Have you got some good news for me this morning?"

"I have great news. The DNA on the samples that the hospital rape kit obtained and the DNA from the coffee cup and other things you gave us all matched that of one Thomas Nelson Key."

"Fantastic. Thanks Casey."

Grey hung up the phone and turned to Fred and said, "We got him Fred. Let's get Tammy in here."

He dialed Barbara Mills number and told her she needed to bring Tammy in immediately to look at some pictures and possibly identify her abductor.

"Really? We'll be there just as soon as I can pick her up and get there. Thank you so much."

It wasn't long before Barbara and Tammy arrived at the Police Station and were welcomed by Grey and Fred.

Grey said, "Tammy, we have some pictures we would like for you to look at and pick out anyone that you might recognize. Can you do that for me?"

"Yeah, I guess so."

A photo lineup had been prepared for her that consisted of two pages. There were twelve pictures on each page with Tink's on the second page next to a picture of an almost look-alike undercover detective.

"Okay, Tammy, sit right here and look at these pictures. Take your time and if you see anyone here that you recognize, point him out to me, okay?"

"Okay."

She began with the first page and didn't see anyone she knew, and then Grey turned to the second page, and hardly before she looked at any of them she pointed out Tink and said, "That's Tink right there."

"Are you absolutely sure Tammy?"

"Do you think I would spend all that time with somebody doing terrible things to me without knowing what they looked like? Of course I'm sure. That's Tink. Do you know where he is?"

"Yeah, we know where he is, and we're going to arrest him. Thank you for your help, Tammy. You can go now, and we'll be in touch."

Chapter Eight

As soon as Tammy and her mother left the station, Grey said, "Fred, let's go get this Low-Life."

"I'm ready."

They didn't know where he was, so they called Henry Morton to find out. "Mr. Morton, this is Detective Yokley. How are you today?"

"I'm fine. Are you still after Tink?"

"Not for long. Mr. Morton, do you know where we can find him today?"

"Yeah, he's doing a job out on Westwood Avenue. Do you know where that is?"

"We can find it. Thanks. Mr. Morton, I think I should to tell you that we're going to arrest Tink, and it's unlikely he'll be back at work for a long time."

"Are you serious? What did he do?"

"Mr. Morton, it looks like he kidnapped and raped a sixteen-year-old girl."

"That's unbelievable. Detective Yokley, Tink's a married man. Are you sure?"

"Yes sir. We're sure."

"Would you do me a favor?"

"If I can. What is it?"

"He should be finished with the job he's on by two-thirty or three o'clock. Could you possibly wait until he's finished with it before you arrest him? The mill was late getting the carpet to us and the customer has threatened to cancel, and they will if we leave the job only half done. If you will wait until he gets through, I will greatly appreciate it."

"Yes sir. I guess we can do that."

"Thank you very much. Do you think he'll be able to get out on bail?"

"No sir; I seriously doubt it. He committed a very serious crime. Of course, I'm not the judge or jury, but it's my gut feeling that he won't be getting out—ever."

Henry said he thought Tink would be through with the job he was on by two-thirty or three o'clock, so Grey and Fred drove out to Westwood Avenue and got there around one-forty-five, just in case he got through early. They saw his van and drove down the street about a hundred yards where they parked and waited for him to come out.

At ten minutes 'til three they saw him come out of the house where he had been working and immediately started their car so they could go arrest him. Then Fred said, "Grey, why don't we follow him to Morton Flooring and arrest him there? If we arrest him here, we'll have to have his van towed, and if we arrest him at Morton's it'll save his wife a little bit by not having to pay for a towing bill."

"Good idea, Fred. Let's do it that way."

They watched closely while he loaded up his tools and a couple of bags of scrap carpeting and followed at a distance until he pulled into the parking lot at Morton Flooring. As soon as he parked and got out of the van the two detectives pulled up beside him, and Grey said, "Hi Tink. Finished for the day?"

"Yeah, and I'm just about worn out. What are you fellows doing here. Aren't you getting tired of following me around?"

"Yeah, kinda, but this is the last time we'll have to do it. Tink, you're under arrest for the kidnapping and rape of Tammy Mills. Turn around and put your hands behind you."

"Are you serious?"

"We're very serious."

Fred took a piece of paper out of a small folder in his pocket and began reading. "Thomas Key, you have the right to remain silent. Anything you say can and will be used against you in a court of law. You have the right to an attorney. If you cannot afford an attorney, one will be appointed. Do you understand these rights?"

"Yeah, I understand them."

When he finished reading him his rights, they put him into the back of their car.

When they reached Police Headquarters, they took him inside and began the process of booking him.

Tink asked, "Can I call my wife?"

Fred answered, "In a little while, when we finish."

They fingerprinted him, took his picture, gave him some prison clothes and told him to change into them. When they finished everything they had to do to book him they let him use the phone. Instead of calling a lawyer, he called his wife.

"Hello."

"Ryan, Honey, I'm in jail and I need for you to call a lawyer."

"You're in jail? What did you do?"

"They think I kidnapped and raped a young girl. Will you call a lawyer for me?"

"Did you do it Tink?"

"You know me better than that. No I didn't do it. Now, will you call me a lawyer?"

"I don't know one; do you?"

"Not really. I guess you can look in the yellow pages or better yet; call Jenn and see if she knows one. Just please try to find one and have them come get me out of here."

"Why do they think you kidnapped someone?"

"I don't know. They've been harassing me for about a week now. When I get out I may sue 'em."

"Okay; let me get off so I can try to find someone. Where can I call you?"

"I doubt if they'll let me get any calls. When you find a lawyer, tell him I'm at the Douglasville Police Department. He'll probably have be the one to contact me, and oh yeah; Ryan, I love you."

"I love you too."

There was a pause, and then Tink said, "Hey Ryan, I just thought of something."

"What?"

"You know if we hire an attorney it will cost us a lot of money, but if we tell them we can't afford one and can get the Court to appoint one, we won't have to pay anything. Some of those guys charge as much as six hundred dollars an hour, and we sure can't afford that. I think we probably can qualify for one. They told me I have to go to Court in the morning, so don't try to find anybody. I'll just tell them we can't afford a lawyer and let them appoint one for me."

"Are you sure? What if they don't give you a good one?"

"It won't matter. I'm innocent and all I have to do is tell the truth, and they'll let me go. He won't have to be Perry Mason."

"Okay; if you're sure."

Trying to hide his fear from Ryan and not wanting her to hear all the charges against him, he said, "Ryan, Honey, I think maybe you shouldn't come to Court in the morning They're going to try to make me look as bad as they can, and there's no telling what they're going to say, so I just wish you wouldn't come and hear all that. You need to be home for the kids anyway, don't you?"

"Well, I need to be with them, but I need to be with you, too. I'll have to think about it."

"Okay Baby; they're making me get off the phone, so I'll talk to you later. Love you."

"Love you, too," and they hung up.

When they had finished talking, a very large man who looked to be around six-feet-four and weighing about two hundred and sixty pounds came to get him and escorted him to a supply room where he was told to pick up a mattress and then took him back inside the jail to a cell where the man locked the door. Tink had never been in jail before, but had watched a lot of detective and crime TV shows and movies, and when the jailor closed the door and locked it, the sound was unlike anything he had ever heard on a program. It was terrifying.

After an hour or so the giant Jailor came to his cell to get him, and he took him back up to the Detectives who had arrested him.

Tink was a fairly nice-looking guy and had a good personality, but knowing what he did to Tammy made Fred and Grey look at him with contempt.

Grey said, "Hi Tink. Are you settled in?"

"I guess."

Being very sarcastic, he asked, "Are your accommodations comfortable? Do you need anything?"

"Yeah; I need to go home."

"Well, I'm afraid that's not in the cards right now. Tink, Detective Melwiki and I need to ask you a few questions about the time you spent with Tammy Mills."

"I'm not answering anything until I see a lawyer."

"Do you have a lawyer?"

"No, not yet."

"Didn't you call one when you used the phone earlier?"

"No, I called my wife."

"Is she going to get you a lawyer?"

"No, we don't know any and besides, we can't afford one."

"Well, you've got to have one. Is the Court going to have to appoint one for you?"

"I guess. I can't afford one; I know that."

Since he said he wanted a lawyer, according to law, the Detectives couldn't question him, so they called the jailor and had him take him back to his cell.

His cell had two bunks, but there was no one else in there with him until late that night. He was scared just being in jail, but he began to calm down a little after they served him his supper. He missed eating at the regular dinner time because he was being booked, so they had to bring his food to him later.

His meal consisted of what was supposed to be chicken with rice, about two spoonsful of cold green beans, a cold, dry piece of bread, and a small plastic cup of Jello. He took one bite of the chicken and spit it out and did the same with the green beans. He managed to get the rice down, and after nearly choking on the bread he ate the Jello. He put the tray on the small desk and waited for someone to come get it which they did soon after he finished with it.

He heard a lot of men talking, yelling, and laughing somewhere and thought there must be a place where the inmates went to socialize, but he hoped he wouldn't have to; he just wanted to stay in his cell by himself. No one ever came to offer to take him to where the others were, so he just sat on his bunk and thought about what was going to happen to him. Finally, he laid down and after what seemed like forever he drifted off to sleep.

After about two or three hours of fitful dozing, he was awakened by the large jailor opening the cell door and ushering an extremely mean-looking character into the cell.

Tink raised up and said, "Hi, I'm Tink," and the man just grunted.

He asked the man, "What's your name?"

"Tony." Then Tony said, "Buddy, you're going to have to move. I can't sleep on the top bunk."

"Sorry, I can't either," Tink replied.

"Well, you had better learn how. Get your ass up and get on top. I really don't feel like having to fight with you right now. I'm tired, drunk, and sick, and I want to go to bed, so get your ass up."

Tink looked him in the eye and realized he probably was no

71

match for him and conceded. He got up, pulled his mat from the lower bunk and put it on the top one. Without a word he climbed up on top and laid down and wondered if he did the right thing. He was no push-over himself, but when he looked at Tony he realized that there are people that shouldn't be messed with, and Tony looked to be one of those.

As he lay there he tried not to dwell on his encounter with Tony, but instead he thought about what was going to happen to him the next day. *Will they get me a lawyer first thing? Will he or she be any good? Will Ryan be there? Boy, I miss her. I don't see how they can prove I'm guilty since I was with her and the kids the night they say the kidnapping took place. Think positive, Tink. It'll all work out.*

In the midst of all his thinking, he drifted off to sleep and slept until they woke him up at five o'clock the next morning. Through the door the jailor yelled, "On your feet. Breakfast in thirty minutes."

Tony mumbled, "I'm gonna sleep in this morning. Call me later."

The jailor opened the cell door and walked over to Tony's bunk and yanked the cover off of him and said, "I said on your feet. Breakfast is now in twenty-five minutes. You don't want to be put in Isolation on your first day here at the spa, do you Tony?"

"Naw, I guess not. Okay, I'm getting up."

The jailor looked at Tink and said, "Key, you've got a Court date at ten thirty. You'll have to ride with the others when they go and the van will leave here at seven forty-five. Be ready."

At five-twenty-five they came to get Tink and Tony to escort them to the dining room where there were eight tables with eight seats at each one. Tony acted as if he would be Tink's friend and look after him, and Tink was grateful for that because there weren't any nice people in the place, and he was glad to have an ally. He found out from Tony that he, Tony, had spent over half his adult life in jail and had built up a reputation of being one tough individual.

The prisoners filed into the dining room in single file, sixteen at a time, and took their seats. White prisoners sat together as did Blacks and Hispanics. The Blacks were called Mayates, and each group was careful to sit with their own. If a seat was empty at a table and say a White prisoner had to sit at a Black table, he was careful to not even ask someone to pass the salt or anything else. Failure to keep that distance could result in a serious fight.

Going through the line, each man picked up a tray and went through the serving line. Someone had put a sign behind the servers that said *Eggs Benedict*, but they looked like instant eggs that someone had attempted to cook. Whatever they were, they were inedible. In addition to the eggs benedict, there was a small helping of grits, a piece of fried bologna, a piece of dry toast, and a pre-packed butter and jelly. The coffee tasted like it was brewed with grounds that had been in the pot for several days with new grounds added each day, but as pretty much a coffee addict, Tink managed to drink it. It reminded him of old episodes of *Gunsmoke* that he'd seen where Chester made the coffee at the jail and always made it with old grounds and just added new ones on top of them each time.

In a few minutes the guards told everyone in Tink's group of sixteen that it was time to go back, so they got up and walked single-file again back to their cells. Once there, Tink and Tony managed to engage in conversation, and Tink found that Tony was not such a bad guy after all; in fact, he was glad he found him.

The prisoners that had to go to Court were handcuffed and led to a door at the rear of the jail, and at precisely seven forty-five the van pulled out and headed to the Courthouse. Six prisoners; four men and two women had Court appointments, and they were all put in holding cells inside the Courthouse until their turn to go before a judge.

Their crimes varied from shoplifting to armed robbery to kidnapping and rape, for which Tink was being accused. His crime was by far the worst of the six, and his appointment was scheduled for last because it would more than likely take quite a while for the arraignment.

The cases in front of him finished early, and the court clerk called him early; actually at nine-thirty. When he walked into the courtroom, to his horror there sat Ryan, his wife. Even though she was his wife, he was embarrassed for her to hear all that he was being accused of. The clerk read the charges against him, and the first question the judge asked him was, "Young man, are you already represented by an attorney?"

Tink replied, "No sir."

"Do you want to apply for a court-appointed lawyer?"

"Yes sir."

Then the judge paused while he looked over the spectators in the room and asked, "Are there any attorneys present?" Two men and one woman raised their hands.

Judge Oliver looked at the woman and asked, "Ms. Ashman, will your case-load allow you to take an additional case?"

"Yes, your honor."

"Very well, step forward."

She got up out of her seat and walked to the front of the courtroom, and Judge Oliver introduced her to Tink. He then said, "Mr. Key, Ms. Ashman is very good at what she does, and I urge you to listen to her. The charges against you are very serious, and if you want to have any chance at all of winning your case, I advise you to listen to her."

He then addressed Ms. Ashman. "Ms. Ashman, are you free right now to assist Mr. Key with the balance of this arraignment?"

"Yes, your honor. I can help him."

"Do you need a short recess to discuss his plea and the charges against him?"

"That would be a big help, your honor."

"Would twenty minutes be enough?"

"Yes sir, that should be plenty."

"Very well. Court is in recess until ten fifteen."

Tink and his new attorney went into a small room off the courtroom to talk. A guard stood outside the door just in case Tink tried to get cute and run.

"My name is Regina Ashman," the attorney said to Tink. "What do you go by, Thomas?"

"No ma'am. Everybody calls me Tink," he answered.

"That's cool," she said. "Now tell me, Tink; how did you get in to this mess?"

"I'm not sure. Some girl was kidnapped and raped, and she said somebody called Tink did it. The Police think it was me, but I didn't do it."

"Do you have an alibi?"

"I do for the night she said she was held."

"Where were you that night?"

"I was with my wife and kids at a restaurant."

"Really?"

74

"Yeah. My wife can tell you."

"Did you tell that to the Police?"

"I did, and they checked with the restaurant, and the restaurant verified we were there, but they still charged me."

"Hmmm, there must be something else going on here. Well, let's see what we can do about this. The judge is going to ask you how you plead. What are you going you tell him?"

"I'm going to tell him I'm not guilty."

"Okay. We had better get back in there; it's almost ten fifteen."

When they returned to the courtroom the Assistant District Attorney was already back, but the judge hadn't returned yet. Tink and Regina took their seats, and in just a minute, the judge came in. The Bailiff told everybody to rise, and as soon as the judge was seated, everybody else was told to be seated.

The judge asked Regina, "Ms. Ashman, did you and your client discuss the charges against him and decide on a plea?"

"Yes, your honor."

"Very well. Mr. Key will you stand up, please?"

Tink stood up and Judge Oliver asked him, "Mr. Key, how do you plead?"

"Not guilty, sir."

Judge Oliver said, "Okay. Trial will be set for October twenty second. That's two months from today. Is that alright with you Ms. Ashman?"

"Yes sir. That will be fine."

"How about you, Mr. Bradford?"

"That's fine, your honor."

The Assistant District Attorney then stood up and said, "Your Honor, the people request no bail for the defendant."

At which time Regina said, "Your honor, the defense asks for a low bail. The defendant has no prior record, is gainfully employed, and is a happily married family man. He is definitely not a flight risk."

The ADA then said, "Your Honor, those things are well and good, but due to the seriousness of the charges, the people feel there is a definite risk of flight, and we ask for no bail."

The judge answered, "The Court tends to agree with you, Mr. Bradford. Bail will be set at five million dollars."

Tink's mouth fell open, and he looked at Regina in shock.

"Five million dollars? What does that mean?"

"It means you will have to pay ten percent of that amount to get out of jail. Have you got five hundred thousand dollars? If not, then I'm afraid you'll have to stay in jail. I'm sorry."

Chapter Nine

Tracy and Jerry had been discussing their future together and since they were both in their mid-thirties, they thought it would be best if they began trying to start a family right away. What brought the subject up was the fact that Tracy had an appointment with her Gynecologist for her annual checkup the following Friday.

She had to fly out the day after their discussion and was scheduled to be back on Thursday before her Doctor's appointment on Friday. She and Wendy had pretty much been able to work it out whereby they would always fly together and room together wherever they went. On that particular flight, they went back to Paris, and while there, they worked on a plan for the four of them; them and their husbands, to make the trip they had talked about earlier.

They scoured through brochures in the hotel lobby and talked to hotel employees that could speak English trying to find fun things to do when they brought Jerry and Tom with them.

Wendy said, "There are so many neat things to do here I don't think we need to have any set plans for when we all come, do you?"

"Probably not," Tracy said, and then she spotted something. "Look here, Wendy. Here's a package of three things that sound like a lot of fun. It's kind of expensive, but I think it would be worth it."

"What is it?"

"Let me read you what it says." She began with *Experience the romance of Paris with an unforgettable night out that combines three of the top tours in the City of Lights. Visit the iconic Eiffel Tower lit up against the night sky, and cruise down the Seine for a riverside view of the city's famous monuments. Choose from dinner at the tower's chic 58 Tour Eiffel restaurant or a gourmet meal aboard a dining cruise. Cap off the night with a Parisian cabaret show at the Moulin Rouge nightclub, complete with Champagne.*

"I don't know about you, but that sounds really good to me. What do you think? Do you think Tom would like to do something like that?"

"I know he would. Do you think Jerry would?"

"Probably; if he thinks I would like to. He tries to act as if he likes whatever I like, whether he does or not, but I feel sure he would like to do that."

"Okay then. Let's plan on it. We know enough other things to do that we can keep busy when we bring them. Besides, we don't have to be busy every minute while we're here. I want to have some quality time with my man when I bring him to a lover's paradise like this. Don't you agree?"

"I absolutely do. In fact; I'd rather spend more time with Jerry than anything else that Paris has to offer."

"Me too. I mean with Tom, though. I guess all we need to do now is set a date, right?"

"Yep. When we get back let's check our schedule."

As soon as the gals got back to Atlanta, they checked the calendar for their scheduled flights for the next month and found that they were not scheduled to fly anywhere for more than a week the second week of the month.

Wendy said, "That looks like a pretty good time to me. What do you think, Trace?"

"Looks good to me. Let's run it by the guys and see what they think."

They did, and after checking their schedules both guys said that would be good for them. Both were mildly excited, but neither was as excited as the girls were, but in order to show a sign of togetherness, they showed what they thought their wives wanted to see.

"Jerry, have you ever been to Europe?"

"No, have you? I've never been many places outside of the Southeast."

"Well, I've been to a lot of the states, but never out of the country. I'm kinda looking forward to going to France."

"I am too, but with all I've got coming up, business-wise, I'm having a hard time showing it."

"Well, it'll still be here when you get back."

"I know, but I just don't want to be thinking about it while I'm cruising down the Seine."

"Tracy will keep you too busy for that."

"You're probably right. It's going to be a great trip; I guess I'm just a little pre-occupied."

Early the next morning, Wendy called and asked, "Hey Trace,

have you got time to go to the airline office today to try and schedule our trip?"

"I might can this afternoon, but I've got a doctor's appointment this morning. Will this afternoon work?"

"I guess so. What time?"

"I should be through at the doctor's before noon, so I'd say any time after that."

"Would we be safe saying two o'clock?"

"I think so. You just want to meet at the office at two?"

"Yeah, let's do that."

"Okay, I'll see you then."

Everything worked out just right and when they went to the airline office, they were able to get their tickets and make all the arrangements for their trip.

****

Jerry went to his office Friday morning to work on the mountain of preliminary work having to do with the apartment complex he was going to build for Frank Thomas. Around ten o'clock his phone rang, and Beverly, his office girl answered it. He heard her say, "Yes, just a moment, please," and then she called him. "Jerry, it's Melissa from Frank Thomas's office."

Jerry picked up and said, "Good morning Melissa. What's happening?"

"Hi Handsome. I'm just staying busy. What's happening with you?"

"Well, right now I'm sitting here trying to see the top of this mountain of stuff I have to do in order to get started on Frank's apartment complex."

"It sounds to me like you need to relax a little. Maybe a drink would help after you get off this afternoon. Interested?"

"That sounds really good, but I think Tracy has some plans for us tonight. Maybe I'll have a drink wherever we go."

"Is Tom going with you?"

"Yeah, he and Wendy, his wife."

Coldly she said, "I really hope you all have a good time."

"I'm sure we will. Are you calling for Frank?"

"I am. Hold on a minute."

In just a few seconds Frank was on and said, "Jerry, hi. How're you doing?"

"I'm doing just great, Frank. I hope you are."

"I am. Listen, the reason I called is to ask you something. Have you ever heard of a program called *Off-Site Precision Layout Pro?*"

"No, I can't say that I have. What is it?"

"It might be something you'd be interested in taking a look at. It was developed by Charlie Simmons, one of my clients, and it looks like it would work when you get ready to layout the apartments."

"What does it do?"

"It's something you do on a computer. It takes blueprints and can someway layout an entire complex without having to use tape measures and run strings the way you have to do now in order to layout a building or buildings. Instead of having to use two or three men to do a job, you only have to have one, and it's unbelievably fast. With this thing you can have the whole job laid out while you're just thinking about what to do the old way.

David, the guy who invented it, is trying to get some financing from us, and he'll be here Monday. Would you want to come by and meet him and take a look at his program? I think you might be interested in using it."

"By all means. What time Monday?"

"Eleven o'clock. Will that work for you?"

"That's perfect. I'll see you Monday."

The weather was beautiful all weekend and Tracy and Jerry spent quite a bit if time Saturday doing some much needed chores, including skimming some of the ugly algae off the lake. Tracy couldn't let the weekend pass without spending some time with Cantress, so she saddled her up and took a ride around the farm when she and Jerry finished most of their chores.

A portion of the farm, around the house, was made into a yard or lawn, and either Jerry or the man who worked for him mowed it each week with a lawn mower. The remainder was bush hogged once every month or six weeks, and the entire farm looked like a picture in a magazine, especially the part around the horse pasture. The barn was faced with a pretty shade of vinyl siding and it looked like something straight out of House Beautiful. It certainly didn't look like a horse barn.

Saturday night they invited Jack over for supper. Tracy had found a deal on some filets, so they grilled them and had a baked potato and salad, and everyone enjoyed themselves. Jerry had become an expert with the grill. He liked his steaks medium-rare and Tracy liked hers medium, and he had learned how to make them come out just the way they liked them.

Ever since Tracy had begun to date Jerry, her Dad had been encouraging her to start back to church, but up to that point she had only gone with him occasionally. Jack left to go home a little after nine, and to his delight, Tracy told him that she and Jerry would meet him the next morning and attend church with him. She had been brought up to go to church every Sunday, but after she grew up and got out on her own, she didn't go as often as she should, and Jack was pleased that she and Jerry were going to come and go with him.

Jerry was pretty much in the same boat. He and his family went every Sunday, and he, like Tracy, sort of quit going after he got out on his own, and especially after he moved to Atlanta. He was converted as a teenager, and even though he had not been active in church for a while, he still considered himself to be a Christian.

Tracy, on the other hand, had never made a profession of faith, so she was going to be a little harder to get back in the swing of going to church than Jerry.

They met Jack outside the front door of the church the next morning and attended worship. After church they went to a great Mexican restaurant about three blocks from the church, and when they finished lunch Jack went home as did Tracy and Jerry. Sunday afternoons were pretty much reserved for naps at the Martin household, and after changing clothes and settling down in front of the TV, it wasn't long before they were both asleep.

Tracy woke up before Jerry, and while she was piddling around the house, she heard the little ring of Jerry's Text. He didn't hear it since he was asleep, so Tracy went over to see if she could tell who it was from. She didn't want to open it, so she just looked at the limited amount of message showing. The main thing she saw were the words *new number* and *Melissa*.

She couldn't understand why someone named Melissa would be sending him her number since she didn't know of anybody they knew named Melissa.

That Text remained in her mind until Jerry woke up. He didn't immediately check his phone, and she didn't want him to know that she peeked at it, so she didn't say anything. In a little bit she saw him pick up his phone and bring up the Text, but she still remained silent about it. After checking the Text, Jerry put the phone in his pocket and never did say anything about it, and Tracy's curiosity was about to get the best of her.

After the large lunch they had, they just wanted to snack for supper, so that's all they did. She had a bowl of cereal and Jerry fixed a peanut butter and jelly sandwich with a glass of milk.

They watched TV until around ten o'clock and then went to bed. The Text was never mentioned.

Jerry let Tracy sleep the next morning since she didn't have a flight. He shaved, showered and got dressed in nicer than usual clothes and left without even having a cup of coffee. He knew there would be coffee at his office, so he stopped and got a couple of steak biscuits and took them with him.

He had a meeting at eleven o'clock at Frank's office with Frank and a fellow named Charlie Simmons to see a computer layout program that Charlie had developed.

He arrived at the bank a little before eleven and went straight up to Frank's office. Charlie had come at ten o'clock since he had a meeting with Frank at that time, and Jerry assumed it had to do with the financing of Charlie's new invention, so he took a seat in the outer office with the receptionist. It wasn't but a couple of minutes until Melissa came and sat down with him.

"Hi. Did you just get here?"

"Hi, Melissa. Yeah, I just beat you by a minute or two. How're you doing?"

"Good. Did you have a good weekend?"

"It couldn't have been better. How about you?"

"Boring, just like all weekends. One of these days I'm going to find someone to help liven things up for me."

"Well, keep looking. You'll find him."

"I don't know about that. I need to find somebody like you. I'll bet you could really liven things up. Whatta ya think?"

"You've got the wrong guy, Melissa. I'm already spoken for."

Before the conversation could go on Frank's secretary told them they could go in.

Frank introduced Charlie to Melissa and Jerry, and Jerry was sort of surprised when Frank introduced him as *my partner*. He thought, *I hope he really does think of me as his partner*. Charlie seemed to be in a really good frame of mind, and Jerry thought, *this guy is too happy to have been refused his financing. Frank must have come through for him.*

Jerry was only average when it came to computers, and a lot of Charlie's stuff looked pretty much like Greek to him, but Melissa seemed to pick up on it immediately. After a lengthy demonstration by Charlie, and after several times letting Jerry try some of the exercises himself, Frank asked, "Jerry, what do you think?" "I don't know. Seeing Charlie do all this makes it look simple, but when I do it, it shows you what a dummy I am when it comes to computers, and I think there are probably more people like me than there are like Charlie. I'll have to think long and hard before I'm ready to spend all that money on something I'm not sure I can operate."

Frank asked, "What about that, Charlie?"

"Jerry it's really not hard. I'm sure you can do it with just a little practice."

Jerry replied, "Charlie, you're probably right, but I have got so much on my plate right now, I don't have the time to spend practicing a new computer program."

Frank interrupted with, "Melissa, you seemed to understand what Charlie was doing. Did you?"

"Yes sir. It looks fairly simple to me."

"Do you think you could operate the system?"

"I'm pretty sure I can."

Frank said, "Tell you what Charlie; let the three of us talk about it and I'll call you. I've got to say I like it, but I'm not a construction guy and Jerry is. Give us some time to kick it around a little and we'll be back in touch."

Then Charlie said, "Mr. Thomas, I understand where Jerry is coming from on this. You've got to remember that I'm a contractor, too, and this is why I created this."

"Jerry, if you decide you want to buy this, I'll either come myself or send someone to work with you and stay with you however long it takes until you're comfortable with the program. I promise you that once you get used to it you will wonder how you ever got along without it, and it's going to save you a ton of money."

Once more Frank said, "We'll talk about it and I'll be in touch with you."

"Okay. Thank you, Mr. Thomas, Jerry, Melissa. It has been a genuine pleasure. Jerry, don't let this pass you by. You're soon to be one of the largest and best contractors in this part of the country from what I hear, and you need this program."

"Okay Charlie, I'll think about it, and like Frank said, we'll be in touch. It was nice meeting you."

After Charlie left, and Jerry and Melissa were still in Frank's office, Frank said, "Jerry, as a financial guru, it sometimes takes a lot to convince me that something is really worthwhile and worth investing in, but I'm convinced that Charlie's program is all it's cracked up to be. I hope you'll seriously consider buying it.

"Charlie said that you'll soon be one of the largest contractors in the country, and he's right. I haven't said anything about what I'm about to say to anyone; not even Melissa, but my partners and I are going to begin construction on a large, a very large shopping mall in the near future, and we want you to be our General Contractor. Are you interested?"

His mouth flew open, and he said, "Am I interested? You bet I'm interested. I've never built anything of that magnitude, but my Dad has, and I know he would be happy to join forces with me to build you the biggest and best shopping mall in Georgia. Yes sir; I'm very interested."

"Who is your Dad," Frank asked.

"Bob Martin in Chattanooga. Have you ever heard of The Shepherd Apparel Group?"

"Everybody has heard of Shepherd Apparel."

"Well, he built all of their plants except the original one plus just about everything else the Shepherds have in addition to many other large commercial projects in East Tennessee and North Georgia and Alabama. If you look up General Contractor in the dictionary, you'll probably see his picture."

"That's interesting. So you're a chip off the old block."

"I guess you could say that. When you get ready, I'll ask him to come down and let you meet him; that is, unless you would rather he not be involved in the build.

"Oh no; that's fine. If you would feel more comfortable having him with you, that's fine. Just remember that it's you we'll be looking to as the *Head Honcho.*"

"I understand, but he has so much more experience than I do I would really like to have him as a backup."

"If he has as much on the ball as you do, we'll be lucky to have him."

"Thank you. By the way; I don't think you said where the mall is going to be."

"We have bought two hundred acres in Douglas County and plan to build it over there. Our plans now are to have it compare, size wise, to the Mall of Georgia over in Gwinnett County. Our friend Melissa here will hire people who have access to the largest retailers in the country to, hopefully, bring them in to our mall."

"What will be the name of it?"

"It's not set in stone yet, but we're thinking it will be *Douglas Mills.*"

"Good name. I like that."

Frank said, "As you know from being a builder, there are many things to be done before construction can start, even on a small project, so while we're going *full-steam ahead*, it will be a while before the first nail is driven. Jerry, this might be the perfect project for something like Charlie Simmons Lay Out thing."

They talked for a few more minutes and Jerry looked at his watch. It showed ten after twelve, and he asked Frank, "How about some lunch, Frank?"

"Thanks, but I promised to go eat barbeque with my wife and one of her friends. Can I have a raincheck?"

"You sure can. I've got plenty to do, and I need to get back to my office, so maybe I'll just grab a take out and go back and eat at my desk. Do we need to meet again this week?"

"I don't know yet. If we do I'll have Melissa give you a call."

"Sounds good. I'll see you later, and Frank, I guess I'll get one of Charlie's Lay Out things if I can get someone to work with me on it."

Melissa piped up and said, "I'll help you," and Frank said, "There you go; problem solved."

That wasn't what he wanted to hear, but he had already opened his mouth, and was trapped.

Melissa then said, "I don't have to meet Frank's wife, so I'm free. You want to have lunch with me? I enjoyed the Olive Garden when we went there before. Why don't we go there? It shouldn't take too long. I know you've got a lot to do."

Trying to be agreeable and diplomatic he said, "Okay, let's go," and they hopped into her sexy gray BMW and took off.

While they were in the restaurant, they had just begun to eat when Jerry looked up and coming toward him was Tracy and Wendy. He was just thankful that Melissa didn't have her hands on him and hoped Tracy didn't see her put her hands on his a few minutes earlier.

"Hi Sweetheart, hi Wendy. Want some lunch? Oh, Trace, this is Melissa Morris. She is Frank Thomas's Assistant. Melissa, this is my wife Tracy and our friend Wendy Sharpe. You all sit down. Have you had lunch?"

Tracy said, "Yeah, we had what you're having. I wish we had seen you in time; you could have bought our lunch."

In their years of being Flight Attendants, they had been trained to smile regardless of the circumstances, and they did a beautiful job of doing that, but under Tracy's smile she was thinking back to the text she saw on Jerry's phone the afternoon before as well as wondering what he was doing sitting there having lunch with Melissa.

They talked for just a couple more minutes and then Tracy and Wendy got ready to leave. Tracy told Jerry as she was leaving, "Don't eat too much; we'll probably have to eat out tonight. Wendy is wearing me out, and I'll probably be too tired to cook."

"That's fine. We'll go somewhere. This soup and salad will be gone by supper time. Besides, I have more good news to tell you."

Melissa said, "Tracy, it was sure nice meeting you, and Wendy, it was nice meeting you too."

Tracy and Wendy responded with similar comments and left the restaurant. Tracy was quiet after their encounter, and Wendy said, "Boy, you've got quiet all of a sudden. What's wrong?"

"Oh nothing."

"Nothing my foot; this is Wendy you're talking to. Now tell me what's wrong."

In an irritable voice she said, "I said nothing is wrong."

"Whoa. Have it your way, but I know better."

"It's that girl with Jerry. I don't know about her. Yesterday afternoon, while he was asleep, she sent him a text giving him her new phone number and now she's with him at Olive Garden. Did you see her put her hand on his at the restaurant?"

"No, I didn't see them at all until we ran into them as we were leaving."

"Why would she text him on Sunday if she knew she was going to see him on Monday? It doesn't make sense."

"Well Tracy, Jerry said she is somebody's assistant. Who is Frank?"

"He's the head of the bank and the one that's giving him all that business I was telling you about."

"Well if she's his assistant, then their lunch must have to do with business; don't you think?"

"I hope you're right. Come on, let's go to the Mall. Dillard's is having a big shoe sale."

"I know I'm right. I know Jerry even better than you do, and I know he wouldn't do anything to mess up his relationship with you, so just relax, okay?" She paused and then said, "I don't need any shoes."

"Well I do, so come on. You'll probably find something you like."

Melissa and Jerry finished their lunch a couple of minutes after Tracy and Wendy left, and Melissa drove Jerry back to his car. The meeting with Jerry's wife calmed her down some, and there was virtually no flirting on the way back. She parked in her parking space and they got out. She said, "Jerry, thanks for lunch. I enjoyed it. We'll have to do it again."

Jerry replied, "I'm sure we will. I enjoyed it too."

He walked to his pickup and drove straight to his office. As soon as he went to the rest room, he went into his office and picked up the phone. He heard it ringing and on the other end a voice answered, "Good afternoon; Martin Construction Company."

Jerry said, "Hi Kelli, it's Jerry. Is my Dad there?"

"He is. Hold on a minute, Jerry."

Bob picked up and said, "Whatta ya say, Jer?"

"Hi Dad. How're ya doing?"

"I'm good. Since you're calling me in the middle of the day maybe I should be the one asking how are you doing, so, "How're you doing?"

"I couldn't be better."

"How's my beautiful daughter-in-law?"

"She's great. We want to get up there as soon as we can, but things are so busy right now, I don't know when that will be. And that's why I'm calling, Dad. I'm hoping you can help me on a huge job that I just got this morning."

"What in the world is it?"

"Do you remember me telling you that I got the financing on my proposed White Rock Estates neighborhood that I've been wanting to build, and that that led to my getting a job to build a large high-end apartment complex."

"Yeah, I remember."

"Well, this morning I had a meeting with Frank Thomas, the banker that did the other things, and he told me that he and his partners are going to build a huge shopping mall, and they want me to be their General Contractor. Dad, I've never built anything anywhere near this magnitude, and I told Frank that I would like to get you to help me, and he said I could. I'm just hoping that you might have some time that you can at least help me get started and give me advice on things I don't know about. Will you help me, Dad?"

There was silence on Bob's end of the phone for several seconds and Jerry asked, "Dad, are you there?"

"I'm here. I'm just thinking. Of course I'll help you any way I can, but I will need a whole lot more information. When do you think you'll know more?"

"I don't know. This was just sprung on me this morning. I'd say I won't know anything much for at least a week, and it could be as long as a month. This is going to be a really large mall. Frank indicated that it would be equal to if not larger than the Mall of Georgia, over in Gwinnett County, which is the largest in Georgia."

"Well, I'd say you've hit the jackpot with this Frank Thomas. How did you find him?"

"That's an interesting story. Do you remember a year or so ago when some kids seriously damaged one of my houses?

"I remember."

"Well, there were two sixteen-year-old boys and a fifteen-year-old girl, and the amount of damage made it a felony. I felt sorry for them, and the Lord made me feel that I should help them, so I was able to convince the judge to let them work out the damages by working at some of my houses until their sentences were paid, and this has been going on now for over a year. Their parents were extremely grateful because their felony conviction will be wiped out when they finish.

"Now here's the part that lets you know that the Lord works in mysterious ways. As you know, I've been trying to get my neighborhood financed for more than a year, and the other week the guy I've been working with at the bank told me that the amount of money I wanted was above his authorization, and I would have to talk to someone higher in rank than him. Well sir, he set up an appointment for me to meet Frank Thomas, who is the CEO of the bank. I had met Frank the night the kids were arrested and then again at the kids' trial, but I didn't have any idea that he was Chairman of the bank. When I walked into his office and saw him I nearly fainted.

"I made my presentation to him and he approved the financing based on my figures and the presentation, but his gratitude for my helping his son didn't hurt either. The reason I got the apartment job was because he knows the apartments I built somewhere else and was impressed with the quality and workmanship."

"That's quite a story. I'd like for you to tell it to Monty Shepherd sometime; he would like that."

"I'll be glad to tell him. Have him give me a call. Okay, Dad, I feel much better knowing you will help me on the mall. I'll let you get back to work, and I'll call you the minute I know more, okay?"

"Okay Son. I love you."

"Love you too."

Chapter Ten

There were only two weeks remaining until the two couples' big trip to Paris, and Jerry was working like a mad man to get things done before he had to leave. It was hard for him to get excited about the trip due to the extra ordinary amount of work that had to be done, but when he thought about how thrilled Tracy was about going, he pushed on.

One thing that took a huge load off his mind was when he met with the Douglas County Water Authority; he was told that the County would run water and sewer lines to his White Rock Estates neighborhood, and that eliminated a major obstacle in the start-up process of the project.

He had taken a set of blueprints to one of the large surveying companies in the Atlanta area, and they were getting ready to begin surveying and lining out where each house was to go. The plans were to begin with two houses; one a model home and the other a nice spec home equal in appearance and style as the model home.

At the same time, all the permits and other *red-tape* items had come through for the apartment complex, and Frank was beginning to push him to get started on it. Receipt of the permits brought up something that he wasn't dreading, but not looking forward to either, and that was having to make a decision on the Off-Site Precision Layout Pro. He talked to Frank about it and told him he was going to call Charlie Simmons, and that seemed to please him.

"When are you going to call him?' Frank asked.

"This afternoon or tomorrow; why?"

"I remember him telling you that he would either come or send someone out to help you get started. I thought since she seemed to pick it up pretty well when he was here, that I'd send Melissa out to see what she could learn and at the same time be able to help you when you get ready to put it into use. Do you have a problem with that?"

Trying not to sound negative, he said, "No, I don't have a problem. I just don't know if I'll need her."

"Maybe you won't but sometimes two heads are better than one. Don't you agree?"

"I agree. I'll call you when I find out when Charlie's coming."

"Good, but you don't have to call me. You can call her directly."

"Okay. I'll be in touch."

When he hung up he thought, *Darn it. Why can't things be simple? Oh well, I guess there's nothing I can do about it, and Frank is so high on her I dare not offend him or her. I wonder if he is messing around with her. It sure would be tempting. Nah, I doubt it, but you can't ever tell about people. Jerry, just mind your own business, and let everybody else mind theirs.*

He looked in his desk drawer and found Charlie Simmons' card. He dialed Charlie's number and when he answered he said, "Charlie, this is Jerry Martin. How are you doing?"

"I'm doing great, Jerry. How about you?"

"I'm good. Listen Charlie, I'm getting ready to start on the apartment complex for Frank Thomas, and I thought I would like to take another look at your layout thing. What do I need to do?"

"That's wonderful news, Jerry. Just tell me when and where you want me to come, and I'll be there and help you get started."

"Okay, how about Friday morning. That way, if I'm smart enough to pick up on the operation I can have the weekend to study and practice with it."

"That sounds like a great idea. Jerry, don't be afraid of this program. I promise you that once you get the basics it'll be a piece of cake. What's the address?"

Jerry gave him the address and said, "Oh yeah, Charlie; Frank wants Melissa to be there when we start so she can get efficient with it, too. I'm not sure why, but with the business he's giving me I'm not going to question him." Then jokingly he said, "Maybe he's going to help me buy it."

"Charlie came back with, "You never can tell. What time, Jerry?"

"How about nine o'clock?"

"Great. I'll see you then."

It was Wednesday when he made the arrangements with Charlie, and he was tempted to wait until late Thursday to call Melissa in hopes that by giving her such a short notice she wouldn't be able to go, but when he thought about how Frank was so definite about her going he thought he had better go ahead and call her. He looked up her number and dialed.

"Hello, this is Melissa."

"Melissa, hi. This is Jerry."

"Whatta ya say Jerry?"

Without engaging in any small talk Jerry came right to the point. He said, without calling her by name again, "Frank wanted me to call you and tell you that Charlie Simmons will be at the apartment complex Friday, and he said he wanted you to come too, so I'm calling."

Pausing for just a second by Jerry's all business demeanor she said, "Friday? What time?"

"Nine o'clock."

"Okay, I'll be there. Hey Jerry, is something wrong?"

"No. Everything's fine; why?"

"Well, you seem so distant this morning, I just thought there might be something wrong."

"No, I'm just real busy. Gotta go. I'll see you later."

"Okay, hon. Bye."

Jerry arrived at the site early Friday morning to get ready for Charlie. Charlie showed up between eight thirty and eight forty-five, and Melissa got there right at nine. Charlie and Jerry had already started on one of the layouts when she got there, and they didn't stop to rehash what they had already done; they just let her try to pick up where they were.

Maybe it was the outdoor atmosphere or maybe it was because he had already seen the program work, but whatever it was, Jerry had almost an immediate grasp of the Layout Pro. After a short instruction period Charlie turned him loose with it, and he was amazed at the Layout Pro and what it would do and what he could do with it. When he finished a portion, Melissa asked, "Boy, Jerry, you sure caught on fast; can I try it?"

Jerry hated to turn it loose, but since Frank had sent her out there, he felt he had to let her. He backed away and walked over to his pickup and got a drink of water while she took the program through its paces. In a few minutes he walked back over and said, "Okay, Missy, let me have it back now. I want to see if I can get this first building laid out before Charlie has to leave."

Charlie said, "Jerry, I'm yours for the day if you need me, so don't worry about holding me up."

"Thanks Charlie."

By then it was eleven o'clock and he was making amazing progress laying out the first building. The only thing was, Melissa was standing shoulder to shoulder with him while he did the various exercises, and on several occasions she would put her arm around his shoulder and say something like, "Atta boy, Jerry" or "Way to go." Once, when he had made a particularly difficult move, Charlie came over and patted him on the back and shook his hand, and at the same time, Melissa put her arm around his shoulder and said one of her atta boys.

That time, Tracy had just arrived and was walking toward them and saw what Melissa did. They had their backs to her, so nobody saw her coming, and Melissa's move angered her. When she reached them, Jerry was the first to see her and he said, "Hi Sweetheart, I wasn't expecting to see you out here."

Without displaying her usual smile, she glanced at Melissa and said, "Apparently not."

Before anything else was said, he said, "Honey, this is Charlie Simmons. He's the one that developed the layout thing I was telling you about, and you've met Melissa." He pointed out what he had done and said, "I know you don't know anything about building, but look at what I've done this morning," and he and Charlie pointed out some of the things.

She said, "I'm impressed." Letting her eyes quickly glance at Melissa again she asked, "Did you do this all by yourself?"

Charlie interjected, "Yes ma'am. He did the whole thing by himself. You've got a smart fellow here."

She said, "I know," and then she asked Jerry, "Can I see you for just a minute?"

They walked up toward her car, and she said, "Wendy and I are going shopping for some things we need for our Paris trip, and I want to pick up some things for you. Do you know of anything you need?"

"No, I can't think of anything."

"How about a new swim suit?

"I doubt we'll be doing any swimming, will we? If we do, I have one that's plenty good to take."

She named off some other things; some he wanted and some he didn't. When she got ready to leave he said, "I appreciate your coming out here to ask me these things, but why didn't you just call me?"

"I tried, but you didn't answer."

"Darn! I must have left my phone in the truck. I'm sorry."

Being very catty, she said, "Maybe I should get your girlfriends number. I can call her when you're not available. I understand she has a new number."

"What's wrong with you Tracy? I've never seen you act like this before. She's out here because Frank sent her out her. I certainly didn't want her."

"Well you sure didn't pull away when she put her arm around you."

"I'm not believing this. Do you honestly think there's something going on between us?"

"You tell me."

"I'll tell you this, young lady. There is absolutely nothing going on. She's Frank's assistant, and he thinks the world of her, and she's going to be around as long as I'm doing business with him, unless she quits or he fires her. I have told her that I am and will be totally true to you, and that's all there is to it. I admit she's kinda flirty, but she knows the score, and you certainly don't have anything to worry about. Now, does that help?"

"I guess."

"I love you Trace."

"Me too. I'm sorry."

She moved over to him and gave him a kiss and said, "I'll see you tonight."

"Okay, don't cook. We'll go out and grab a bite if you want to. I'm so excited about the progress I'm making on this new equipment, we may need to go out and celebrate."

As soon as Tracy left, Jerry went back to the Layout Pro and by lunchtime he and Charlie thought he knew enough to continue on his own. "Would you like to keep the Pro and work with it over the weekend?"

"That would be great. Maybe I'll come out tomorrow and see what I can do with it." Jokingly, he asked, "You're not going to leave the country this weekend are you?"

"Smiling, Charlie said, "No, I'll be around if you need me."

"Great. I hope I won't have to call you, but just in case, it's good to know I'll be able to."

They began packing up, and Charlie didn't have anything to put in his truck since Jerry was keeping the Layout Pro, so he got in his pickup and left.

As Jerry and Melissa were leaving, Melissa asked, "Jer, do you want get to some lunch?"

"Not today. I've got a lot to do, and I'll probably just pass on lunch, but thanks anyway."

She looked at him and asked, "Did your wife say you couldn't eat with me?"

When she said that, he saw red. He looked at her, squinted his eyes and said, "Don't you ever say anything like that to me again. I do what I want to do when I want to do it. If I wanted to go get lunch, I would, and if I didn't want to go, I wouldn't. Today, I don't want to go. I've got too much to do."

She wished she hadn't made that comment and knew she made him mad, so then she just said, "Okay, some other time."

Without saying anything else, he got into his pickup and left; squealing his tires as he scratched off.

Deciding that he was hungry after all, he pulled into the Old Smokey's Barbeque to grab a bite of lunch, and when he got inside he was surprised to see Frank and another bank employee eating. They had just arrived and invited him to sit with them. "Hi Frank; you're a long way from your stomping grounds, aren't you?"

Before answering, Frank said, "Jerry, I'd like to introduce you to William Younger. William works with us and is our resident expert on construction."

Jerry shook hands with William and said, "It's nice to meet you William," and then asked Frank, "Do you eat out here often?"

"Not at this one, but we eat at the one close to the bank pretty often." Sensing that Jerry was wondering why he was there he said, "I want to show William where our apartments are going to be, and while we're in the area, I want to show him where the White Rock neighborhood is going to be."

"That's great. Is there any way I can help you?"

"No, no. We're just sort of sightseeing, and I know where both projects are, so you won't have to go."

"Okay. I met Charles Simmons at the apartment site this morning and believe it or not, the operation of his Layout Pro came to me just like I had been using it for a long time, and I've decided to buy one. He left the one we worked with this morning with me, and I'm going to practice with it over the weekend. It's quite a deal. I'm glad you put me in touch with him."

"I thought you'd like it. Did Melissa go out, too?"

"Yes sir. She did."

The waitress brought their food while they were talking, and they pretty much began devoting all their efforts on eating the delicious pork barbeque. The outside meat was especially good.

After eating, Frank picked up the check for all three, and they parted ways; Frank and William to the building sites, and after some thought, Jerry went home early. He wanted to spend as much time with Tracy as he could, and since it had been such a good day up to that point, he wanted to be with her, especially after the little blowup at the apartment complex that morning.

Tracy wasn't home when he got there, so he took advantage of the time and went out on the porch and took a nap. Tracy came home around four o'clock, and the noise her car made driving in woke him up. When she got out of the car she came around to the porch and gave him a big kiss and then sat down beside him.

She said, "I wasn't expecting to see you this early. Is everything alright?"

"Yeah, everything is great. I had a great morning, and then Frank Thomas bought my lunch, so I figured I was on such a good roll I'd come home to be with my Honey, but my Honey wasn't here."

"Sorry about that. I was being a good wife and buying my husband some things to take on our trip. What are we going to do for dinner?"

"I don't know. I'm not very hungry; are you?"

"No I'm not. Wendy and I had a Frap about two thirty, and I'm still full."

"I've got a suggestion."

"What?"

"Let's go to a movie and eat afterwards. If we have popcorn we might not even want anything later. Whatta ya say?"

"Sounds like a plan to me. Let's do it."

It was only a few minutes after four, so they rested for a while, had a Margarita, and left home in time to make the seven o'clock movie.

Just as Jerry had predicted, they had popcorn at the theater and didn't want anything to eat after the movie, so they went home.

Tracy had to leave on a flight to Rio the next morning, and that meant leaving Jerry by himself all weekend. She kissed him bye and left home around seven o'clock and told him she would see him Tuesday.

After she left he killed some time around the house and around nine-thirty he decided to take the Layout Pro and go to the apartment site. He set up the equipment and began going through dummy drills and was doing really good on most of the exercises, but there was one thing that he could not make work, no matter how hard he tried, so he thought he would just have to call Charles on Monday to get him to help him through it.

Around eleven o'clock he heard a car door shut, and when he turned around to see who it was, he saw Melissa coming toward him. He thought, *now what is she doing here and how did she know I was going to be here?*

When she got to where he was she said, "Hi."

"Hi," he answered. "What are you doing out here?"

"Well, I didn't have anything to do and I thought you might be out here, so I thought I would come and see what you are up to."

"I'm just putting this piece of equipment through its paces."

"Are you learning it pretty good?"

"Pretty good, but there's one thing I can't seem to get the hang of, and I guess I'll have to call Charles Simmons to help me."

"What is it?" she asked.

He showed her what he was having trouble with, and it just so happened that that problem area was one that she knew how to do. She told him how to set the thing up, and to be sure he was doing it right, it was necessary that while he held a certain part in place that she put her arm around his shoulder to reach something else.

When she did that, the thing did exactly what it was supposed to do, and he said, "Thanks. Maybe I can do it now."

She said, "Let's try it again just to be sure."

"Okay," so he got into the same position he was in before, but instead of Melissa putting her arm around his shoulder, she stood behind him that time and put both arms around him to reach the machine. When the exercise was over, Jerry put his hands down, but Melissa held her arms around him for several seconds; maybe ten to fifteen.

"Thanks, Melissa, that's a big help."

"Glad I could be of some help. Do you want to try it one more time?"

"Do you think I need to?"

"Practice makes perfect, they say."

"Okay, one more time."

That time, when Jerry put his hands on the machine Melissa put her arms around him at first and rested her head on his back, but didn't reach for the machine. She just stood there hugging him. He didn't pull away and said, "You sure do smell good."

"Do you like it? I thought you would. I put it on just for you. Where's your wife this morning?"

"She's on her way to Rio."

Melissa perked up and asked, "How long will she be gone?"

"'Til Tuesday."

"Until Tuesday? We can have a lot of fun between now and Tuesday can't we?"

'Melissa, I've told you; I'm not cheating on Tracy. I love her, and I'm not going to do anything that would hurt her. You're a good-looking, very desirable woman, and believe me, I'm tempted, but with the help of God, I've got to resist, and I hope you'll respect that."

"Okay, but just think about what you'll be missing every time your wife is away on one of her trips."

She was still standing behind him with her arms around him, and before turning him loose, she took her right hand and turned his head toward her and gave him a kiss; not a long sensual kiss, but a short one packed with meaning.

"I've got to go," he said.

"What's the matter? Are you afraid you might do something you really want to?"

"No, I've just got to go. Thanks for showing me about the problem with the Layout Pro. I think I've got it now."

"Okay, but if you should get lonesome tonight you know how to reach me."

"I won't get lonesome. I'll be working with my horses, and you don't get lonesome when you're around them."

Okay, Cowboy; maybe I'll see you Monday. You have a nice and lonely weekend."

"See ya, Melissa."

Jerry got into his pickup and headed home, but all the way he was thinking about the kiss that Melissa gave him. He prayed a silent prayer and said, *Father, please help me. Please remove the temptation that's been put before me and help me resist it. You know I want to be loyal to Tracy, and with your help I will, but Lord I need your help. I ask this in Jesus' name. Amen.*

The weekend went well. He rode his horse for a long time Saturday afternoon, and called Jack to see if he would like to go out and eat. And then he met Jack Sunday morning and went to church with him, and every time a thought about Melissa would get into his mind he would pray about it. After church, he took Jack out to lunch and then went home and slept a big part of the afternoon.

On Monday morning, Jerry got up real early and went to his office. Since they were leaving Thursday for Paris, it was going to be a three-day-week, and he had about a hundred days of work to do.

One of the first things he did when he sat down at his desk was to go over reports from the previous week's work, and he noticed that the three teenagers would be ending their sentences later in the week, so he made it a point to go out to the job to see them later that morning.

Before he left the office, he called Frank to see if he could come by his office and task with him, and Frank said he could come by around two o'clock if that would work for him.

He gathered some things together and went out and got into his pickup and drove to the only house that he still had under construction. He wanted to see the three teens and talk to them.

Gathering them around him after he got through talking to Bobby Kunkle, the foreman, he told them, "Do you all know what week this is?"

Reed said, "I believe it's our last week of work on our sentence."

"You're right. You finish up Thursday, and I want to compliment all of you for doing a good job. I know it hasn't been very enjoyable, but it could have been worse, couldn't it?"

They all said it could have been.

Jerry continued, "Since you've all hung in there and showed responsibility for your actions, I'm declaring your sentences complete at the end of work today, and I'm going to pay you for the rest of the week as a sort of bonus. Is that okay with you?"

The two boys grinned and said, "Yes sir. Thank you."

He noticed that the two boys seemed to be really happy that their sentence was over, but he couldn't help but notice that Tammy looked sad.

"Stony, you told me one time that you would like to come to work for me. Are you still interested?"

"Yes sir, I sure am."

"All right. When I finish out here in a few minutes, catch up to me and we'll talk about it."

"Thank you, sir."

He and Stony got together in a few minutes and he hired Stony to come work for him as an apprentice carpenter.

When he walked into Frank's office at two o'clock, Frank welcomed him and then asked, "Is there something special that you need today, Jerry?"

"On no sir. Since we're going to be doing a lot of work together I just felt that I needed to tell you that I'll be gone on Thursday and Friday of this week, but I'll be back Sunday."

Frank said, "You work for yourself, so you don't have to check in with me on your comings and goings, but I appreciate it. Why are you going to be off; are you going somewhere?"

"Yeah, Tracy has been wanting to take me to Europe for a while, and she has made arrangements for us and another couple to go to Paris for a couple of days. I know I don't have to ask permission or anything like that, but since we are going to be working together I just wanted to let you know why I was going to be off. By the way, I took the Layout Pro back to the apartment complex Saturday and pretty much figured out how to work the darn thing. I had a problem with a particular operation, and Melissa happened to come out, and she knew how to do what I didn't, so your comment about two heads being better than one was right on in that case."

"I'm glad to hear that. Paris, eh? Well I hope you guys have a great time."

"Frank, I plan to start laying out the first two buildings on the apartments Monday. You're ready, aren't you?"

"I'm ready and can hardly wait. I may see you out there Monday."

"Great, I'll see you then."

Back at the office making plans for next week, the phone rang at four-twenty-five. It was Frank. "Jerry, it's a good thing you came in when you did."

"Why, what's wrong?"

"Nothing's wrong, but I just got a call from our Architect, and he and his team wanted to come down Thursday and meet with all of us. I told him our General Contractor would be out of the country Thursday and couldn't make it and after arguing for a while, I was finally able to convince him that we couldn't see them until sometime next week. He wanted me to call you and have you postpone your trip."

"Thanks, Frank. I appreciate that. This trip means a lot to Tracy, and I would hate to disappoint her."

"Glad we could get it worked out. You owe me one, and oh yeah; do you think your Dad could come down for the meeting on Tuesday? This is apparently an important deal from the way they talked."

"I'm sure he can. I'll call him right now."

"Thanks, Jer. Have a great time on your trip, and Jerry, I think we should get together Monday and go over our plans. We want to know what we're talking about when the Architects get here Tuesday."

"No problem. I'll see you Monday."

He immediately called Bob and told him about the meeting with the Architects next Tuesday, and Bob said he could be there. "Would you and Tracy object if I come down Monday and spend the night?"

"Dad, you know you don't have to ask that. We'd be glad to have you. Come on down."

"Okay, I'll see you Monday night."

"Great. See ya."

While he was on the phone with Bob, Beverly stuck her head in the door and waved bye as it was five o'clock. He waved to her and wished he had had her stay for a few minutes to go over some things he wanted to have her do while he was gone. *Oh well; I'll tell her in the morning,* he thought.

The next day was spent laying out everything he wanted done while he was away, and he hoped he hadn't left anything out. He finished the day around three o'clock and headed home to clean up the house because Tracy was due home around five.

They were so glad to see each other when she got there, and he poured her a glass of wine while they relaxed. Almost immediately, she asked, "Darling, do you think there's any way that you could leave on Wednesday afternoon? If you can, we can catch a 767 at three-twenty and get to Paris at five-thirty Thursday morning. The 767 is such a comfortable airplane, we should be able to sleep all night going over. That way, we can have all day Thursday in Paris instead of only part of the day, and that will give us three full days in the city of love. Wendy is going to ask Tom, and she thinks he will be able to. What do you think?"

"I think I can do anything for you. If you want to leave Wednesday afternoon, then that's what we'll do."

The four of them got to the airport about two-thirty Wednesday afternoon, and since Tracy and Wendy were airline employees, they had to go through a security check, but not like the general public. One of the comps of being an airline employee was getting free tickets to just about anywhere in the world.

They were booked in Coach class and Wendy and Tracy's seats were next to each other. Tom was in the aisle seat next to Wendy, and Jerry was across the aisle in that aisle seat and technically next to Tom.

The seatbelt light was on, so they all fastened their belts, and then, right before time to take off, Becky, one of the flight attendants, motioned for Wendy to come up to where she was standing. When she got up there, Becky said, "Wendy, First Class is not full. Would you guys like to come up here?"

Well, she didn't have to ask twice. Wendy immediately went back to their seats and told the others to get up; they were flying First Class. They tried to keep the other passengers from hearing what was going on, but were sure they didn't do a very good job of keeping it quiet.

There is absolutely no comparison between Coach and First Class. The seats are so much wider and more comfortable plus First Class has several perks that the other classes don't have. All four were very thankful for the upgrade.

There were several choices of movies to watch, and Wendy and Tracy watched a love story while Jerry and Tom watched a western.

Destiny

After the movie, Becky began serving dinner, and that night it was filet mignon with baked potato and asparagus topped off with banana pudding.

Being so used to flying, Wendy and Tracy slept like babies, but Tom and Jerry didn't do so well. They were both awake about as much as they slept; in fact, neither one of them got to sleep until around four o'clock, and when the girls woke them up at five, they were sleeping really good. Each one had a cup of coffee before they landed, and said they would eat breakfast after they got to the hotel.

All the planning that Wendy and Tracy had done was perfect. They knew exactly what they were going to do and when they were going to do it, and it was an outstanding trip for the four of them. Although they stayed busy most of the time, there was still plenty of romantic time for the couples to spend with each other.

On Thursday afternoon, when Melissa couldn't get in touch with Jerry, she asked Frank if he had seen him. "Didn't he tell you?"

"Tell me what?"

"He and his wife and another couple have gone to Paris for two or three days. I'm surprised he didn't tell you."

She looked shocked and then said, "I guess he figured it wasn't any of my damn business," and she stomped out of Frank's office.

Frank looked kind of surprised at her reaction and watched her walk away.

Friday was the big day for the Paris visitors. That was the day they were to take the three top tours in the City of Lights.

They went to the starting point and Tracy said, "Remember when I read about these to you, Wendy?"

"I sure do, and it looks as if the brochure was right, doesn't it?"

They cruised down the Seine for a riverside view of the city's famous monuments and had their choice of dinner at the Eiffel Tower's chic 58 Tour Eiffel restaurant or a gourmet meal aboard the dining cruise. They chose the cruise ship meal. Then they went to the Eiffel Tower as it was lit up against the night sky, and finally they capped off the evening with a Parisian cabaret show at the Moulin Rouge nightclub, complete with Champagne.

Romance had to take a back seat after the busy day they had, and after getting back to the hotel and sitting in the lobby for a little while, they decided that the next day would pretty much be a day of rest. There would be a little sightseeing, but mostly they would rest in anticipation of the busy day the girls had planned for Saturday.

Wheels were up at seven o'clock EST Sunday morning for the trip back to Atlanta for a scheduled arrival time of nine-thirty Sunday night, and as luck would have it, they got to fly first-class the way they did when they came over. It wasn't nearly as hard to sleep going back as it was when they came over. Reality had set in for Jerry, and he was both dreading and looking forward to the meetings on Tuesday. Dreading because he was afraid the Architects would be afraid he was too inexperienced to do such a huge job, but looking forward because he knew he could do it.

The big plane landed in Atlanta right on time, and by the time they got their luggage and said their goodbyes, they got home a little before eleven.

Tracy and Jerry slept in Monday morning and didn't get up until after eight o'clock. They were both beat after their whirlwind trip to Paris, but Jerry knew he had to get moving. He called Frank to see what time he wanted him to come in, and Frank said to come in around noon and they would go to lunch and spend the afternoon together.

At lunch, not much business was discussed, but a lot about Paris, and at one point, Frank talked about the main reason he wanted to meet ahead of the meeting the next day. He said, "Jerry, I wanted for us to get together before our meeting tomorrow to air out a couple of things. The main reason being, are you absolutely sure you can deliver on the mall project? If you're not, I need to know right now because there are other people involved. I'm not in this alone; there are investors, and the fact that you are so small has been mentioned. I have seen your work, and I have full confidence in you, and I just wanted to be sure you feel the same way."

Jerry put on his *game-face* and said, "Frank, can I tell you a short story?"

"Please do."

"When I was in high school I was a pretty good football player and several colleges began looking at me as early as my sophomore year, and in my junior year the amount of recruiters increased substantially. I was really getting good, and then in my senior year I quit growing at six feet and two hundred pounds, and the recruiters stopped coming around for the most part, however, there were still a few. I managed to get a scholarship to Georgia, as you very well know, an SEC school. I signed the "Grant-In-Aid and reported to practice in July before classes started in late August.

"When I walked out on that practice field the first day I was scared to death because I was so much smaller than all the other guys that were out for my position, but you know what Frank? I told myself that I was the toughest, meanest, baddest guy on the field, and I went out to prove it. Not only did I make starter my freshman year, but in my senior year I was elected Captain, and I made second team All SEC.

"That's who I am, Frank, and that's the way I try to operate my business. I know I'm small, but I'm the toughest so-and-so on the block, and when I start something, I finish it. Now to answer your investors' concerns; tell them they don't have to worry; they have a winner working for them."

"That's a great story, Jer. I'll be sure to pass it along. I told you that I'm not in this alone, but I didn't tell you that I own controlling interest in our company, so don't worry. As far as I'm concerned, you've got the job."

Thanks Frank. I won't let you down."

"I know you won't. As I told you, I've seen your work, and I have full confidence in you, and I just wanted to be sure you feel the same way, and Jer, I don't know if you've thought about this in these terms, but when you complete the job you're going to be a millionaire several times over."

"Wow! No I haven't thought about it in those terms. Wow!"

They left the restaurant and returned to the bank. After they went to the restroom they went into Frank's office and continued their conversation.

Frank took the lead and said, "Jerry, I know you know most of what I'm about to say, but I think I need to bring it up. I tell this to every builder whose projects I finance, and I've said it so much, it probably sounds like I'm reading it. I'm by no means a builder of anything; I'm just a lowly banker, but I have had a lot of experience financing building jobs; both large and small, and what I'm about to say applies to every business; not only the construction trade, and that is Project Management.

"You may ask, what is Project Management? The management of construction projects requires knowledge of modern management as well as an understanding of the design and construction process.

Construction projects have a specific set of objectives and constraints such as a required time frame for completion. While the relevant technology, institutional arrangements or processes will differ, the management of such projects has much In common with the management of similar types of projects in other specialty or technology domains, such as aerospace, pharmaceuticals, and others.

"Generally, project management is distinguished from the general management of corporations by the mission oriented nature of a project. A project organization will generally be terminated when the mission is accomplished.

"Specifically, project management in construction encompasses a set of objectives which may be accomplished by implementing a series of operations subject to resource constraints. There are potential conflicts between the stated objectives with regard to scope, cost, time, and quality, and the constraints imposed on human material and financial resources. These conflicts should be resolved at the onset of a project by making the necessary tradeoffs or creating new alternatives.

"Jerry, I could talk about this until next week, but I think you know what I'm saying. You've got a good head on your shoulders and the experience necessary to know how and when to apply these things. I hope I didn't bore you with all this."

They began to do some other things, and once, while they were going over some things still in Frank's office, Melissa came in with some papers for Frank to sign and just barely glanced at Jerry and didn't speak. Jerry said, "Hi, Melissa," and without looking his way she answered coldly, "Hello," and that's all she said. When Frank finished signing the papers, Jerry couldn't resist saying, "It's nice to see you Melissa." She gave him an icy look and left and wasn't seen again the entire afternoon.

Jerry thought, *she must be mad about something to not even speak. How can I be so lucky?*

When they finished their talk, Jerry was getting ready to leave, and Frank said, "I hope I haven't bored you to tears this afternoon, but it has been my experience that Project Management has to be in the fore front of every business, and you're getting ready to begin something where Project Management is going to play a very vital role."

Jerry replied, "You didn't bore me at all. This was a big help. I guess I already knew a lot of these things, but I had never had them brought up and emphasized the way you did today. Thank you, and Frank, you're not a lowly banker. I think you're someone other businessmen can look up to."

He left Frank's office, and when he had gone just a few feet, he turned around and stuck his head in and said, "Frank, I've decided to put White Rock on hold until I finish the mall. I don't want any distractions on either one."

Frank replied, "Good Boy; wise decision."

Chapter Eleven

In anticipation of the meeting Tuesday, Bob Martin, Jerry's Dad, arrived Monday afternoon and stayed with Tracy and Jerry. Tracy fixed a delicious meal, and the three of them very much enjoyed each other's company as well as the good food.

After dinner, Jerry and Bob went to the den and talked about the mall and all the other things that were to go along with it. At one point Bob asked Jerry, "Son, you're sure you can handle all that aren't you?"

Real seriously, Jerry looked at his Dad and said, "You too?"

Bob said, "Me too what?"

"It seems as if nobody thinks I can do a big job. Dad, have you ever known me to not be able to finish anything that I started?"

"No, I guess I haven't. I'm sorry, Son. I guess this thing is too big for me to think about. I've built some pretty big things, but what you're getting ready to do is mind-blowing, and I know you will do a great job."

"I hope we will do a great job together; you and me."

Bob looked real serious for a few seconds, and then a smile came across his face. "I wonder if you're expecting more from me than I'm able to give."

"I might be; I hope not. Do you know what Frank told me this afternoon?"

"What?"

"He told me that when I finish this project I will be a millionaire several times over, and Dad, you can share in a large part of it if you're willing."

"All this sounds good, but you've got to remember; I have a good sized business that I have to look after in Chattanooga. We're only a couple of hours apart, but that's a long way when you're talking about working with two separate companies. I want to help you, and I intend to help you, but I can't just up and leave to come down here on a full-time basis."

"Tell you what, Dad. Let's wait until after the meeting tomorrow, and we'll see what you think, and then we'll talk about it, and you can make a decision then."

"Fair enough. Tracy, what do you think about all this?"

"It sounds too big for me to comprehend. I'm just going to keep flying and leave all this building stuff up to my resident expert. I do hope you will seriously think about moving down here because you and big Jer here need each other full time."

After more talk and some TV shows that were not too interesting, the three got ready for bed. Just as Jerry was about to turn off the lights in the den, the phone rang. He picked up and said, "Hello."

On the other end was Barbara Mills. Jerry?"

"Yes, who is this?"

"It's Barbara Mills, and I'm wondering if we might meet sometime tomorrow. I really need to talk to you."

"Barbara, I'm going to be in a meeting all day tomorrow. Would Wednesday work?"

"Yeah, that'll have to. Could we meet early?"

"Whenever you say. What's wrong, Barbara?"

"I'd rather wait and tell you when we meet. How about we meet at the Cracker Barrel out here close to where I live?"

"Sounds good. Are you still working?"

"Yeah, so it will have to be early."

"Why don't I meet you at seven o'clock Wednesday morning?"

"Okay, I'll be there."

"Are you sure you don't want to tell me what's going on?"

"I'd rather wait."

"Okay. I'll see you Wednesday morning. Good night, Barbara."

"Good night and thank you."

Tracy didn't sleep well for thinking about an upcoming flight to Ecuador, a country where she hadn't been before, and Bob and Jerry had a hard time sleeping because the shopping mall was front and center in their minds.

The meeting was set for ten o'clock Tuesday morning in the Conference Room at Frank's office. Jerry and Bob arrived about ten 'til and waited in Frank's outer office until Melissa came out to get them right at ten. When they went into the conference room, everybody was already there, and Frank indicated that they were waiting for them. That sort of ticked Jerry off because he was there ahead of time, and for some reason, Melissa just made them sit outside and wait until the exact time the meeting was scheduled. He thought, *I don't know what I've done, but she's sure mad about something.*

Frank introduced Jerry to Clark Randle and Steven Carroll of Carroll and Randle Architects from right there in Atlanta. Jerry then introduced Bob to everyone, and they began the meeting. Jerry was a little surprised when he first saw Clark and Steven because they didn't look much older than him, and from what he had heard, they had done several awesome projects, including a couple of shopping malls.

Frank began the meeting by telling the reason for the meeting and laying out what will have to take place to make the mall become a reality. He stressed the importance of the architects' role and turned the floor over to Clark Randle.

Clark began by saying how happy he was to be chosen to be the Architect for that fine Mall, and then he told what he and his firm would be responsible for, but before he did that he gave a cost breakdown for everything that would be put in the Mall; not a cost of everything, but categories, such as lighting, plumbing, heating and cooling, display fronts and things of that nature, then he went into the architects' responsibilities.

"Our firm will determine the scope of the project and establish a preliminary budget. We will draft a list of proposed work, budget, and outline of plans. We will create the schematic design and draft floor plans with elevation drawings. Then work with any structural engineers and meet with planning agencies to verify any requirements. We will finalize drawings and incorporate all details about materials and finishes, any fixtures or equipment, and all systems in the structure.

"We will serve as project manager and review the plans with any required local agencies while also obtaining necessary permits. At this point we will meet with Martin Builders and select whatever subcontractors will be needed. Many other things will be done by our firm and one of the most important is that we will administer the construction and ensure that the contractors' request for payments are accurate and that all final details are corrected or finished by the contractor."

"Now, what will the General Contractor do?" When he said that, Jerry's ears perked up.

"In a nutshell the General Contractor will provide the services and materials required for the entire job; they will hire the subcontractors according to need and suggest plans and ideas to us or to Mr. Thomas and his group to help them meet goals and finally, they will deliver the final cleanup of the entire job site.

"That's pretty much it. Are there any questions?"

At that point, Frank stood up and asked the same thing. No one had any, so Frank said a few words. "I just want to review for a minute what we are going to do. First, there will be the main Mall and as near as we can tell, it will have somewhere in the neighborhood of one point six million square feet and should cost around seven-hundred and ten million dollars to seven-hundred and twenty-five million dollars.

"That does not include any of the outbuildings. We anticipate there will be approximately fifteen restaurants plus many other businesses such as craft stores, shoe stores, telephone stores, and who knows what else. All in all, I think we're looking at something in excess of a billion dollars. That's a billion with a B."

A couple of times Jerry looked over at Melissa who was sitting next to Frank, and when he would look her way she would look away except once when he looked at her, she was slow to look away. Always one to try to stir something up, he winked at her that time, and a slight smile came to her face when she turned in the other direction.

Frank's secretary had arranged to have lunch catered, and the caterer must have had ESP because he timed his arrival perfectly. Frank stopped talking and the food arrived at the same time.

Everyone got a plate and began spooning food onto their plates as they talked. Jerry and Bob were next to each other, and very quietly Jerry asked Bob, "What do you think, Dad?"

"I think this is going to be major."

"Do you think it's something you want to get involved in?"

"Maybe; we'll just have to see."

"Do you know what, Dad?"

"What?"

"I think I'm going to delay the start of my White Rock project until I finish this. I'm just beginning the apartment complex for Frank, and I have to build that, and I don't want to cut things so thin that I can't do justice to them all. The financing is already approved for White Rock, so I think I'll just wait a while."

"That's probably a wise decision."

While they were talking with each other, Steven Carroll came over and asked Jerry, "Jerry, have you ever built a shopping mall?"

"No, but I'm really looking forward to it."

"What makes you think you can build this?"

His question rubbed Jerry the wrong way, and he was slightly indignant by the way it was asked. He answered by saying, "I don't just think I can build it, Steven; I know I can build it, and I've got an expert here to make sure I stay on the right track."

Steven looked at Bob and said, "Did I understand Frank to say that you're Jerry's Father?"

"You did."

"Are you experienced with something this large?"

"Not a shopping mall, but a lot of huge commercial projects"

Steven asked, "Such as?"

"Are you familiar with The Shepherd Apparel Group up in Chattanooga?"

"I sure am. I've been up there several times. Did you build them?"

"All but the first one."

"Good job. Those are nice buildings."

"There are a lot more besides the Shepherd buildings. I'm pretty sure I know what I'm doing when it comes to constructing buildings, and Jerry here grew up working with me on many of them until he came down here and started his own company. Together, we're going to knock this job out of the park."

When Bob told Steven that, Jerry smiled and almost laughed out loud. He thought, *I hope that means that he's going to become really involved.*

The gathering went on until about three o'clock at which time Frank said, "Gentlemen, I'm going to have to break this up as I have another meeting at four o'clock, and I have to make preparations for it, but I want to mention something for all of you to think about until next week. As you all know we have said we were going to name the Mall Douglas Mills, but I had a thought over the weekend: You may or may not know that Douglasville was originally named Skint Chesnut, and for that reason, I'm thinking about naming it Skint Chesnut Mall. You all think about that this week and we'll talk about it next week.

"Clark, I suggest you and Steven get together with Jerry and Bob in the next day or so and come up with a plan to get this baby started. They all shook hands and agreed to meet the following week.

Jerry, always the antagonist and knowing she was mad about something, caught up with Melissa, put his hand around her shoulder and said, "Melissa, it's always good to see you. I guess I'll see you at the meeting next week."

Pulling away from him and still trying to act mad she said almost inaudibly, "Okay, and oh, I hope you had a good time in Paris."

"We did; thank you."

As he and Bob were walking down the stairs after he said what he did to Melissa, Bob said, "Now tell me again who Melissa is."

"She's Frank's Assistant; excuse me; his Administrative Assistant and she carries a lot of weight when it comes to his business dealings. She and I have had to work together on some things and she's a little flirty, and I've had to set her straight on some things, but she's smart, and I don't want to cause any problems where Frank is concerned, so I just sort of go with the flow. Right now she's apparently mad at me about something; I'm not sure what, and I thought I would just ag her on by saying what I did as we left."

"Oh, just watch her, okay? Sometimes those kinds of people can cause some real problems. What do you think now that we've had that meeting?"

"I think this is going to be a big deal, and do you know what else I think, Dad?"

"What?"

"I don't think it's going to be quite as big a deal on our part as I first thought. After hearing Clark in there and what he said he and his company are going to do, it looks to me like they're going to do most of the heavy lifting, and we can concentrate on the construction part. Is that what you think?"

"Pretty much. They're going to do a whole lot of it; that's for sure."

"Well, they should. I read somewhere a while back that on mall constructions, the architects require approximately seventeen percent of the total building budget. Frank said this project will run around a billion dollars, so you do the math. Did you warm up to the idea of getting more involved after you heard the Architect talk?"

"Maybe a little. Son, you're smart enough and good enough to handle this without my help, but if you feel you must have me, then I guess I can make the effort to at least help you get started. Will that work for you?"

"I guess, but Tracy and I wish you would retire and move down here. You don't have anybody left in Chattanooga, and we don't have anybody down here except Jack, and we think it would be wonderful if you did."

"You make it sound inviting, but Chattanooga's home, and it would be awfully hard to leave. I'll tell you what; I'll think about it."

"Are you going to stay tonight?"

"No, I guess I'll head back north. From the way Frank and Clark talked, I'll be coming back in a few days, so I need to get back home and check on some things."

As they were driving back to Jerry's to get Bob's car they had to ride through some very pretty country, and he commented on how pretty it was, and Jerry smiled and said, "Well, you know how you can see it every day, don't you?"

He didn't answer. He just smiled. When they got to Jerry's, he went in and got his things and put them in his car. Before he left he gave Tracy a huge hug and said, "I love you," and then gave Jerry one and said the same thing. He got in his car and waved as he drove out of the driveway.

Tracy asked how the meeting went and Jerry told her and told her how large the project was going to be. He told her how he hoped his Dad would move down there and become a part of his company, and he told her he thought he would delay starting the White Rock project. Everything he mentioned always led back to the mall, and Tracy could see that he was very excited about it.

"Do you know what, Trace?"

"No, what?"

"It's really true that God works in mysterious ways. You know if those kids had not broken in and damaged that house, chances are that I would not have met Frank Thomas, and now Frank is making it possible for us to be set up for life, financially. I want us to take him and Mrs. Thomas out to dinner one night. I think you'll like him. I met Mrs. Thomas at the Magistrates Office and at Court when the kids were tried, but I don't really know her. When do you leave again?"

"I don't have a flight until Monday."

"Would it be okay with you if I asked them to dinner Saturday night?"

"Of course. Whatever you want to do."

"Great, I'll call him tomorrow. Oh, I nearly forgot; Barbara Mills has got some kind of problem, and I'm going to meet her at seven o'clock in the morning."

"What kind of problem?"

"I don't know. She just said she needs to talk to me and it's important."

"It must be about Tammy."

"I'd say it is. I guess I'll know in the morning."

Barbara was standing outside the Cracker Barrel when Jerry got there the next morning. "Good morning, Barbara."

"Good morning."

"Have you had breakfast?"

"No, not yet."

"Want some?"

"That would be nice."

"Let's go in."

They went in and sat down and Barbara looked at the menu. Jerry didn't have to because he knew what he wanted; the Smokehouse."

After they had ordered, Jerry said, "You sounded upset when I talked to you the other day. Is something wrong?"

"I don't know for sure, Jerry, but I afraid there is. It's a little too early to tell, but it looks like Tammy might be pregnant."

"What makes you think so?"

"Well, she's late for her period, and she hasn't been feeling very well. Her next one is not due for two more weeks, and if she misses that, then we'll be pretty sure that she is."

"Well, we'll pray that she's not, but Barbara, what if she is?"

"I don't know. That's why I wanted to talk to you. You always seem to have the answers to things."

"Let's say she is. Does she know whose it is?"

"It's got to be that animal that raped her. She swears that she hasn't been to bed with anyone else, and I believe her."

"Barbara, you're talking about something that's completely out of my realm of thinking. I'm going to have to have some time to think this through before I can give you any suggestions as to what you should do. You probably know much more than I do about things like this, but I'll be there for you all and we'll do something."

"If she is pregnant, do you think she should have an abortion?"

"No, that's one thing that I know I wouldn't do. In my opinion, that's nothing more than murder, and I couldn't possibly suggest to someone that they kill a little baby."

"That's kind of the way I feel, but we have to come up with something."

"We will. It's still early, so let's see what develops."

"Okay. Thank you, Jerry. I always feel better after I talk to you."

They finished their breakfast as they talked, and Jerry asked, "Are you ready to go?"

"Yeah, I've got to get to work. Thank you again for letting me talk to you. I don't know what Tammy or I would do without you."

"You're welcome. You know where I am any time you need me. Try to relax. She might not be pregnant, but if she is, we'll figure out something. Tell Tammy I said hi."

He left the Cracker Barrel and drove to his office. Beverly had just arrived there and was making a pot of coffee when he walked in. "Good morning," he said.

"Good morning. Did you sleep well last night?"

"Yeah, why?"

"I thought with all this building you're getting ready to do that your mind would be so clogged that you couldn't sleep. You're here early. Is something special happening today?"

"No, I met someone for breakfast and came on in after we finished. Did I tell you that we got the new shopping mall job?"

"We got it? Wonderful! No, you didn't tell me. I know you have been talking about it, but I didn't know there was a chance you would get it."

"There's going to be a tremendous amount of planning, not only for the mall, but for the apartment complex as well. I've decided that I'm going to put White Rock on hold until the mall is finished."

"You are? I thought that was the most important thing in your

116

life. I'm surprised you're putting it on hold. You're still going to build it aren't you?"

"Oh yes. I just don't feel that I can do justice to three large projects at the same time; it's actually going to be hard to do justice to the mall and the apartments, but I think I can do it. My Dad is going to come down and help some, and that will be a big help.

"Beverly, we're probably going to have to hire a lot of people and we might even have to hire another person here in the office. I don't know that for sure, but it's a possibility."

Tracy had wanted to know why he was going to meet Barbara, so when he got settled in the office and was sure she would be up he called her. "Hi Sweetheart, are you up?"

"Yeah, I'm just having a cup of coffee while I watch the news. What's up?"

"Well, you wanted to know what Barbara wanted to talk to me about, and I thought I'd call and tell you. She's afraid Tammy's pregnant."

"You're kidding."

"No, I'm serious. She thinks it's the guy who raped her because Tammy swears she hasn't slept with anybody, and that guy is the only one she has been with."

"What's she going to do?"

"Well, first of all, they're not absolutely certain she's pregnant, but she's late. Her next period is not for two more weeks, and if she misses that one her mother will take her to the doctor. Just pray she's not."

"Okay; I'm glad you called. Do you have a busy day?"

"Yeah, I'm up to my ears in planning for the mall plus I've got to really get to work on Frank's apartments. I'd like to be pretty far along with them before we get absolutely covered up with the mall."

"Well, there's no doubt you can do it, and being a little facetious she said, "If you get too bogged down, I'm sure you can always get Melissa to help you out, can't you?"

"You're a certified S A, did you know that?"

"What's an S A?"

"You know what an S A is."

"No I don't; tell me."

"S A is short for smart-ass."

"Oh, I should have known that might be what it was."

117

"I've gotta go. See you tonight. I love you, S A."

"Love you too."

As soon as he hung up with Tracy, he called Frank and was surprised that the call went straight through. Usually his calls were intercepted by his secretary first.

"Good morning, Frank. How are you? This is Jerry."

"Good morning Jerry. What's up?"

"Frank, the reason I called was to see if you and your wife would like to go out to dinner Saturday night. You haven't met Tracy, and although I have met your wife, I don't really know her and would like for the four of us to become friends. If you don't have any other plans we would really like to take you out."

"Thank you, Jerry. That sounds wonderful, and I'm all for it, but like most married men, I'll have to check with my *social secretary* to be sure we don't have any prior plans, but right now I'd say we can go. Can I call you back in a little while?"

"You sure can, and I hope you can go."

Frank called back in about thirty minutes and said he and his wife would love to go to dinner with them, and they decided to meet at the Knight's Table in Atlanta at eight o'clock Saturday night.

Jerry worked in his office until lunchtime and then went by his remaining residential job and picked up Bill Case, his main Superintendent. He took the Layout Pro with them and went to the apartment site where they began to layout buildings for the complex. The more he worked with the Layout Pro the better he got at it, and before long he had Bill trying his hand at it. All in all, it was a very productive day.

When they finished, he had to take Bill back to the residential job where he picked him up, and that gave him a chance to talk to him because it was about thirty to forty-five minutes from the apartments.

"Bill, I'm glad we had this chance to spend some time together. I need to talk to you about something."

"What is it, Boss?"

"Have you heard any rumors about there going to be a new shopping mall in Douglasville?"

"I've heard a little bit, but I just figured they're rumors."

"Well, they're not rumors. It's a reality, and believe it or not, Martin Builders is going to be the General Contractor. I'm postponing my White Rock Estates project and everything else I've been working on except for the apartment complex that's already out of the ground, and when we finish that, all my efforts will be directed toward the mall. This is going to be a billion dollar project; that's billion with a B, and I want to count on you to be my main man."

"Jerry, I've never worked on anything that big. Do you think I can do it?"

"Neither have I, but I think you're just as tenacious as I am, and between the two of us, my Dad, the Architects, and a good group of subcontractors, we can knock this thing out of the park."

"What all will we be doing?"

"As the General Contractor, we are responsible for the construction itself even though most of the work may actually be undertaken by a number of specialty subcontractors. We're going to give you the title of Construction Manager, and as so, you're going to have a multitude of responsibilities. You will work with the subcontractors, and sometimes you'll have to be mother to them to make sure they all get along.

"As manager, if you see anything that you feel should be changed, you can propose design and construction alternatives and analyze the effects of the alternatives on the project cost and schedule.

"You will coordinate the purchase of material and equipment and the work of all construction contractors. You will also coordinate payments to contractors, changes, claims and inspection for conforming design requirements, and finally you will perform other project related services as required by the owners. Do you think this is something you would want to do?"

"Jerry, I'd love to try, but again, do you think I'm able to do it?"

"I know you're able to do it; that's why I want you. If you take this job, if you don't already have them, you'll need to get a pair or two of some new khakis, a couple of new shirts, and some cool looking shoes because these people believe in meetings. I'm telling you that because when you go to a meeting in the Chairman of the Board's office at the bank, you don't want to wear muddy boots and jeans with holes in 'em."

"When will we start on this, Boss?"

"We've already started. The surveying is finished, and grading is still going on, plus a couple of plumbing contractors are doing the preliminary plumbing work as we speak. Meet me at my office in the morning and we'll go out there and you can take a look at it."

Chapter Twelve

On Saturday night Tracy and Jerry arrived at the Knight's Table at about ten 'til eight and waited inside for Frank and Marilyn. Jerry's secretary had made reservations for eight o'clock, and at five 'til, Frank and Marilyn arrived. They were shown to a table, and a very handsome and efficient waiter went over and introduced himself as John and asked if they would like something to drink.

Jerry, acting like the gentleman he was, held his hand out and said, "Marilyn."

Marilyn then ordered a Vodka Martini and Frank said, "I'll have the same." And then Jerry held his handout to Tracy and she said, "I'll have a frozen Margarita," and Jerry said, "I'll have one on the rocks."

While they waited on their drinks they made small talk the way strangers do, and then Marilyn told Jerry, "Mr. Martin, I can't tell you how much I appreciate what you did for Reed and his friends. You were an angel in disguise."

Jerry responded with, "You're very welcome. They're good kids and I remember how it was when I was a kid. There were times when I wished someone would come to my rescue, and please, Marilyn, call me Jerry," and looking at Tracy, he said, "and call her Tracy."

Marilyn acknowledged Jerry's instructions and directed her next comments to Tracy. "Did I understand Frank to say that you're an airline Flight Attendant, Tracy?"

"Yes, I am."

"That has always sounded so intriguing to me. I'll bet you're gone a lot aren't you?"

"Yes, I'm gone quite a bit, but not as much as you might think."

"Where do you fly?"

"I fly pretty much all over the world. Nearly all my flights are international flights. I'm going to Ecuador Monday."

"How long will you be gone down there?"

"I'll be back Wednesday night."

Marilyn was fascinated with Tracy and her flying and couldn't get enough of hearing about the interesting trips that she was constantly going on.

In the meantime, Frank and Jerry were carrying on a conversation of their own, mainly about football. Frank was a *dyed-in-the-wool* Alabama supporter while Jerry was just as strong a supporter of Georgia. Frank jokingly said later that it was probably a good thing that Jerry wasn't an Auburn supporter or else he'd have to cancel his business with him.

They had one more round of drinks, and then they ordered dinner. They drank their drinks while they waited on their dinner, and the conversation was relaxed and comfortable. Jerry was glad to see Tracy and Marilyn getting along so well, and he felt real good about the whole evening.

Later in the evening, still exploring each other's lives, Jerry asked, "Is Reed your only child?"

Frank answered that. "No, we have two daughters. Reed is in the middle. Our oldest is at Alabama and the youngest is still in high school. And you know Melissa; she's my niece. Her mother was my sister and she passed away a few years ago, and we sort of adopted her. She has become almost like another daughter."

"I didn't know she is your niece. I have been wondering if there wasn't some family connection there."

"Yep, there is."

"Well, Reed started at Alabama this year, didn't he?"

"He sure did. A chip off the old block."

Jerry said, "Darn, I guess I wasn't around him enough to convince him to go to Georgia." They all laughed.

Marilyn asked, "Do you two have children?"

Tracy answered, "No, not yet, but we're hoping. We've only been married for about a year, and that's something we're working on."

After the talk about children, the women kept up the subject, but the inevitable talk about building and malls and apartments began with the guys with Frank taking the lead. "Are you still feeling good about our projects, Jerry?"

"Yes sir; more than ever. My superintendent and I went out to the apartment site yesterday and started laying out some of the buildings, so it won't be long 'til you will see some evidence that there will actually be buildings there.

"Excellent; that's what I like to hear."

Finally, Jerry called the waiter for the check, and after he took care of it the four of them began saying their goodbyes. In a few minutes they left the restaurant and went to their cars to go home.

On the way, Tracy said, "Jerry, I liked the Thomas's, and I think Marilyn and I could become friends."

"I'm glad because it looks as if we're going to be thrown together for the next umpteen years."

"You know, when Marilyn and I were talking about kids, it made me more anxious to have a baby."

"Well, we're trying."

"I know, but we're not having any luck. I think I'll call for an appointment with the doctor when I get back next week."

"I thought you just went to the doctor."

"I did, but it was just for a routine checkup. I think I need a complete physical just in case there's something wrong that's keeping me from getting pregnant."

"It would be nice to have some little Martins running around the house, wouldn't it?"

"Yeah, and have all of them look just like you."

The two Margaritas and the delicious dinner at the Knight's Table made them want to go to bed soon after they got home, and they both slept like babies all night.

****

Three Weeks Later

Jerry didn't realize just how many meetings he would be in when he agreed to build the shopping mall. Bob had come down from Chattanooga each of the last two weeks for meetings with the architects, Frank, and the investors. Each meeting had been necessary, although at the time some of them didn't seem so.

At the first meeting, Frank had mentioned naming the mall Skint Chesnut Mall, since Skint Chesnut was the first name of Douglasville. At the second meeting, he mentioned it again, and there were no objections, so since he had controlling interest, that's what they were going to name it.

Between Jerry and Bill Case and their use of the Layout Pro, all the buildings in the apartment complex were laid out and ready for the footings to be poured. The next step was the foundation and preliminary plumbing and then the road paving. Once the plumbing was complete, framing could begin on the first two buildings.

Melissa had begun to be constantly under foot. Whenever Jerry went to the apartments, Melissa went, too. If he went to the mall site, there was Melissa. Every time, she said there was something she had to do concerning the particular job, and always she made it a point to be close to Jerry and managed to touch him as often as she could. She would brush up against him, put her hand on his arm or shoulder, or if they were looking at blueprints or something else, she would have her face up close and sometimes even against his.

He tried very hard to keep his distance, but the cologne or perfume that she used smelled so good, it was really hard for him to pull away from her. They began to have lunch together more and more often, and in some cases, when he had to go somewhere, she would ride with him in his pickup without any objection from him. At the end of some days, he would think something like, *Boy, she smells good, but I've got to cut this out. While she's so desirable I can't afford to get mixed up with her. This has got to remain strictly business, besides I can't do Tracy that way.*

He had been so busy out in the field that he hardly had time to go to his office except for late in the afternoons. Most of the time he left his cell phone in the pickup so he wouldn't be interrupted from something important. On one particular day, when he returned to his truck and checked his messages, there was one from Barbara Mills asking him to call her. He thought *Uh-Oh, this might not be good.*

He punched in her number and when she answered he said, "Hi Barbara. This is Jerry. What's up?"

"Jerry, I'm so glad you called. Tammy missed her period again this month, and I feel almost sure that she's pregnant. I don't know what to do and I thought you might be able to tell me."

"Barbara, the first thing you need to do is take her to the doctor and see what he says, and then if she is, in fact pregnant, you can decide what to do then. Barbara, you know I'm here to help you, and I guess I can make suggestions, but what you and Tammy do will ultimately have to be your all's decision. I can't make it for you."

"I know, but you seem to always know what's best, and we depend on you so much. Just please help us to know what we should do."

"Take her to the doctor as soon as you can, and if he says she's pregnant, then call me and you and Tammy and Tracy and I will get together and try to come up with something. I want Tracy involved because she's a lot smarter about these kinds of things than I am."

"All right, but I don't know if anybody's smarter than you are, Jerry."

"I assure you, Tracy is."

"Okay, I'll make an appointment and call you after we see the doctor."

"How's Tammy doing with this?"

"She's worried sick. She says if she's pregnant she's going to get an abortion."

"I hope she'll change her mind about that. That baby is a part of her, and we don't want to kill it."

It was almost quitting time when he talked to Barbara, and after he talked to her, he went by his office for a few minutes and then went home. Tracy was there and they were glad to see each other; really glad to see each other. So glad, in fact; that they went to bed for a while before supper.

When they got up and were trying to decide what to do about dinner, Jerry told her about Barbara's call.

"What are they going to do? She asked.

"I don't know. Barbara wants us to help them make the decision about what to do, and I told her we could only make suggestions, but they would have to be the ones to decide what they are ultimately going to do."

Tracy said, "Isn't it something? Tammy's afraid she's pregnant, and here I am, wanting to get that way but can't. There's something wrong with that picture. Maybe the session we just had worked."

"Maybe so. Keep your fingers crossed. We might have to have another session tonight, just in case."

"We might have to."

The next morning Bob came down from Chattanooga to go with Jerry to meet with Clark Randle and Steven Carroll, the architects for the mall. Frank had made the conference room at the bank available to them and there was nothing else scheduled for the room that morning, so they didn't have to rush.

After Sandra, Frank's secretary, had served coffee, tea, or whatever to each attendee, they all sat down and Clark took the floor. He and his staff had created a schematic design of the mall and drafted floor plans with elevation drawings. Steven passed a copy to Frank as well as one to Jerry.

Clark then went over the drawing and explained various details. He said they were to have meetings with a team of structural engineers later in the week and would also meet with the State of Georgia and Douglas County Planning agencies to verify any requirements. The architects asked if they could have another meeting the following Monday because at that time they should have all the drawings finalized and could incorporate all the details about materials and finishes, any fixtures or equipment, and all systems in the structure.

He then addressed Jerry and Bob and said that after the next meeting they would be ready to select sub-contractors, and unless there was a reason not to, they should be selected at that time.

The meeting lasted a little over an hour, and when they had finished, Bob said, "Fellas, thanks for the insight into several things about the mall. If you don't need me any longer, I'm going back to Chattanooga. There are some things there that need my attention. What time do I need to be here next Monday?"

They all looked at each other, and then Frank said, "How about the same time as this morning?"

"That'll work. I'll see you then."

He shook hands with everybody and Jerry walked him out. "Dad, why don't you come down Sunday and spend the day with us, and then you will already be here for the meeting Monday?"

"I don't know; maybe I will. I'll call you before then."

"Be careful going back. I love you."

"Love you too."

Bob left and Jerry went back in. A couple of the investors had gone by that time, and only Frank and the two architects were left. Frank picked up the phone and told Melissa to bring him something, and she didn't take but a minute to do it. When she came into the room she scoped it out as she walked toward Frank with the papers. She didn't ask Frank if he needed anything else; she just went to where Jerry was standing and stood beside him. She made it a point to sway slightly and unnoticed, so she could touch him when she did. He took a step sideways when she did it the second time.

In a few minutes the architects left, leaving only Frank, Melissa, and Jerry. Frank then left and said, "I'll see you Monday, Jerry," and Melissa and Jerry were alone in the conference room.

Jerry said, "Well, I've got to go. I'll see you, Melissa."

"Don't go. Why don't I take you to lunch?"

"It's too early for lunch, Melissa, but maybe another time."

"We could go in my office and talk until it's time for lunch."

"Don't you have work to do?"

"Nothing urgent; besides I'd rather be with you. You can teach me about building things."

"Good try, Melissa, but I've got to go."

"Where are you going?"

"I'm going to my office right now, and then this afternoon I'm going out to the apartment site."

"Maybe I'll see you out there."

"Whatever. I'll see ya."

While he was at his office, he called H.R. Ingle, a friend of his who owned Ingle Electric, and asked if he was interested in doing the electrical work for the apartments he was getting ready to build, and H.R. said he was definitely interested, so they agreed to meet around two o'clock at the site that afternoon.

When Jerry drove up, Melissa was sitting in her Beamer waiting for him. *I can't believe this,* he thought. He got out of his pickup and went over to her car and asked what she was doing out there.

"I told you I'd probably see you out here, didn't I?"

"Yeah, I guess you did."

While they were talking, what looked to be a brand new Ford F-150 pickup drove up with two men in it. The writing on the door said INGLE ELECTRIC COMPANY. H.R. and his son, Rich got out and walked over to where Jerry and Melissa were talking, and Jerry introduced them to her.

Rich had graduated from Georgia Tech with a degree in Electrical Engineering and after working for a few years as an engineer at a high-tech company in what is known as Research Triangle Park, near Raleigh, North Carolina, he felt the pull of Atlanta and his family and came home and went into business with his dad at Ingle Electric. Since he had been back, he had been able to help land some pretty lucrative contracts for Ingle Electric due to his engineering background. He was a little younger than Jerry and had never married. He was considered by many of the local women as an exceptionally good catch.

H.R. told Jerry, "Tell me again what you've got going on here."

Jerry walked over to his truck and took out some blueprints and opened one of the sheets. "We're going to construct an eight building, sixty-four unit apartment complex with lighted tennis courts, a nice pool with a lot of lighting and all the bells and whistles of a first-class residential center. Since we've worked together before, I thought you should be the one to do the electrical work. Money is not a problem for the people who hired me to build it as long as what we do is a good value."

As he talked, H.R. and Rich looked over the prints.

Rich was a very handsome young man and one could tell he spent a lot of time at the gym, and the whole-time Jerry was talking to them, Rich's good looks weren't lost on Melissa.

At one point, Jerry said, "Come on; let me show you around," and they began walking over the grounds of the site. Jerry and H.R. led the way with Rich and Melissa following. Rich began a conversation with her, and the more they walked the farther behind they got.

Rich asked, "How long have you been working for Jerry?"

"Oh, I don't work for Jerry; I work for his boss."

"Really? Who's that? I thought Jerry owned the company."

"He does own Martin Builders, but I work for the people who own the apartment complex."

"Oh, I see." Smiling, he asked, "Well why are you out here; just keeping an eye on Jerry?"

She laughed and said, "You might say that."

And then Rich said, "Well, he's a lot to keep an eye on. I've known him since I was in school. When he first started Martin Builders, he got my dad to wire some houses he was building, and their friendship grew from there. I was helping dad on weekends when I wasn't in school, so I got to know him pretty well, and he's a real pistol. He's a really good man, full of self-confidence, so try not to ever get on the wrong side of him."

"I've already found that out. Are you married, Rich?"

"No, I'm single. Are you married?"

"No, still looking. Do you have anyone special?"

"Nope, do you?"

"Not yet, but I've got my eye on someone."

"Why just your eye on him?"

"Well, currently he's not available."

"Is he going to be available?"

"Yeah; he just doesn't know it yet."

"I don't understand; is this guy married?"

'Let's change the subject. What do you like to do in your spare time?"

Before he could answer, H.R. called to him and said, "Rich, are you ready to go?"

"Yes sir, I'm ready. Melissa, it was nice meeting you. Maybe we'll see each other again sometime."

"I'm sure we will. If you all will be working with Jerry, I'll probably be close by. I'll see you."

They walked together to where the pickups were parked, and H.R. and Rich left. After they had gone, Jerry asked Melissa, "What did you think about Rich?"

"I thought he was nice."

"You need to work on him; he would be a good catch for you."

"Thank you, but I don't need to find a good catch."

"Whatever you say. I'm finished out here for today, so I'm going to take off. See ya"

"Where will you be tomorrow?"

"Don't know yet. I might be in the office all day."

"I hope I get to see you sometime."

"Melissa, look; you don't need to see me every day. Why don't you call Rich Ingle, and see if you two can go to lunch or something?"

"I'd rather go to lunch with you."

"Melissa, back off. I've told you where I stand, and I haven't changed."

That remark made her a little mad, and she frowned and said, "I'm leaving. Good bye."

Chapter Thirteen

At almost exactly six-thirty Jerry's phone rang, and it was Barbara Mills. "Hi Jerry, it's Barbara. How are you?"

"I'm fine, Barbara. How about you?"

Without answering his question, she asked, Jerry, could you come over here?"

"I'm afraid I can't right now, Barbara. This has been a rough day, and I just have got home and put a casserole in the oven. Could I see you in the morning?"

"I really would like to see you tonight if possible. Could I come to your house?"

He didn't know what to say other than, "Yeah, I guess so."

"Could you give me your address? I have a GPS, and I can set it."

"Okay," and he gave her his address and directions to his house."

"Barbara, how about giving me an hour or so, will you?"

"Yeah. How long will it take me to get there?"

"I'm guessing forty-five minutes. Just wait about thirty minutes to leave, okay?"

"Okay. Thank you for seeing us, Jerry."

"You're welcome."

After they hung up Jerry thought, *did she say us? Tammy must be coming with her. Uh-Oh, she must be pregnant. I don't know what they think I can do. Oh well, if I can help by talking to them I'll do it.*

He saw their car as it came down the driveway, and he went out to meet them as they came upon the porch. "Hi, Guys. How are you all doing?"

Tammy answered, "Don't ask."

"Come on in," and he held the door open for them.

When they had gotten inside, Jerry asked, "Can I get you something?" and they both said, "No, thank you."

Tammy sat in one of the recliners and Jerry sat on the loveseat facing them. Instead of Barbara sitting in the other recliner, she sat down on the loveseat with him. In order for her to look at him when she talked she had to turn her body toward him, and when she did she was right in his face.

He pulled back from her and asked, "Do you gals have a problem?"

"Yeah, we do. Is Tracy here?"

"No, she's on a flight."

"Tammy went to the doctor this morning and our worst fears were realized; he said she's pregnant, and we don't know what to do. That's why we wanted to talk to you."

"Well, what do you want to do?"

Barbara said, "Like I said, we don't know."

"Tammy, you're the one who's affected by this. What do you want to do?"

"I think I should have an abortion, but Mama doesn't want me to."

"I agree with your Mama. You don't want to murder a little baby, do you?"

"Not when you say it like that."

"Have you thought about maybe going to one of the homes for unwed mothers?"

"I'm not sure what that is and where is one?"

"Well, ever since you and I talked, Barbara, I got to thinking about one of these homes, so I did some research and found that there are several in the State of Georgia. There's one here in the Atlanta area that sounds awfully good, but you might rather go to one out of town. I found one in Savannah and one in Macon and another down in Tifton. The first one I looked for was the Florence Crittenden home, here in Atlanta, but they are no longer in business. When I read about the others, they all look really good and based on the way they operate, I think you would be happy at any of them."

Tammy said, "You mentioned the way they operate; what does that mean?"

"I printed out some literature on some of them, so let me read a little bit about Kindred Spirit in Atlanta. This home merged with City of Refuge, and this is part of what I read. I'll give you this information before you leave. Here's a little bit of what it says." *Kindred Spirit is designed to be a safe haven for young expecting mothers. Out of a partnership with Grady Hospitals and Emory*

Hospital, the residents receive proper medical care, including prenatal care, delivery, and postpartum. Best of all, the mother gets to stay in school and can stay at Kindred Spirit for up to a year after the baby is born. "This is just a small portion of what it says about that place, and again, it's in Atlanta and you might rather go out of town to get away from your friends if you don't want them to know your situation.

"There are several more, but I think this is my favorite because of the Christian atmosphere. Here's what it says." *The Living Vine, a Christian maternity home in Savanna, Georgia is designed to be a sabbatical for expectant mothers. Believing that these women and their unborn children have been created for a special purpose in the Kingdom of God, our program is orchestrated so residents can focus on their relationship with Christ, while sequestered from the world.* "These are only two, and you can pull up more on the internet and choose the one you like best. You asked me what you should do, and I'm by no means an expert on matters like this, but I think if I was in your place that I would seriously think about doing something like this. What do you think, Tammy?"

"I don't know. If I had to choose one of these, I'd take the one here in Atlanta. That other one sounds too religious, and I'm not very religious."

Jerry said, "A home for unwed mothers is by no means your only option; that's just something I thought of and thought it would give you some peace of mind as well as the medical attention you're going to require. You can always stay at home, but if you do that, you're going to have to face all your friends. If you want to keep your pregnancy secret, staying at home might not be the best option.

"Now, there's another thing you're going to have to think about. You don't have to do it right now, but soon you're going to have to decide what you're going to do with the baby when it's born. You can always keep it, of course, or you might want to put it up for adoption. If you think you might want to put it up for adoption, then it's not too early to start thinking about what you're going to have to do in order to be sure your baby will have a good home. Tammy, these are not easy decisions to make, and they don't have to be made tonight, but they're things that will have to be decided on pretty soon."

"I think I would just rather get an abortion, and then it would all be over."

"I pray you will change your mind about that. It will definitely not be all over. If you kill that little baby you're going to have to live with that for the rest of your life, and that has got to be an awful burden to carry. Promiser me you'll think about the other options we talked about. Will you do that?"

"I'll think about them."

"Good girl. Well ladies, is there anything else we need to talk about? I hope I've given you some things to think about."

Barbara stood up and said, "You've been a big help, Jerry. Thank you. Tammy, we need to go," and Tammy stood up.

"She asked Jerry, "Can I use your bathroom?"

"Right through that door on the right."

While she went to the bathroom Barbara moved in close to him and said, "Thanks again for your help. I don't know what we'd do without you. Can I hug you?"

"You can."

She put her arms around him and squeezed, and then tilted her head back a little to where she was nose to nose with him and kissed him right on the lips. It wasn't a long passionate kiss; it was short, but long enough for him to feel her tongue. She let go immediately and stepped back without taking her eyes off of him. She smiled as if to say I've wanted to do that for a long time.

Being very cool, Jerry took it in stride and smiled back. He thought, *Uh-Oh. What's going on with this* just as Tammy came out of the bathroom.

She came back in to where they were and stood beside her mother. They thanked Jerry and said good bye to him and left to go home, but on the way to the car, Barbara turned around and smiled.

Jerry went in and got ready for bed and had a hard time going to sleep for thinking about what just happened with Barbara. Finally he dozed off and slept until time to get up the next morning.

When he woke up he lay in bed for a while thinking about the event with Barbara the night before. He didn't know exactly what to do because she and Tammy had grown to depend on him so. He thought, *that Barbara is a lot of woman. If it wasn't for Tracy I think I could have a good time with her. Based on last night, I think she's ready.*

Finally, he got up, fixed some coffee, got ready and went to work where things didn't start out very well.

Soon after he got to his office a fellow came in with a paper. It was a subpoena for him to appear in court at the trial of Thomas Nelson Key; better known to him as Tink. He wondered why they would want him because he didn't know Tink; in fact, he had never even seen him. He had only heard about him through Barbara and Tammy. He guessed it was because Tammy worked for him at the time she was abducted.

He thought, *I don't need this with all I've got to do. Hopefully, it won't take too long. How do I always manage to get caught up in things that don't concern me anyway?*

The trial was scheduled for two weeks from the following Monday, and since they were having meetings nearly every Monday he thought he should call Frank and alert him to the situation.

He dialed the bank and punched in Frank's number, but instead of Sandra, Frank's Secretary, answering, Melissa answered. "Frank Thomas' office, may I help you?"

"Why are you answering Frank's phone," Jerry asked.

"Well, hey Big Boy; Sandra had to be out today so I'm acting Secretary. What's up?"

"I need to talk to Frank; is he in?"

"He is. Just a minute."

"Hello, Frank Thomas."

"Good morning Frank; Jerry."

"Good morning Jerry. How are you?"

"I'm good. Listen Frank, I need to tell you something and part of it is confidential."

"It sounds as if you have a problem."

"No, no, I don't have a problem, but someone that you and I both know has one, and it might temporarily affect me and the mall."

"Well what is it Jerry?"

"Frank, do you remember Tammy, the girl that was with Reed and Stony the night they went in my house?"

"Yes, I remember Tammy."

"Well, I don't think I told you, and you might not know that Tammy was abducted a while back and was taken to an out-of-the-way place and raped several times."

"My gosh; that's terrible; no I didn't know about it."

"Yes, it is terrible. The good news is they caught the guy that kidnapped and raped her, but the bad news is she's pregnant from it. Her abduction is the reason I'm calling you."

"I don't understand."

"I'm not sure why, but the guy that kidnapped her goes on trial two weeks from Monday, and I've been subpoenaed to appear. Since we have been having meetings each Monday, I thought I should alert you to this because I will have to miss if we have one scheduled that day."

"Well, if the architects want to have one that day, we'll see if we can schedule it for another time. I appreciate your calling to tell me this, Jerry. Is there anything you can or will tell me about this situation? I'm interested because she's a friend of Reed's, and I know you tried to help her like you did Reed and Stony. I remember that she had an attitude when the break-in and everything happened. Do you think she instigated the abduction because of the way she was?"

"No, I don't think so. This happened on the last day the kids worked to satisfy their sentences. Reed and Stony finished up first, and you or somebody picked them up. Tammy didn't finish until later that afternoon, and my foreman took her to a convenience store so she could call her mother because her cell phone was out of battery. When she tried to call her mom on the payphone at the store she got her voice mail, and a seemingly nice young man offered to take her home and now, as Paul Harvey used to say; you know the rest of the story. Frank, I'd appreciate it if you would keep this between you and me. It will probably be in the papers when the trial starts, but I don't want to be the one to start the story. You know, since I've been subpoenaed it could be that Reed and Stony will be too since they had connections with her."

"You may be right."

Unbeknownst to Jerry and Frank, Melissa was listening in and heard the whole conversation. She was slightly shocked because even though she was almost like Frank's daughter, he had never confided in her about how he and Jerry first met, and she certainly didn't know anything about Reed breaking and entering somewhere.

When he finished talking to Frank, he hung up, and in about two minutes, his phone rang. Beverly answered and told him it was Melissa.

"Hi Melissa."

"Hi Big Fella. Whatcha doin?"

"I'm getting ready to leave for a meeting. What do you need?"

"Oh, I don't need anything; I just thought we might have lunch. Interested?"

"I can't today, but thanks anyway."

"You've got to eat. Where's your meeting?"

"It's at Jeff Clem's office."

"Who's Jeff Clem?"

"You're not nosy, are you?"

"No, I just want to know who Jeff Clem is."

"He's a lawyer."

"Why are you meeting with a lawyer; are you in some kind of trouble?"

"Good bye Melissa," and he hung up on her.

Before she had time to call back he got up and told Beverly he was going to Jeff Clem's office to sign the papers and pay for the land he was buying for the White Rock Estates neighborhood. "If Melissa Morris calls back and asks any questions, you can tell her where I am, but you don't know why I'm there, okay?"

"Okay; will you be back today?"

"Don't know for sure; probably."

He left and drove into Douglasville to Jeff Clem's office and met with Virgil and Frances Lowe and their Realtor, Becky Tate. There were a tremendous amount of papers to sign and by the time all three signed every paper, more than an hour had transpired.

When he walked out of Jeff's office, none other than Melissa was parked next to him in the small parking lot. His first reaction was surprise, then anger. He walked to the driver's side of his car and talked to her over the top.

"What in the name of common sense are you doing here?"

"Well, I just wondered what kind of lawyer Jeff Clem was and where he was, so I decided to investigate. After I got out here I realized it is lunchtime, so I wanted to offer to take you to lunch. Is that so bad?"

Walking around the front of his car to Melissa's side of hers he said, "Melissa, I don't know what you're up to, but I don't like it. You have no business following me, and I have told you basically the same thing before. Now I'm going to get in my car and go back …"

She curled up her lip and tried acting like a child and interrupted saying, "You don't like me? I'm just trying to be your friend. You act as if you don't like me."

"I like you fine, Melissa, but friendship is not what you're after. I've told you over and over that I'm not going to cheat on Tracy, and that still goes, so you might as well back off and in the future, you should make any contact you have with me strictly business. Do I make myself clear?"

She returned to her regular self and said, "Perfectly, but you've got to realize that the way I feel about you can't be strictly business. Before my mother died she taught me to always fight for whatever I wanted, and Big Boy, that 'whatever' happens to be you."

Before he could respond to her ridiculous statement his cell phone rang. "Hello, this is Jerry."

"Hi Jerry; Tom."

"Tom, whatta ya say, Buddy?"

"I don't say much; I just thought I'd call and see if you might be interested in going out to Cowboys tonight and have a couple of drinks. Wendy is gone a lot and I'm usually not very lonesome, but this time I am, and I thought it might be nice to have some company. We haven't been to Cowboys in a long time, and I thought it might be a nice change. Whatta ya say?"

While Tom talked, Jerry was getting into his truck, and when he was inside he closed the door and continued talking.

Melissa stood outside the truck, and while Jerry was inside talking, she was able to hear some of what he was saying. She picked up on the word Cowboys and that was enough for her.

When he finished his conversation with Tom, he started the truck, put it in gear and drove off, leaving Melissa standing there. The last thing she heard in his phone conversation was "I'll see you at eight."

On the way back to the bank, she thought about the way Jerry scolded her for showing up at Jeff Clem's and realized she might have been too forward when she told him what she did about his being her 'whatever'. She had no plans to ease up one bit on her quest for him, but decided to play it a little cooler.

When she got back to the bank she called her friend, Kim, and asked her if she would like to go to Cowboys that night. Kim said she would, and Melissa told her she would meet her there at seven-thirty. She wanted them to be there when Jerry and Tom came in so they might not think that they were chasing after them. She wanted it to look as if their being there was just a coincidence, but her being there so early was a dead give-a-way to her motive because at places like Cowboys, most people don't show up until ten o'clock or after. The bands don't even start playing until after nine. Jerry and Tom were only going there to have a drink and to provide company for each other since their wives were gone; not to dance or anything else except for maybe to listen to the music after it started.

At five after eight Melissa saw her target coming in the door and told Kim that they would soon have company, but before the guys could decide on a table, Jerry spotted her and told Tom, "Tom, there's someone here that I don't want to see. Would you mind if we go somewhere else? Maybe we can go to M.J.'s or The Upper Level. Do you mind?"

"No, that's fine with me. The Upper Level is nice; let's go there," and they left with Melissa in shock that they would do such a thing.

The Upper Level wasn't very far from Cowboy's, so they left Jerry's truck there and went in Tom's car. Melissa knew Jerry's truck but not Tom's car, and when she went outside she saw the truck parked in the lot and she had no idea where they went.

Jerry explained the situation to Tom as they drove to the Upper Level, and Tom understood because he had been with him that night at Oak Grove.

The next morning Jerry had to go to Frank's office to go over some things concerning the apartments, and when he got into the office, before he and Frank could get started on their business, Melissa stuck her head in the door and told Jerry, "Jerry, before you leave, would you mind stopping by my office? I need to go over something with you."

Jerry said, "Okay," then he and Frank went over the things that he had come for. When they finished, Jerry said he had to go, but Frank reminded him that Melissa wanted to see him. "You two are working good together aren't you, Jerry?"

Jerry wanted to tell him about how she was throwing herself at him, but he just said, "Yeah, we're doing okay."

Frank said, "Well, you really have an ally there. All she talks about is you, and according to her, you can do no wrong. Keep doing what you're doing. It can't hurt having her on your side."

He took a deep breath and headed for her office. He was dreading what was next. When he reached her office she said, "Good morning."

"Good morning."

"Did you have a good night?"

"Yeah; my buddy Tom and I got together and had a couple of drinks since both of our wives are out of the country."

"Where did you go?"

"We went to a little place that's quiet and out of the way; a place that Tom likes." He tried to keep from giving her the name in case he needed to retreat there again. "What is it that you wanted to go over with me?"

"Oh, nothing now. I was able to take care of it."

Not a word was mentioned about the night before. He knew she had seen him, but he hoped that maybe she wasn't sure that he had seen her.

Chapter Fourteen

Monday, Two Weeks Later

The trial of Tink was scheduled to begin at nine o'clock and it seemed everyone connected to it was there; including a lot of spectators.

Jerry was right when he said Reed Thomas and Stony Gray would probably be subpoenaed and of course, Tammy Mills, who was a central figure in the trial.

When Jerry and Tracy arrived, the courtroom was filling up. Frank Thomas and his wife along with the parents of Stony Gray were already seated, and there was just enough room at the end of their row for the two of them. Their seats were on the side behind the prosecutor along Barbara and Tammy and several other people, but the side behind the Defense was packed.

What Jerry and the others had forgotten was that a jury had to be selected and the crowd behind the Defense was made up of potential jurors.

At nine o'clock sharp, the Bailiff called the courtroom to order and gave the purpose for the trial. When he told everyone to be seated the judge spoke. It was the same judge that presided over Tink's preliminary hearing, judge Marcus Oliver. He began by having both lawyers come to his bench, and then he told everyone in the courtroom that they would then begin selecting a jury.

During his comments, he used the term *Voir Dire* two or three times. Jerry whispered to Frank, "What does Voir Dire mean?"

Frank answered and told him in a whisper that, "*Voir Dire* figuratively means 'to speak the truth.' In common practice, *voir dire* describes the process of questioning potential jurors by the judge or the lawyers.

When Judge Oliver finished his remarks he told Tom Bradford, the Assistant District Attorney, to call the first potential juror. All the potential jurors had numbers, and he called number one. He asked the man a series of questions and was satisfied with his answers and told the judge that the Prosecution accepted the man.

And then he invited the Defense Attorney, Regina Ashman, to

question the man. She asked a set of completely different types of questions than the D.A. asked, and she told the man that she would ask him five questions, and his being selected as a juror would depend on his answers.

She began by asking, "If you were my client, would you be completely comfortable having you as a juror on this case?"

Without hesitation, the man answered, "Yes Ma'am."

Then she asked, "Can you think of anything in your own life that reminds you of this case?"

"Yes Ma'am."

"What and how?"

"Well, nothing reminds me of this case except I have a daughter the same age as the girl who was raped."

Regina turned to the judge and said, "Your honor, I know we're not in trial yet, but I object to the term, "The girl who was raped. This has not been proven."

"So noted. Please continue."

Regina went on. She asked the man, "Is there anything that you have seen or heard that would make it hard for you to guarantee to judge my client the same as the other side?"

"No Ma'am."

"Is there anything you'd prefer to discuss in private?"

"No Ma'am."

"Is there anything we haven't asked you that you think we should know?"

"No Ma'am."

"Thank you, sir." Then she turned to the judge and said, "Your Honor, the defense rejects this person."

The judge said, "Very well," and told the man, "Sir, you may be excused. Thank you for coming."

He then told Tom Bradford, "Mr. Bradford, call your next prospect."

Number two was called and both sides approved him. Numbers three and four were women and both sides approved them also. And then number five was called. The Prosecution had no objections to him, but when Regina asked the second question, Can you think of anything in your own life that reminds you of this case, he said "Yes ma'am, a few years ago my sister was raped, and I'm pretty sure I would remember that when it comes time to judge this guy."

"Thank you, number five. You're dismissed."

Number six was an elderly woman that indicated she had pretty much made up her mind about the defendant, and she was dismissed. Numbers seven, eight, and nine were all dismissed for one reason or another, and it was noon; lunchtime.

Judge Oliver called a recess until one o'clock at which time Frank told Jerry, "The way this is going, I don't think they will empanel a jury in time to start the trial today, so I'm gonna leave and come back tomorrow," and when he said that, Stony's parents left, too, but Barbara Mills stayed. She didn't want to leave Tammy there by herself.

Jerry asked her if she and Tammy would like to go with him and Tracy to the little sandwich shop across from the courthouse, and they readily accepted his invitation.

When court resumed at one o'clock, they took up where they left off before lunch. Judge Oliver said, "Mr. Bradford, I think we're up to number ten so you may call him or her."

Tom thanked the judge and called number ten, a black, middle-aged woman, and both sides approved her. Going on through the afternoon, several more potential jurors were called, and after nearly depleting the supply, the twelfth juror was selected; a young man who was number thirty-four.

Judge Oliver said that since it was so late in the day they wouldn't start the trial until nine o'clock the next morning and dismissed the court.

The same people were present on Tuesday morning that were there on Monday except for Tracy and the jury pool that wasn't selected, making the crowd a whole lot smaller. Tracy had to fly to Paris that morning.

At exactly nine o'clock the Bailiff called the court to order, and when he had finished, Judge Oliver told the Bailiff to read the charges again. After he finished reading the charges Judge Oliver asked Tom Bradford, "Mr. Bradford, do you want to make an opening statement?"

"Yes, I do, your Honor; thank you." He got up and began speaking to the jury. "Ladies and gentlemen, this case is really cut and dried. We intend to show that this man (pointing at Tink) used his superior strength to kidnap a young high school girl and do terrible things to her. While she was his captive, he drove her to a

142

desolate area in the county and raped her multiple times. He then kept her captive overnight in a box and the next morning took her to that same area and raped her two more times. We're going to ask that you find him guilty of these charges. Thank you."

"Do you want to say something, Ms. Ashman?" Judge Oliver asked.

"Thank you, your Honor." She looked at the jury and said, "Ladies and gentlemen we intend to show that the charges against the defendant should be dismissed. You will see that the defendant and the girl did have sexual relations, but that it was definitely consensual. The defendant admits that he was wrong having relations with the girl because of her age, but it was not rape. Thank you."

Judge Oliver then said, "Mr. Bradford, call your first witness."

The lawyer said, "The state calls Miss Tammy Mills."

Tammy was sitting behind the prosecutor's table holding her mother's hand, and when Tom Bradford called her, she squeezed Barbara's hand, looked at her with a sense of dread on her face and got up. She walked the few steps to the witness stand and was told to put her hand on the Bible and swear to tell the truth.

"Miss Mills, please tell the court how you came to meet the defendant on the day in question."

Tammy told them how Bobby Kunkle had taken her to the convenience store when she finished work because the battery on her phone was dead. She told them how she tried to call her mother on the pay phone at the store, but got her voice mail, and how Tink was standing behind her waiting to use the phone, and how he offered to take her home in his van after he hung up.

"Did you willingly get in his vehicle?"

"Yes sir. How else could he take me home?"

"What happened after you got in his van?"

"He asked me where I lived. He didn't know where it was, but after I told him other places it is close to, he said he knew where it was. He started out, but was going in the wrong direction. When I told him we were going wrong, he said he wanted to take me for a little ride."

"What happened then?"

"He drove a long way and finally we came to a place where there were no houses or anything close by. He stopped the van and grabbed me and tried to kiss me."

"Did you let him kiss you?"

"Are you kidding? Heck no. I wasn't going to let him kiss me."

"What happened then?"

"He made me take my clothes off, and then he raped me."

"How did he make you take your clothes off? Did he just tell you to take them off?"

"No. He had hold of me, and while he held me he undid the buttons and zippers on my jeans and top, and then he reached around me and unfastened my bra. And then he pulled my panties down and got on top of me."

"Did you resist him?"

"I fought real hard, but he was too strong for me. When he was on top of me I tried to relax as best as I could because I thought it might not hurt as bad if I could relax.

"What happened when he got through?"

"Nothing. We sat there and he tried to convince me that I enjoyed it, then in a little while he did it again."

"You mean he raped you twice?"

"Yes sir; that day."

"What do you mean that day?"

"He raped me two more times the next day."

"Do you mean he kept you overnight?"

"Yes sir."

"Where did he keep you?"

"He had a big wood box in his van, and he put me in it and locked it."

"Do you mean he kept you in a locked box all night?"

"Yes sir."

"Do you know where you were?"

"No sir, and after he raped me the second time and put me in the box, it felt like we were riding, but I have no idea where we went."

"When you stopped riding, what did you think was going to happen to you?"

"I thought he was either going to kill me or else I thought I might die in that box."

"Did he unlock the box when you stopped riding?"

"No sir; he didn't unlock it 'til the next morning."

"Do you mean you spent the night locked up in a box?"

"Did you scream or yell for help while you were locked up?"

"I tried, but I soon figured out that with the thick carpet that it was lined with nobody could hear me, so I just laid there and did something I hardly ever do; I prayed."

"How long were you in the box?"

"I don't know, but I know it was all night."

"How do you know if you couldn't see out?"

"I know because when he put me in there it was late in the afternoon; it was starting to get dark, and when he opened it, it was morning, and he had stopped at McDonalds and got us a biscuit."

"Where were you then?"

"At the same place we were at the day before."

During her testimony, Frank's wife said softly, "Unbelievable; you poor baby."

The prosecutor continued. "What happened after you ate the biscuit?"

"He raped me."

"Did you fight him when he took your clothes off?"

"No; they were already off."

"What happened then?"

"He raped me."

"Are you telling the court that this man raped you four times? Why do you think he stopped?"

"Because a truck with some survey men drove up, and I guess it scared him. Right before they came I told him I had to use the bathroom, so he tied a rope around my neck and held onto it while I got out and peed. When he took off and started back to where he let me out, he said I could get dressed, and I did."

"How did you escape?"

"I didn't really escape. He let me out, but I can't tell you where."

"Did he threaten you any way when he let you out?"

"No, he just stopped the van and said get out."

He then looked at the judge and said, "I have no more questions."

The judge looked at the defense counsel and asked, "Ms. Ashman, do you want to cross?"

"I certainly do," and she got up and walked to the witness stand and said, "Good morning, Tammy."

Halfway under her breath, Tammy said, "Good morning."

"You don't mind if I call you Tammy, do you?"

"No."

"Okay Tammy, you testified that my client raped you. Isn't it correct that you made the first move to encourage Mr. Key to take you out?"

"No, he offered to take me home when I couldn't get in touch with my Mom."

"Isn't it true that when you finally convinced him to let you go with him that you suggested he take you to the place where you say he raped you."

At that point, Tammy burst into tears and shouted, "NO, I'M TELLING THE TRUTH. HE RAPED ME AND I DON'T CARE WHETHER YOU BELIEVE ME OR NOT. I'M NOT GOING TO ANSWER ANYMORE OF YOUR STUPID QUESTIONS," and she got up from the witness chair and started to walk away.

Judge Oliver said, "Bailiff," and the Bailiff intercepted her as she was trying to leave the stand. And then the judge told her, "Young Lady, this is a courtroom; not a place where you can come and go as you please. You will sit still and answer the questions that are asked you until you are dismissed. Is that clear?"

Some of her previous attitude came out, and she answered, "Yeah, it's clear, but she's lying."

Several of the jurors looked at each other during the exchange.

Judge Oliver said, "Okay, Ms. Ashman, you may resume."

Regina then asked Tammy, "Isn't it true that after that first night, you had Mr. Key take you to a friend's house where you spent the night and then pick you up the next morning and take you back to the spot where you two were intimate the day before?

"Absolutely not."

"Tammy, isn't it true that the sexual relations you had with Mr. Key were consensual?"

Yelling at Regina again, she shouted, "HOW MANY TIMES DO I HAVE TO TELL YOU? NO."

"Thank you, Tammy. No more questions."

The judge asked Tom Bradford, "Redirect?"

"Yes sir, thank you."

"Tammy, would you mind telling the court again where you spent that night when Mr. Key was holding you?"

Regina Ashman, in almost a shout, said, "Objection; this has already been asked and answered."

Judge Oliver said, "Ms. Ashman, I'm going to allow it. You may answer Miss Mills."

Tammy said, "I spent the night in that big box he locked me in."

"So you didn't spend the night with friends?"

Looking disgusted with the question she said, "How could I. I was locked in a stupid box."

"Thank you, Tammy. You may step down. Your Honor, I call Mr. Jerry Martin."

Jerry was sworn in and took his seat in the witness chair. Attorney Bradford said, "Mr. Martin, will you please tell the court what you do for a living?

"Yes sir. I own Martin Builders. We are building contractors."

"How you are acquainted with Tammy Mills."

"She worked for us for a while."

"Does she still work for you?"

"No sir. She was on a temporary, part-time basis, and her job finished up."

"Was she fired?"

"Oh, no sir. Like I said, she was on a temporary basis, and her work just ran out."

"Thank you. I have no more questions for this witness."

"Ms. Ashman, do you have any questions for this witness?"

"Yes sir, I do." She asked Jerry, "Mr. Martin, under what circumstances did Tammy Mills go to work for you?"

"Well, I had three houses under construction, and I had some part-time work available, so I hired Tammy and a couple of other high school kids."

"Did she come to you and fill out an application for work?"

"No. I had met her earlier, and I offered to let her come work for me."

"Mr. Martin, isn't it true that the only reason Tammy was working for you was to satisfy a sentence set down by the court for felony breaking and entering and felonious damage to property?"

"I guess so, but I'm the one whose property she damaged, and I'm the one who asked the court to let her work out her sentence by working it out at my construction sites."

Tom Bradford objected to that line of questioning and said her court sentence didn't have anything to do with this case. Before the judge could rule on the objection, Regina said, "It goes to show her character."

Judge Oliver said, "Sustained."

Regina said, "You said you hired Tammy and a couple of other high school kids to work part time for you. Were the other kids working off sentences, too?"

"Objection."

"Sustained."

When the judge sustained the objection, it pretty much assured that Reed and Stony would not be called as witnesses, and Frank let out a sigh of relief.

Regina then said, "I have no more questions for this witness."

"Mr. Bradford, call your next witness."

"The Prosecution calls Detective Grey Yokley."

The lawyer began his questioning. "Detective Yokley, how and when were you first in contact with Tammy Mills?"

"Her mother and Mr. Martin came into our office and filed a missing person report on Tammy, at which time I put out an Amber Alert. The next day we received a call from a Ms. Solaben Patel at the West End Grocery saying she had Tammy there, and that she said she had been kidnapped and raped. One of our officers picked her up and brought her into our office."

"How did she appear when she got to your office?"

"Surprisingly good, except for bruising on her arms."

"What do you think was the cause of the bruising?"

"It appeared that she had been held by force, thus causing the bruising, and she confirmed that that indeed was the case."

"What did you do then?"

"We took her to the hospital to be examined and have a rape kit done."

"What were the findings at the hospital?"

They found that she had been raped."

"Did you begin an investigation at that time?"

"Yes sir, we did."

"Were there clues that you could follow? And if there were, what were some of them?"

"Well, Tammy gave us a wealth of information, and we acted on much of that. Our Forensic people did an outstanding job of tracing threads and hair and other things, and the combination of everything led us to Mr. Key."

"Thank you, Detective. That's all I have."

"Ms. Ashman."

"I have no questions for this witness, your honor."

"Very well. Mr. Bradford, call your next witness."

"Your honor, the Prosecution rests."

"Ms. Ashman, call your first witness."

"Thank you, your Honor. I call Mr. Robert Kunkle."

"Bobby was sworn in and Regina said, "Mr. Kunkle, do you work for Martin Builders?"

"Yes ma'am."

"What do you do for them?"

"I'm one of their job foremen."

"Were you working on the day of the alleged kidnapping?"

"Yes ma'am."

"Do you recall anything different happening with Miss Mills that day?"

"Yes ma'am; she was working part time and her job finished up that day. She tried call her mother to come get her when she got off, but her phone battery was dead. I took her to a convenience store and let her out so she could call her mother on a pay phone."

"Did you wait to see if she reached her mother?"

"No, and now I wish I had."

"Did you ever see the defendant with Miss Mills before that day?"

"I never saw the defendant, period. Today is the first time I ever laid eyes on him."

"Thank you, Mr. Kunkle." She looked at the judge and said, "No more questions of this witness.

The judge asked, "Mr. Bradford, do you want to question this witness?"

"No sir; I have no questions."

"Call your next witness, Ms. Ashman."

"The defense calls Mr. Robert Treadwell."

"Mr. Treadwell, do you own a convenience store that goes by the name of Speedy's Quick Stop?"

"Yes ma'am."

"Are you Speedy?"

"That's what most people call me."

"I won't ask why you have that nickname. Mr. Treadwell, on the day of the alleged kidnapping at your store, did you see anything unusual happening around three or three thirty?"

"No ma'am, I didn't see anything."

"Do you recognize this defendant?"

"Yes ma'am, I've seen him in the store several times."

"Do you know him personally?"

"No ma'am. He just comes in to buy drinks and snacks and things like that."

"And you didn't see anything unusual that afternoon?"

"Did you see Miss Mills that afternoon?"

"I don't know if I did or not."

"Did you see the defendant that afternoon?"

"I'm not sure."

"Then you can't say with certainty that Miss Mills and the defendant left your store together."

"No ma'am."

"Thank you. No more questions."

"Mr. Bradford?"

"No questions."

Ms. Ashman, call your next witness."

"I call Mrs. Ryan Key."

After she was sworn in, Regina asked, "Mrs. Key, what is your relationship to the defendant?"

"I'm his wife."

"How long have you two been married?"

"Nine years."

"Is yours a happy marriage?"

"I always thought it was."

"Mrs. Key, on the night Miss Mills alleges that she was kidnapped, where were you?"

"At home until my husband came in from work, and then we went out to eat."

"Do you mean you and your husband went to a restaurant to eat that night?"

"Yes ma'am, along with our two children."

"Did you notice anything different about his behavior or demeanor that evening?"

150

"No, he was just his normal self."

"When you returned home from the restaurant did your husband remain at home all night?"

"Yes ma'am, until he left for work the next morning."

"No further questions."

"Mr. Bradford, any questions for this witness?"

"Yes sir. Mrs. Key, you said that you and your husband and two children went out to eat the night Tammy Mills was kidnapped, is that correct?"

"Yes sir."

"Where did you go eat"

"To Coxes Restaurant."

"Did you drive your husband's van when you went out?"

"No sir. We drove my car."

"Where was his van?"

"It was parked in front of our house."

"Mrs. Key, do you know if your husband has a large box in his van that's covered with carpet?"

"I think so."

"Thank you. That's all I have."

"Ms. Ashman, call your next witness."

"The defense calls Mr. Arthur Cox."

Arthur Cox took the stand, and Regina asked, "Mr. Cox, what do you do for a living?"

"I own and operate Coxes Family Restaurant."

"Do you know the defendant?"

"I can't say I know him. He comes into my restaurant from time to time."

"On the night in question, did the defendant and his family come to your restaurant to eat?"

'Yes ma'am; they were there."

'Was the restaurant busy that night?"

"Yes ma'am; it was very busy."

"If you don't really know him, and the restaurant was very busy, how can you be sure he was there that night?"

"Because, like I said, we were very busy, and his little girl knocked over a glass of water, and a couple of our people had to stop what they were doing and clean it up."

"Thank you, Mr. Cox. Your Honor, the defense rests."

"Very well. We'll now hear closing arguments."

"Mr. Bradford, you may make your closing statement."

"Thank you your Honor. Ladies and Gentlemen, if there was ever a cut and dried case, this is it. Miss Mills not only picked the defendants picture out of a photo lineup, but fibers from the defendants van were found on her clothes and in her hair, and the icing on the cake was when her DNA was found in his van. This was a horrific crime against an innocent sixteen year old girl, and you shouldn't even have to think about your decision. You must find Thomas Nelson Key guilty of all charges. Thank you."

"Ms. Ashman."

"Ladies and gentlemen, one of the Prosecution's key points was that the defendant was locked in a box in my clients van overnight. That's very strange since my client and his family went out to dinner that same night, and this fact was corroborated by the restaurant's owner, and his van was at home according to his wife. I ask you; how could that happen? Do you think anybody in their right mind would take someone they had kidnapped home with them and then gather his family and go out to eat? Mr. Key admits that he and the young lady had a sexual experience, but here's the key word; consensual. This man is a well-respected businessman with a nice family and has never done anything to cause a black mark to be put on his record. I ask you to find my client not guilty, and let's allow this family to get back to their normal lives."

The judge then charged the jury and gave them their options, and they left the courtroom for the jury room to weigh the evidence and hopefully come to a decision before the weekend.

Jerry thought, *this is Thursday, late morning. Surely, they won't have to debate this all afternoon and all day tomorrow. As the lawyer said, it's pretty cut and dried.*

When the jury went out, everybody got up and began to leave the courtroom. Jerry asked Frank, "Are you going to wait around for the decision?"

Frank said, "No, I don't think so. I've got so much to do at the bank, I'm going to go back. Are you going to stay?"

"Well, the day's half gone now, so I might just hang around for the rest of the day. If they don't come back by the end of the day, I probably won't come back tomorrow." Smiling, he said, "Some people have got me locked into building a shopping center and some apartments, so I'll have to get back to work. This trial has already cost me nearly a week."

Frank smiled and said, "Time's money, isn't it, Jerry?"

"You know it is. Look, tomorrow's Friday and hopefully, my guys have done their jobs this week, but I think you and I need to get our heads together, either tomorrow or over the weekend. I want to give you an update on what we've done so far. Will that work for you?"

"As far as I know now it will. I can't tell you for sure until I get back and see what's been scheduled for me while I've been gone. If I'm not available, you can meet with Melissa, can't you?"

With a frown on his face, Jerry said, "I guess so; if that's what you want me to do, but I would rather meet with you. I feel more comfortable with you."

"Why? Are you not comfortable with her?"

"It's not that I'm not comfortable with her; I just want to deal with the head man, and that's you."

"I understand, but I want you to understand that Melissa is me when you're dealing with our bank and our company. I've given her pretty much Carte Blanc when it comes to making most decisions for us. As chairman of a large bank and head of a large conglomerate such as ours, I can't possibly spread myself so thin that I can handle everyday decisions, so I have to have people to handle things for me. Naturally, I'll still make the major decisions, but you'll have to work a lot of things out with her.

"Another thing, Jerry; I've worked with you enough to know that you have a cool head on your shoulders, and you're sharp enough to make routine decisions yourself, so you really don't need me or Melissa, for that matter. If you run into something major, then call Melissa and if she thinks it necessary, she'll have you come see me. Does that make sense?"

"I just hope I satisfy you."

"I'm sure you will. Of course, we'll still be having our weekly get-togethers with the Architects, and that will put us together pretty often."

"Yeah, I didn't think about that when I said what I did. Everything's great."

"Do you want to grab some lunch while we're here?"

153

"Yeah, that sounds good. How about that little place across the street?"

"That'll be fine. I ate there Monday, and their hamburgers are good."

While they were at the diner, Frank asked, "Is Tracy out of town?"

"Yeah, she's in Paris. She's supposed to be back tomorrow afternoon."

"Well, you and Tracy and Marilyn and I need to get together again pretty soon. Marilyn had a great time when we went out before, and has mentioned doing it again several times."

"We did, too. I'll tell Tracy, and maybe we can do something in the next couple of weeks."

"That sounds great; just let me know."

In a very few minutes after they finished their lunch, Frank said, "Well Jerry, I've got to get out of here. I'll see you later."

"Okay. Thanks for the lunch."

Chapter Fifteen

After Frank left, Jerry noticed that the diner wasn't full, so he stayed at his table and made some phone calls because he didn't think the courtroom would be open yet. He ordered a Coke refill and spent another thirty minutes before leaving. He walked back across the street and entered the court house, and then took the stairs to the third floor.

Entering the court room, he saw six or eight people; three he knew and the others were people he had seen during the trial but didn't know them.

Tammy and Barbara Mills were there, and he wondered if they had sat there the whole time after the jury went out without having any lunch. The other person he knew slightly was Henry Morton, the owner of Morton Flooring and Tink's boss. He threw his hand up and waved to the ladies and walked over to speak to Henry.

"Hi Henry. You haven't been here for the trial, have you?"

Not real sure who he was talking to, he said, "Hi. No, I haven't. Tink works for me as an independent contractor and he has been one heck of an employee, and I just hated to see him go through what I assume the trial put him through. Someone called and told me the jury is out, and I wanted to come see what happens. Knowing Tink the way I do, I can't believe he would do what they're accusing him of doing."

Well, I think he did, Henry. See that girl sitting over there with her mother? She's pregnant, and she says Tink is the father. She swears she has not had sex with anybody else except for him when he raped her, and apparently the blood tests back her up."

"Wow! Looks like she has a strong case, doesn't it?"

"I'd say she does."

"How long do you guess the jury's going to be out?"

"That's the sixty-four dollar question. Of course, nobody knows, but I did hear some lawyers talking among themselves, and they think that since the case against him is so strong they won't be out too long. I hope they have a decision today because I don't need to be here tomorrow; I've got so much work to do."

"You look familiar. Aren't you a builder?"

"Yeah; I own Martin Builders. I had your company do the flooring in a couple of my houses a while back."

"That's right, I thought I recognized you. You're Jerry Martin, aren't you?

"I am."

"Well, it's good to see you, Jerry. Did I see your name on the sign where the new White Rock Division is going to be built?"

"You did, but I've had to put that on the back burner for a little while. I've got two more jobs that have to take precedence over White Rock."

"They must be awfully big to come before that. Can I ask what they are?"

"One of the jobs is not that big; it's a large high-end apartment complex, but the other is a *doozy*. Have you heard about the large shopping mall that's going to be built in Douglasville?"

"I've heard rumors of one going to be built."

"It's more than a rumor; it's a reality, and my company is the General Contractor."

"Wow! You're going to have to have a lot of flooring in that, aren't you?"

"Probably more than you've ever done at one time."

"How big is it going to be?"

"Over a million, seven hundred thousand square feet. It's going to be pretty close to the size of Mall of Georgia."

"Do you think I might be able to get in on some of that?"

"Maybe, but we're a long way from needing flooring right now."

"How about the apartment complex? Have you committed to the flooring on that yet?"

"Not yet; are you interested?"

"You bet I am. Could I come by your office and talk to you about it?"

"Yes sir, but not tomorrow; maybe one day next week."

"Great; I'll call you and set up a time. By the way, where are the apartments going to be?"

"In the Cowart Lake area. Do you know where that is?"

"I know exactly where it is. I'll call you the first of the week and maybe we can set up a time, okay?"

"Okay; I'll look forward to it."

"Jerry, it's none of my business, but can I ask what is your connection to this trial?"

"It's a long story. Tammy, the girl who was raped, worked part time for me, and I've become fairly close to her and her mother."

"Oh."

About that time, the Bailiff came into the court room, and someone asked him if the jury had come to a decision yet, and he said, "I think so. The Judge will be in in just a few minutes."

Jerry went up to speak to Barbara and Tammy, and said, "It looks as if it won't be much longer. I thought I heard the Bailiff say he thinks the jury has come to a decision. I'll see you all later." And then he went to where he had been sitting throughout the trial and sat down.

In about twenty minutes the judge came in and the Bailiff told everybody to rise. When the judge was seated, the Bailiff told everyone to be seated.

Judge Oliver told the audience, "I've been told the Jury has reached a verdict," and then he told the Bailiff to "Show the good people of the Jury in."

The Jury filed in and took their seats, and then Judge Oliver in his down-home, laid-back way asked, "Mr. Foreman, have you all come to a decision?"

"Yes, we have your Honor."

"Pass it to the Bailiff, please."

The Bailiff took the piece of paper and handed it to the judge. The judge read it and handed it back to the Bailiff who in turn handed it back to the jury foreman.

The judge then told the foreman, "Mr. Foreman, will you please read the verdict?"

The foreman stood and read, "Count one; kidnapping in the first degree; we find the defendant guilty. Count two; felony statutory rape of a child in the first degree; we find the defendant guilty: Count Three; felony statutory rape of a child in the first degree; we find the defendant guilty: Count four; felony statutory rape of a child in the first degree; we find the defendant guilty: Count five; felony statutory rape of a child in the first degree; we find the defendant guilty."

"Thank you, Ladies and Gentlemen. As soon as court ends for the day you will be dismissed with the gratitude of the court and of the State of Georgia," and then he said, "Court will be dismissed for the day and will reconvene Monday morning at nine o'clock at which time attorneys for both sides can speak as well as the defendant and victim, if they so choose before sentencing. I now declare court adjourned."

After court had ended, Jerry caught up with Tammy and Barbara. He asked to whoever wanted to answer, "Well, what did you think?"

Barbara said, "I had hoped it would go this way; that man did a terrible thing to my baby."

Tammy said, "I hope he gets the electric chair."

"Well, that won't happen," Jerry said. "This was not a capital case, but he'll probably get a real stiff sentence. The law doesn't condone messing around with minors, and when rape is involved, they really come down hard on the rapist. I wasn't planning to be here after today, but I think I'll come Monday to see what the judge gives him. I've been so busy lately that I haven't been in touch with you the way I should; Are you all doing all right?"

Barbara said, "Yeah, we're doing okay. We're going to contact one of the unwed mother's places pretty soon, and we'd sure like your opinion on which one. I know we talked about it before, but we didn't decide on anything for sure, and we need to make a definite decision. When do you think you might be able to help us?"

"I don't know when I could help you in a daytime, but I'm free most nights. Call me one night ahead of time, and I'll come over, and we'll get our heads together."

"Thank you, Jerry. We always like for you come over. I guess we just feel more secure with you around."

"Okay, I've got to go. I'll see you here Monday."

"Bye, Jerry."

"Bye."

Most of the day was gone when Jerry left the Courthouse, but he wanted to see what progress his people had made on the apartments in his absence, so he drove out to the site and was very pleasantly surprised at what he saw. He thought to himself, *Man, maybe I need to be gone more often. That Bill Case is a good one; in four days he made a bunch of pipes and some concrete look like two buildings. I'm going to be sure and tell him how glad I am with what he and the guys did. Maybe they don't need me as much as I think they do.*

When he left the building site he headed toward home, and about half-way there his phone rang. He looked at the caller ID and it said Melissa Morris and her number. He thought, *what now* and answered, "Hi Melissa. What's up?"

"Oh nothing; I just thought you might like to have some company for dinner since Tracy's gone. What do you think?"

"Sounds nice, Melissa, but you know where I stand on things like that."

"What I'm talking about is very innocent. I'm lonesome, and I know you must be, too. You can even invite your buddy, Tom, and we can go somewhere where there are a lot of people and it's well lighted. I just want some company tonight. Pleeeze."

"Melissa, you make it hard to say no, but I've got to. I just can't do Tracy that way, but thanks a lot for asking. I'll see ya next week."

"All right, but sometime you're going to be sorry you missed out on being with me. I can make you forget your troubles if you'll let me."

"I don't have any troubles, Melissa. Look, I'm pulling in my driveway now, so I'm gonna hang up. I'll see you."

"Bye."

He parked his pickup and went in the house and fixed himself a Margarita. He turned on National Geographic and sat in his recliner and sipped on it until he fell asleep. He slept for about a half hour and then went to the kitchen to see what he could fix for supper. When he opened the fridge it was almost bare, and he thought, *I should have agreed to meet Melissa. I wonder if it's too late to call her now.* Then he thought, *bad idea; I'll find something. Maybe I'll run up to the 129 Café. At least I won't be with Melissa.*

Tracy was scheduled to be back from Paris late Saturday afternoon, so when he got up Saturday morning, he washed his dirty dishes, vacuumed the floor and did his best to make the house look decent for her welcome home. He went to the store and bought some steaks, baking potatoes, and packaged salad with three kinds of dressing. He wanted everything to be nice for her so she wouldn't have to do anything when she got there because he knew she would be tired.

She got home around six thirty, and immediately after fixing the two of them a Margarita, he lit the grill and did a great job fixing the steaks. His years as a bachelor had come in handy. They enjoyed an outstanding meal and after spending some quality time together, they went to bed and slept until time to get up and get ready for church Sunday morning.

Jerry debated with himself about going back to the court house Monday morning, and when Tracy said she would go with him, he decided to go.

They arrived at the court house a little before nine, and when they got to the courtroom the Bailiff was getting ready to start the proceedings. Most of the same people were there that had been at the trial except for Frank and Marilyn and Stony's parents. Henry Morton was even there.

The Bailiff called the court to order and Judge Oliver came in. As soon as the judge came in, two deputies escorted Tink in handcuffs with a chain around his waist and the handcuffs hooked to it. They didn't want to take any chances on him getting away.

After he sat down, Judge Oliver addressed the court. He said, "The reason for our being here today is to pass sentence on Mr. Key after he was found guilty by a jury of his peers, and in addition, the court will hear statements from the attorneys, the defendant, the victim, and family members of the victim and defendant, if any of them want to speak."

He addressed the Assistant District Attorney first. "Do you have anything you want to say, Mr. Bradford?"

"No, your Honor. Thank you."

"Ms. Ashman?"

"Yes, your Honor. I realize the jury found my client guilty of the charges against him, but they made a terrible mistake. Mr. Key made a mistake, and he admits he made a mistake by having sex with a minor, but your Honor, there was no rape committed. Mr. Key has never even had a speeding ticket. He is a model citizen. He owns his own business and is a well-respected family man. We ask that you show mercy so he can continue to provide for his family and continue to be a loving husband and father."

"Mr. Key, do you want to speak to the court?"

"No sir. Ms. Ashman pretty well covered it."

"Miss Mills, is there anything you'd like to tell the court?"

Tammy stood up and said, "I'm just glad they found this thing guilty. He's ruined my life, and I hope he rots in jail. You probably can't tell it, but I just found out I'm pregnant with his baby."

"Thank you, Miss Mills. Mrs. Mills, do you have anything to say?"

"No sir."

Judge Oliver then said, "Very well. Mr. Key, will you please stand?"

Tink stood up with his attorney, and the judge said, "Thomas Nelson Key, having been found guilty on all charges, I hereby sentence you to sixty-five years to life in the State Penitentiary. The only reason I'm not sentencing you to life without the possibility of parole is because you showed enough decency to release this child instead of killing her. Court is dismissed."

When Judge Oliver announced the sentence, Tink's knees buckled, and the two deputies grabbed him and sat him down in a chair until he recovered enough to be lead out of the courtroom, and at the same time, Ryan Key, Tink's wife, burst into tears and cried aloud. It was a very serious and touching scene for a few minutes.

Tracy and Jerry were really glad to get outside as were Barbara and Tammy. The atmosphere inside the courtroom was hard to describe. Seeing a man basically lose his life for something that didn't have to happen affects people.

Jerry remembered hearing his preacher say that sin not only affects the sinner, but it affects others as well. Tink's sin not only affected him, but it ruined his wife's life as well as their two children's. It also messed up Tammy's life as well as her mother's, and no one knows how it will affect the life of the unborn child until years later.

The four of them stood and talked for a while after court, and then Jerry said, "Well folks, I've got to get to work. Trace, what are you going to do today?"

"Wendy and I are going shopping. Would you like to get together with her and Tom tonight?"

"Probably; I've got a lot to do. Let me call you. Barbara, Tammy, have you all thought any more about what we talked about the other night?"

"Yeah, and we think we'll see if Tammy can get in the home here in Atlanta."

"That's great. I'm very happy for you. If there's anything I can do to help you, call me."

"You've done so much already, I hope we won't have to call on you much more."

"Well, I'm here if you need me."

161

"There is one thing, Jerry; I hate to ask, but do you think you could help us figure out how to go about getting Tammy in the home?"

"Yeah, I'll help you with it. When do you want to do it?"

"How about tonight?"

"Tonight's out. You heard Tracy say we're getting together with our friends tonight. How about tomorrow night?"

"That will be good. How about seven o'clock?"

"I think that will work. I'll call you if I have to make a change."

"Thank you, Jerry."

With that, they broke up; Jerry to his office, Tracy to the mall, Tammy to school, and Barbara to work.

When Jerry got to his office he tried to call Frank, but he was gone all day, so he tried the next morning. That time, Frank answered with, "Frank Thomas."

"Good morning Frank," Jerry said.

"Good morning Jerry."

"I won't keep you; I just wanted to tell you that Tink Key got sixty-five years to life."

"Wow! They really threw the book at him, didn't they?"

"Yeah. The judge told him that the only reason he didn't sentence him to life without the possibility of parole was because he had the decency to turn Tammy loose rather than kill her."

"Well, I appreciate your calling to tell me this. Have you got a busy day today?"

"Very busy. I've got to try to play catch up after losing so much time last week. Have a great day, Frank."

"Thank you. You too."

After he hung up with Frank, he called Tracy. "Hi Beautiful, did you sleep well?"

"Like a log. How about you?"

"Same way. I always sleep good when you're laying beside me. Look, the reason I called is to see if you would like to meet your husband for lunch."

"I'd love to, but don't you remember? I have to go to the doctor."

"Darn! I forgot that. Oh well, we'll just eat together tonight."

"I can go to lunch tomorrow. I'm not flying out until Thursday."

"I can't. I've got a meeting with Frank and the Architects

162

tomorrow, and if it's like all the other meetings, it will run through lunch, and then tomorrow night, I promised Barbara Mills that I would come over there to help them figure out how to get in one of the unwed mother homes. You can go with me if you want to."

"We'll see. I probably wouldn't be much help on something like that."

"Okay, I've got to get to work. I'll see you tonight. Love you. Oh, call me when you get out of the doctor's office."

"Okay. Love you too."

The rest of the day went well. It seemed to him that he could see the progress on the apartments by the hour. He was so busy that he didn't notice that Tracy didn't call him, and later, about four o'clock, he realized that he had left his phone on the console in his pickup. He checked his calls, and sure enough, there was a missed call from her, but he decided to just wait until he got home, and he would talk to her then. There was also a missed call from Melissa which he was glad he missed.

Tracy was at home when he got there, and what was becoming a usual thing, Jerry fixed Margaritas for them both. When they sat down to enjoy them, Jerry asked, "Well, what did the doctor say?"

"He can't tell me anything for sure until he gets the results back on the tests that he ran. He did say that from what he saw, there should be no reason for my not getting pregnant. He said, however, that the internal injuries I suffered when I had that wreck could possibly be a problem, and he will know more when he gets the test results back, and Honey, do you know what he told me?"

"What?"

"He smiled at me and said, I know you probably won't want to do what I'm about to suggest, but I suggest you all just keep trying as much as you can, and who knows what might happen?" She smiled at him and asked, "Do you want to keep trying, Jerry?"

"Can we wait until we finish our Margaritas?"

She laughed and said, "Well, if you're going to play hard to get, I guess so."

When they finished their drinks, they became pretty lovey-dovey and went into the bedroom and did what the doctor told Tracy to do. And then, they got dressed and went out to eat.

Chapter Sixteen

The next morning, Jerry was up early and went to the apartments to give Bill Case his instructions for the day, and then he ran by his office before going to the bank for his meeting. He was planning to build and finish the first two buildings first and then the next two and then the next two and so on. They weren't very far on the first two, but he felt that they should go ahead and start some of the work on the next two because when some operations were done simultaneously there would be considerable savings.

Bob wasn't there for that meeting because the Architects felt that it wasn't necessary for him to drive down from Chattanooga, but they nearly inundated Jerry with all sorts of things. It was a little after three when the meeting broke up and he went back to his office where he went over the notes he took at the meeting. Having to go to Barbara and Tammy's at seven o'clock was really inconvenient because since it was nearly five o'clock then, if he went home he wouldn't get there until almost five thirty, and he would almost immediately have to leave because they lived about forty-five minutes away, so he called Tracy.

When she answered he said, "Hi beautiful; what's up?"

"Nothing; just sitting here waiting for you. I'm about ready for one of your good Margaritas. Are you going to be late?"

"I'm afraid so. Do you remember that I have to go to Tammy and Barbara's tonight?"

"Yeah, I remember."

"Well, I'm still at the office and if I come home I'll just have to turn right around and leave for their house, so I think I'll do better to stay here until time to go over there. I suggest you go ahead and eat, and I'll eat when I get there. Is that okay with you?"

"Not really, but you've got to do what you've got to do. What time do you think you'll be here, and I'll have your supper warm for you?"

He thought for a minute and said, "If I don't get held up for something, I'd say I'll be there between eight thirty and nine."

"Poor Baby; that's an awfully long day."

Always the jokester, he said. "Well, we Supermen can handle things like that."

"Okay Superman; I'll see you later."

Jerry became impatient and even though he wasn't to be at Barbara and Tammy's until seven, he decided to go on out early, and he arrived there at six forty. Barbara came to the door with a drink in her hand and said, "Hi Jerry. Come in."

He walked into the living room and Barbara said, "I haven't been home too long and thought I would fix some Whiskey Sour to relax after a rough day. Do you want one?"

"No thank you."

She walked up to him and held her drink up to his lips and said, "Taste this," and he did.

"He said, "Boy, Barbara, that's really good."

"Let me pour you one. I fixed a whole pitcher."

"Okay, but just one. Where's Tammy?"

She answered as she was pouring his drink. "Oh, she called from school and asked if she could go home with Polly, her best friend, and spend the night. I told her she could because after what she's been through I thought it would be good for her to be around some of her friends. You and I can talk about her situation just as if she were here because we do most of the talking anyway."

"Okay; if you're sure."

She handed him his drink and he sat down on the sofa. She sat in a chair across from him and they sat there and drank their drinks. She hadn't sat there but a couple of minutes before she got up and said, "My glass is empty. Excuse me; I'm gonna get me a refill."

"Sure; go ahead."

She went into the other room and poured her another Whiskey Sour, and when she returned to the living room, instead of sitting back down in her chair, she sat down pretty close to him on the sofa. When she did, he scooted over toward the arm of the sofa, and when he did that, she scooted with him as if she didn't want to leave any space between them.

When she scooted over next to him he looked at her and asked, "What are you doing, Barbara?"

"She looked back at him and said, "Nothing; why would you ask a question like that?"

"Because I came over here to talk about what Tammy is going

to do, and she's not here, and you and I are sitting here up close, drinking Whiskey Sours."

Before he even finished what he was saying, she reached across him and sat her drink on the table, and then when he finished talking, she took the drink out of his hand and reached across him and sat it on the table.

When she sat his glass on the table, instead of completely returning to her seat, she slipped her left hand around his neck and pulled his head toward her. Before he could react, she gave him a really passionate kiss.

He leaned away from her and started to say something, but before he could, she was on her knees on the sofa; leaning over him and kissing him again. That time, he didn't resist, but when she finished, he said, "Barbara, I can't do this."

"Why? Didn't you enjoy it?"

"You know I did; more than you know, but I can't do this to Tracy. When I married her I took a vow that I would be faithful, and I just can't do this to her."

He stood up and looked down at her while she was still seated on the sofa and started to say something, but before he could, she said, "Jerry, my husband and I began having trouble about a year before we divorced, and we've been divorced for almost two years. I haven't been with a man for nearly three years now, and I really need you. Can't you make a one-time exception? I won't ask you anymore."

"Barbara, I'm flattered that you would want me, and I think you're a truly desirable woman, and boy oh boy, you sure know how to kiss, but I guess I've just got too much conscience. I'm sorry."

"I don't guess you'll want to help Tammy and me anymore after this, will you?"

"Barbara, my intentions all along have been to help Tammy, and this doesn't change that. Of course I'll help. You and I just can't fool around. I think I had better come back when Tammy is here, don't you?"

"I guess. I'm sorry, Jerry, and I'm sorry you don't want me, but will you do me a favor?"

"Of course; what is it?"

She smiled at him with a devious smile and said, "Since we can't do anything, and you insist on being true to Tracy, could I kiss you one more time?"

At first he thought, *no,* and then he thought, *boy, this is really fun. She can really kiss,* so he said, "All right; one more time."

She got up and put her arms around him and began an unbelievable kiss. Since this was their last one, she wanted to make it count and in addition to just kissing, she began grinding her body against his, and then he began to grind against her. After a long time, he came to his senses and pulled away saying, "Man, that's hard to leave, but I've got to," and Barbara said, "Just one more time."

"No. That's it." Jerry walked to the door and said, "Barbara, I've got to go as bad as I hate to, but this can't go on. I'm sorry. Call me if you think you and Tammy need me," and he went to his pickup and left to go home.

All the way home he thought about how tempting she was and how much he enjoyed smooching with her, and one time he slowed down and was tempted to turn around and go back, but his better judgement won out.

When he pulled in his driveway, he stopped and turned off the motor and bowed his head. *Heavenly Father, please forgive me for nearly yielding to the temptation that Satan put before me tonight, and thank you for giving me the strength to resist. It sure was tempting to do what Barbara wanted. Satan was strong. Lord, I want to help these people, and if I'm put with them again, I pray that you will help me to be strong against temptation, and please keep Barbara from being the temptress. Thank you again for helping me tonight, and I'm sorry that I almost yielded to Satan's way. I make this prayer in Jesus' name. Thank you again, Lord. Amen.*

He got out of the pickup and went into the house. Tracy was watching TV and said, "I fixed spaghetti and it's still warm. Do you want some?"

"That sounds good; yeah, I'll have some."

She got up and fixed his plate. The spaghetti had cooled so she put it in the microwave for a minute or so. While it was warming she asked, "Would you like some Chianti with it?"

"Chianti! I didn't know we had any."

"I stopped and bought some today when I decided to fix the spaghetti. Do you want some?"

"Yeah, that sounds good."

Tracy put his dinner on the table, poured both of them a glass of wine, and sat with him while he ate. "Did you have a good day today?"

He said, "Yeah, it was good, but when you have to sit through meetings, you feel as if you're not being very productive, but I guess that's all part of it."

Tracy didn't have to leave again until Saturday, and that gave her almost four days to do what she wanted. She was enjoying her time off, and then her doctor's office called Friday morning and said they had received the results of her tests, and could she come in that afternoon; her doctor wanted to talk to her, and of course she said she would be there.

She met Jerry for lunch, and then he went with her to her doctor's office. When they got into his office he talked about different things in medical terms that neither of them understood, and then he gave them the news they were waiting to hear.

"Tracy, we have the results of the tests from the other day, and I'm afraid your chances of getting pregnant are what you might call *iffy*. That is not to say that you can't get pregnant; there are just some things that might make it hard."

"What are they? Are they things that I can do to make it easier?"

"I'm afraid not. Like I told you the other day when you were in here, I think the internal injuries that you suffered in your auto accident are major contributors to the situation, and in my opinion, that is the main reason, but your tests also show some things that definitely contribute. Before I get into the test results, let me ask you this; Do you have regular periods?"

"Yes and no. Sometimes I have like a half a period, but I always have some."

"That's what I thought. There are three things that can possibly affect your periods, thus causing problems with getting pregnant. First is what we call POI, which stands for Primary Ovary Insufficiency. This is a condition in which your ovaries stop producing hormones and producing eggs at a young age; even younger than you. Women with POI do not ovulate regularly, or sometimes not at all, and may have abnormal levels of hormones due to problems with their ovaries.

"Women with POI often have trouble getting pregnant. However, pregnancy is still possible. About 5% to 10% of women with POI get pregnant without medical treatment."

"So you think I have POI?"

"It looks like it, according to the tests. Another test reveals the probability of a condition called PCOS, which stands for Polycystic Ovary Syndrome. The name tells you that it involves the ovaries as well, and it is one of the most common causes of female infertility. The third possibility is something called Uterine Fibroids. Uterine Fibroids are noncancerous tumors that form inside the uterus, and these, too, can cause female infertility.

"Tracy, I'm not confident that any of these three things will cause you to be infertile. Like I said before, I believe the injuries you suffered in your wreck are the main reasons your having such a hard time getting pregnant. You and Jerry just keep trying; you may succeed one day. Any questions?"

"Dr. Dodd, I'm nearly thirty-seven years old now and that's old to bare children. In your opinion, would we be better off if we adopted a child rather than keep trying to conceive?"

"Like I told you, Tracy, you can possibly get pregnant, but with the conditions I described, it's sort of *iffy*. If my wife and I were in your and Jerry's place, I think we would probably explore adoption. That's the perfect solution for many people. In the meantime, you all can have a lot of fun trying."

"Okay, but I've got to say that I'm disappointed, and I know Jerry is, but I guess it is what it is. Thank you, Dr. Dodd."

They left the doctor's office and neither uttered a word all the way to the car. When they finally did get to the car, they got in, and before Jerry started the motor he looked at Tracy and asked, "What do you think?"

"I think we're going to have to do it about three times a day and hope we get pregnant or else resign ourselves to the fact that we might not have any children. What do you think?"

"Naturally I'm kind of disappointed, but I can make it without kids as long as I have you. You're the most important thing in my life," and with a smile on his face he said, "But I do like what you said about doing it three times a day."

She said, "You're a rascal; did you know that, and I love you so much. What would I do without you?"

He started the motor and asked, "Where are we going now?"

She said, "I don't care. I guess we can go home."

And then Jerry said, "Tell you what; it's too late for me to go back to the office and it's too early for dinner. Why don't we go by your Dad's store and visit with him for a little while and then go to the Old Smokey's and get some of their good barbeque? How does that sound?"

"It sounds good. Let's do it," so that's what they did.

When they got ready to leave Jack's store, Tracy asked, "Daddy, we're going to the Old Smokey's. Do you want to go with us?"

"I don't think so tonight. I had lunch there today, and I'm not very hungry. Thanks for the invitation, though."

"Okay, but I wish you would go with us. I've got a flight tomorrow, so I won't see you again until next week. Keep my big boy here straight, and I'll see you when I get back. I love you."

"I love you too. Where are you going this time?"

"I'm going to Rome."

"Sounds like fun. Tell that pilot to be careful."

She grinned and said, Okay, I'll tell him." And then she kissed him and said, Bye, Daddy."

The next morning they were both up early. Tracy had to leave at seven thirty in order to get to the airport in time to do her pre-flight duties before they took off at ten o'clock. While she was getting ready, Jerry cooked breakfast for the two of them, and they ate together.

She left right at seven thirty and Jerry was right behind her on his way to the mall site. The Architects had been working with surveyors for the last couple of weeks and they had things pretty well lined out and almost ready to start laying out the mall itself.

He knew that he would have to have a field office once they started building, so he made a deal with one of the trucking companies to buy a forty-foot trailer to use for that purpose. He hired a painter to paint it and then had a sign painter go by and paint MARTIN BUILDERS on both sides. He had already been out there to decide on where it should be, and he prevailed on the trucking company to deliver it to the site.

He called the guy at the truck line and the guy said they would bring it before noon and wanted to know if he would be there, and he said he would. About mid-morning he looked up and saw it coming at a distance and he was proud as punch when he saw a large trailer with the name of his company on the sides. The driver worked for a few minutes until he got it exactly where Jerry wanted it, and then he unhooked it from the tractor and left.

After he left, Jerry wanted to get inside, but the door latch was so high he had to back his pickup over to it and stand in the bed in order to reach it. The sides of the pickup bed were so high, all he could do was unfasten the latch and open the door a couple of inches, and then pull the pickup away so the doors would open. Once the doors were open, the floor of the trailer was forty to forty-five inches off the ground, and instead of climbing up and getting his clothes dirty, he backed the pickup back again and stood in it and then stepped into the trailer.

He knew he was going to have to do some work on it, but all that made him realize that the first thing he needed were some steps. He needed some tables for blue prints and other things, and he would have some men go out Monday and build those things. He thought, too, that he would call H.R. Ingle and have him or some of his men come out and run some lights; in fact, the lights would have to be put in before the tables and other things were built inside.

He stayed a while longer and planned for the furnishing of the trailer and then left to go home. It had been a long week, and he was ready to relax, but before he did, he wanted to see if H.R. might happen to be in his office. When he called, Rich Ingle answered.

"Hi Rich; Jerry Martin. Is your Dad there this morning?"

"He is. Just a minute."

"Hi Jerry; what's happening?"

"Everything is busy, busy. Listen, I need to hire your company to run some lights in a forty-foot trailer I bought to use as a field office at the mall. Do you think you could possibly do that Monday?"

"I don't see why not. Is the trailer at the mall now?"

"Yeah. I can meet your men out there, and we can decide where to put them, and also, H.R., I need to have power hooked up to Georgia Power's line when you wire the trailer. Can you do that, too?"

"You bet we can, but Jerry, you'll have to contact Georgia Power to work out the details of the hookup. Since you do so much business with them you can probably handle it by phone, and in the meantime, we'll be wiring the trailer. Can you meet my guys out there around eight thirty?"

"That'll be perfect. Thanks' H.R.."

While he was at his office, he called Charles Simmons. When Charles answered, he said. "Charles. Jerry Martin. How ya doing? Listen, I hate to bother you on Saturday, but I need to find out something."

"Okay; what do you need to know?"

"Within the next few days we're going to be ready to start laying out the mall, and I'm wanting to know if my Layout Pro is able to handle something that large."

"Absolutely; in fact, if you'll call me when you get ready, I'll come out and help you get started. It will be no different than the apartments you're building except on a larger scale."

"That will be great if you can help me get started. I was just afraid it might not work for something that large. Thanks a lot, Charles. I'll give you a call. It might be one day toward the end of next week. "

"Okay, Jerry. I'll be happy to help."

"Thanks again. I'll see ya."

When he got off the phone he sat at his desk and drew ideas of what he wanted in the trailer and how and where he wanted everything. After an hour or so, he left and went home to work with the horses.

Chapter Seventeen

Monday turned out to be a *crusher*. First, he had to meet the electricians at eight thirty, and when he called Georgia Power to have the power turned on, he found out that there was no power where the trailer was parked, so he had to go into their office and try to get things worked out. There would have to be major lines run for the mall, and the Architects would have to arrange for that. In the meantime, he needed power to his trailer.

When he found out that there was no power for him, he borrowed their phone book and looked up the number for Carroll and Randle Architects. He found the number and called. Clark Randle was not there, but Steven Carroll was, and he asked to speak to him. When he answered Jerry said, "Steven, this is Jerry Martin. How are you?"

"I'm fine, Jerry. How about you?"

"I'm okay. Listen, I'm trying to set up a field office out here at the mall site, and there's no power out here. I know a lot of power is going to have to be run for the mall, and they tell me there's no order for that. Are you guys the ones to have that done?"

"We are, and we ordered it last week. They're supposed to run a line this week, and then they can branch off the main line to your office."

"Well, they're telling me there's no order. Maybe you need to talk to somebody because I need electricity now."

"Okay, Jerry, I'll call my man and call you back. Where can I reach you?"

"You can call me at this number. I'm on my cell."

He thanked the lady at the office and left to go back to the mall site. On his way back, Steven called and said everything was worked out and he should have power by Wednesday. He wasn't happy with that, but since that's the way it was, he had to accept it.

Since he had been gone, some of his men had shown up and were waiting to find out what he wanted them to do. He had told Bobby Kunkle when he talked to him earlier what he wanted to do and told him to have the guys bring the necessary lumber to do the job, and to bring a ladder or two, but there was a problem; there wasn't any power to run the tools, and they didn't have any hand tools with them.

The only thing he knew to do was to send the men back, and since there were no lights, the electricians couldn't see to work, so he sent them back, too. He called H.R. and apologized, and H.R. said, "No problem. Call me when you get ready."

Since nothing could be done at the mall, Jerry went to the apartment job and spent the rest of the day.

The first two buildings were really taking shape, and the second two were beginning to look a little like buildings. He thought that since things were going to well, it was time to start on the third two.

While he was there, Henry Morton, with Morton Flooring, called and wanted to know if he could come by, and Jerry told him he could, but to make it after lunch; somewhere around two o'clock.

****

Two Weeks Later

Martin Builders was abuzz with activity. The apartments were coming along, and Jerry had decided to go ahead and begin the fourth two buildings, making all eight under construction. The first two were already taking on the look of a showplace, and the second two were showing real progress.

At the mall, all the surveying was finished and the mall itself was being laid out. The plumbing company that Jerry hired was beginning to lay pipes and make the connections for the water and bathrooms and all the other things that would require water when the mall was finished.

One day when Jerry was in his field office trailer looking at some blueprints, Melissa was there, and his phone rang. "Hello, this is Jerry."

"Jerry, this is Barbara. How are you?"

"Hi Barbara. I'm fine, how are you? I haven't seen or talked to you in a while; in fact, I don't guess I've seen you since that night at your place. How's Tammy?"

"She's fine. We've decided that she's going to the Kindred Home for Unwed Mothers."

"Well, I think that's great."

174

"She didn't know if she wanted to or not because of their emphasis on religion, but she didn't want to leave Atlanta, so that's where she's going. I don't know what it cost to go there. I just hope we can afford it. Listen, the main reason I called you was to tell you that Detective Yokley called a few minutes ago and said Tink Key committed suicide last night. He had managed to get a plastic bag and he used it to smother himself. Detective Yokley said that apparently he was afraid that the other prisoners would kill him. They had already been giving him a rough time."

"You don't mean it. Man, that's rough. Well, I appreciate your calling and telling me this. I have wondered how he would make out in there after what he did, and now we know, don't we?"

"Yeah, we know. Detective Yokley said that even though most of the prisoners are hardened criminals and a lot of them are guilty of violent crimes, they don't cotton to a man that molests children, so they really made it hard on him."

"Does Tammy know about it yet?"

"No, she's at school, and I didn't call her. I'll tell her when she gets home."

"I wonder how she'll feel about it."

"She'll probably be happy. She acts like she hates him. Well, Jerry, that's all I wanted. I just wanted to tell you about Tink. I'll see you."

"Wait a minute. Do you all need anything?"

"Not really. Nothing that we can't handle ourselves. I know you don't want to have any more to do with us, so we'll make do."

"That's not true, Barbara. I'm here for anything you might need and you should know that by now. When is Tammy leaving?"

"Pretty soon. She wants to go before she starts showing. I'm going over there one day this week to find out more about it and how much it costs, and then I guess she'll move in whenever they say she can. It's sure going to be lonesome around here when she leaves."

"I know it will. Maybe you can find something to occupy your mind when you get lonely."

"I already have."

"What?"

"You don't want to know."

"Uh oh; I think I know."

"I think you do too. Well, I'll see you, Jerry."

"Bye Barbara. Be sure and call me if I can help you."

"Bye Jerry."

After he hung up he just sat there, staring into space.

Melissa asked, "Who was that?"

Jerry, being very facetious asked, "Didn't I tell you?"

She said, "No."

"Well, it must not be any of your business."

It made her mad and she said, "You're a certified wise ass; did you know that?"

"That's what I've been told."

She then asked, "Who is Barbara?"

He replied, "My girlfriend."

"You're impossible. I'll see you tomorrow. Bye," and she left and slammed the door behind her.

When he heard her car leave, he called Henry Morton.

"Henry, Jerry Martin How're you doing?"

"I'm good Jerry. How're you?"

"Good. Listen, the reason I called is to tell you that I got a phone call a few minutes ago telling me that Tink Key committed suicide in prison last night. Since he worked for you, I thought you'd want to know."

"Darn! I hate what he did, but I thought a lot of Tink. I'm sorry he killed himself."

"I know and I'm sorry. I just wanted you to know. I'll see you Henry."

"Okay. Thanks for calling, Jerry."

Tracy was due in from a trip that morning, and he wondered if she had gotten home yet, so he called his house. No answer; then he called her cell, and she answered.

"Hi Sweetie. Where are you?"

"At the grocery store. It seems like I remember our cupboard being pretty bare when I left, so I'm replenishing it. What are you doing?"

"I'm getting ready to wrap the day up and come see you. Don't cook, and we'll go out and get something after a while. Do you want to do that?"

"That's fine with me. I'm kinda tired."

Having a Margarita first thing when they got home had gotten

176

to be a regular thing when Tracy was in town, and that day was no exception. He fixed enough for each of them to have two, and they relaxed and enjoyed them and each other before they went to eat. While they were at the café, Jerry said, "Honey, Tink Key killed himself last night."

"You don't mean it."

"Yeah, he got hold of a plastic bag and suffocated himself."

"How did you find out?"

"Barbara Mills called and told me. Detective Yokley called her."

"I'm not really surprised because I've heard that prisoners don't accept child molesters, and probably, if he didn't do it himself, one of them would have done it for him."

"You may be right."

They finished eating and went home, and as soon as they got there, Tracy went in and put on her pj's. They watched TV for a little while and then turned in early.

The next day while Jerry was in his office, Barbara called again. "Good morning, Barbara."

"Jerry, you said you would still help us, and I'm afraid we need you. When can we get together?"

"Anytime. Do you want to meet me or do you want me to come over there?"

"I'd like it if you would come over here. Could you come tonight?"

"Will Tammy be there?"

She laughed and said, "Yeah, she'll be here scaredy-cat."

"You're right about that. I'm a scaredy-cat. What time?"

"Seven or eight o'clock; it really doesn't matter."

"Okay. If it doesn't matter, I'll probably be there a little before seven."

Melissa had come to his office early to get information from him about various subcontractors, and when he hung up she said, "Barbara again?"

"Yep. Barbara again."

"I want to know who Barbara is."

"I told you; she's my girlfriend."

"You're ridiculous, do you know that?"

"That's what Barbara says."

Aggravated, she said, "Oh, I'm not even going to talk to you anymore."

Then she said, "She must have called you a scaredy-cat. What was that all about?"

"Just an inside joke."

"Why won't you tell me who she is?"

"Because it's none of your business. She has nothing to do with anything remotely connected to you."

Just then, Beverly came on the intercom and said, "Jerry, there's a Monty Shepherd on the phone for you. Do you want to take it?"

"Absolutely."

"Hello."

"Jerry, this is Monty Shepherd, up in Chattanooga. How're you doing this morning?"

"I'm fine, Monty. How are you?"

"I'm good. Listen, I was with your Dad yesterday, and he was telling me that you're boring with a big auger down there.

"That's right. Things have been falling our way lately, and we're very thankful for everything that's happened."

"Jerry, I don't know how much you know about me, but one of the things I am involved with is the Fellowship of Christian Athletes, and Bob tells me that you have a story that would be interesting to tell at one of their meetings."

'I'm not sure what you're talking about."

"About how you met and got involved with the head of the bank down there."

"Oh yeah. Monty, I found out first hand that God truly does work in mysterious ways. It's an interesting story."

"Look Jerry, we're sending one of our airplanes down there tomorrow to be serviced, and if I hitch a ride on it, do you think you might be able to squeeze in some time for us to get together?"

"Absolutely, I've been wanting to meet you for a long time, and tomorrow will be perfect. What time will you be here?"

"We're supposed to have the plane there at nine o'clock. Anytime after that will be good for me, so whenever you say."

"Why don't I pick you up at the airport and we can spend some time together?"

"That will be good. Come to the area where the private planes are, and I'll see you then."

"I'll be there, and I'm really looking forward to it. See you tomorrow."

That night he told Tracy about Monty coming down the next day and asked her, "Would you like to have lunch with us tomorrow?"

"I'd love to, but tell me who Monty Shepherd is."

"I can't believe this. Monty is only one of the most successful men in the world. He has a company named Shepherd Apparel up in Chattanooga."

"Shepherd Apparel; I know who that is. If you'll look in my closet, you'll find some of their clothes."

"Okay, I'll call you in the morning and let you know when and where. It will be somewhere around noon, okay?"

He had a hard time finding the area where private planes went in and out, but after asking directions twice, he finally found it, and when he went inside, it wasn't hard to figure out who Monty was. He was the handsome guy that looked like a male model and had success written all over him.

Jerry went up to him and asked, "Are you Monty?"

"I am, and you must be Jerry."

When they got to his pickup, he asked Monty, "Is there anything in particular that you would like to do while you're down here?"

"Not really. Your Dad told me about some of the things you've got going on, and I'd just like to see them. I'm a fan of people who are successful and give God the credit. Just take me where you want to."

"Okay, I'll be happy to."

The first place he took him was to the apartment complex. Men were working all over the place, and Jerry pointed out the four stages of two buildings each, and Monty said, "Boy, these are going to be nice. I'm very impressed." They stayed at the complex for about a half-hour, and then out in the country to the White Rock Estates site.

As they drove to the beginning of the site, Monty saw the sign with the name of the development and the name of Martin Builders and commented on it. Jerry turned off the main road and slowly drove down the dirt trail that would one day be a paved road, and he explained everything that was going to be done to make White Rock one of the nicest residential neighborhoods in the entire Atlanta area.

Before they left White Rock, Jerry said, "When we go to lunch, I'll tell you about this. It's the beginning of what my Dad told you would be the story I'll tell you."

"I'm anxious to hear it."

"Monty, I'd like for you to meet my wife, Tracy. Would you mind if she meets us for lunch?"

"By all means. I'd love to meet her. Did you say her name is Tracy?"

"Yeah, Tracy. I'd better call her."

He dialed her number and when she answered, he asked her," Hi Beautiful. How would you like to have lunch with two good-looking men?"

She said, "I'd love to. Do you know where I can find two good-looking men?"

"Very funny. Yeah, I know where you can find two good-looking men, but today, you're going to have to settle for Monty and me. If you're interested, how about meeting us at." He held the phone down and asked Monty, "Do you like barbeque?" and Monty said "Yes." Then he held the phone back up to his ear and said, "Meet us at Old Smokeys in Douglasville in about thirty minutes."

Their timing was perfect. Tracy was pulling into the parking lot just as Jerry was parking. Jerry and Monty went over to her as she got out of her car, and Jerry introduced her to Monty. They went inside and luckily, there was an open booth.

When they ordered and were waiting for their food, Monty asked Tracy what she did while Jerry was working, and when she said she was a Flight Attendant on international flights, a whole new branch of conversation got started. Since Monty's company owned some very high-end airplanes and flew around the world, he knew a lot about them, and since Tracy flew on some of the best planes, they established an immediate commonality. Jerry was sort of left out of the conversation until the food arrived, and then they all stopped to eat. When they were about through, Monty said, "Jerry, you said you were going to tell me a story. Would now be a good time?"

"Yeah, but first, do you want anything else?"

"No, I'm stuffed."

"Okay then. I'm not sure what my Dad told you, but I've been down here building houses for quite a while, and I've been

180

moderately successful. I managed to make a living and a little bit more, but I could never seem to hit the big one that would let me grow to major contractor status. One day. I was down in the country where we went to the White Rock area this morning, and when I saw that land, something just told me that that would be a great place for a residential development, so I began to try and work out something. Long story short, I was able to progress to the point where it was up to the county to decide whether or not they would put in water, electricity, and streets.

"I began talking to the bank about financing the development, but they wouldn't do anything until the red tape was overcome about those things, so I was stuck. Then, about two years ago I had three houses going and one night some teenagers broke into one of them and did a tremendous amount of damage. They tore up nearly all the sheetrock and did a lot of other damage and later that night, the police caught 'em. There were two boys and one girl. I remembered back to my teenage years and felt sorry for them, and when their trial came up I was able to convince the judge to let them work out their sentences by working for me. The terms of the sentences were that they would work them out by working for me, and if they successfully completed them their records would be wiped clean, and we're talking about felonies here.

"Now, back to White Rock. One day, not too long ago, the county came through and agreed to put in water and sewers. That allowed me to go back to the bank, and then when I presented my plan to them, the guy I had been working with said it was too big for him; that I would have to talk to someone up the ladder from him so he made an appointment for me to come back and talk to the big man.

"When I went back, my guy took me upstairs to the man I was to talk to, and Monty, it wasn't just someone a little higher than my guy; it was the Chairman of the Board of the bank. When I walked into his office, I nearly passed out. Do you know who the Chairman was? It was none other than the father of one of the kids that broke into my house. He was very appreciative of what I had done for him and his wife and son, but he is too good a businessman to base his business decisions on personal feelings, but it gave me the ticket to get in to see him.

"He not only liked my presentation for White Rock and

approved the financing for it, but he went out and inspected some things I had built, and he gave me the job of building the apartments we went to this morning. From there, he gave me the job of General Contractor for one of the largest malls in Georgia, which I'm going to show you when we leave here.

"Now, I ask you; do you think that's a God thing or not. I'm convinced it is."

Monty said, "I don't think there is any doubt about it. That's a great story, and I'd like to get you to tell it to some of the FCA meetings I go to. Would you be willing to do that?"

"I would, Monty, but I've got so much on my plate right now, I don't see how I can do it anytime soon."

"Jerry, can I tell you something?"

"Of course you can."

Now, "I think you'll have to agree that somebody running a business as large as ours has got to be busy. You know, I have found out that if I'm working for the Lord, He always helps me find the time, and I don't ever have to let anything go that I thought had to be done. He takes care of it, so I hope you'll think about that."

"I will, and I'll commit right now, so call me when you want me to go to one of the meetings."

"Good boy. You went to Georgia, didn't you?"

"Yeah, I'm a proud Bulldog."

"Well, I'm scheduled to go up there next month to speak at their FCA meeting. Do you think you could go to that one?"

"I don't see why not."

"Great, I'll call you with the date and time."

Jerry said, "I guess we should get out of here and let them have their table back, and I want to show you where the mall is going to be. Are you ready to go?"

Both Tracy and Monty said they were and Jerry asked Tracy if she wanted to go to the mall site with them, but she said no; she would just go back home. He kissed her on the cheek and told her he would see her after work, and then before she could get into her car, he said, "Don't forget, I have to go to Barbara's tonight."

"You do? I didn't know."

"Yeah, she called. Do you want to go?"

"I don't think so. I'll just see you when you get home."

"Okay, I shouldn't be late."

He and Monty got into his pickup and they headed to where the mall was going to be. On the way, Monty said, "Jerry, I enjoyed meeting and eating with Tracy. You've got a winner there."

"I know, and the fact that she's even here is something else that God worked out."

"Why is that?"

He told him how she was in the wreck and how she hung upside down for a week by her seatbelt, and how they had only met the night before she had the wreck. "Monty, I've got a lot to be thankful for."

"I hope you're sharing your stories with other people."

"I am, but not nearly as much as I should. Maybe they will mean something to the FCA students when I get to meet them."

They reached the mall site and Jerry pulled in to where his field office was, and they got out. "Well, this is it," he said, and he began pointing out different things in different directions to give Monty a rough idea of how large the mall would be, because he didn't want to walk the whole site. "You'll have to come back down in two or three months, when we get her out of the ground, and you can tell a lot more about it."

"I will. I can tell it's going to be huge just by the way you pointed it out. Thank you for the tour today, Jerry. I apologize for taking you away from your work for a whole day, but maybe by our building a friendship and a possible business relationship later, we can justify it. Now, if you don't mind, I'll ask you to take me back to the airport. They said the plane would be ready around three o'clock, and it will be that by the time we get there."

Jerry heard Monty tell Tracy at lunch that he was in a 767-400, and he didn't know what a 767-400 was until he got to the airport, and Monty pointed it out as they drove into the parking area. When they pulled into a parking place, Monty said, "Get out, and let's go out to the plane, and I'll give you the thirty-five-cent tour."

When they climbed the stairs, and went inside, Jerry was absolutely blown away. He had never seen anything so lavish. They began the tour in the front where the pilot and co-pilot sit and worked their way to the back as Monty pointed out various things. In one section there was a Multiplex Movie system that holds a thousand movies and twenty-five-hundred CDs. The plane had two bedrooms; a master and a guest room. The master bedroom had a full bathroom with a full-size shower. The galley, or kitchen, was complete, but Monty said they normally have their meals catered when on a long flight. He added that, "It's nice to be able to fix a pot of coffee or warm up something in mid-flight if you want to."

"Monty, I'm not believing what I'm seeing. This is the most luxurious thing I've ever seen. I think if I were you, I'd never get out of it."

"Yeah, you would. The luxury impresses you at first, then when you are constantly flying to London or Tel Aviv or Seoul or somewhere else, it gets to be just a real nice tool that you use to do business. The Lord has really blessed us, and we're always sure to give Him the credit."

"Well, I appreciate you showing it to me. I'll probably dream about it tonight."

"Sometime after you finish the apartments and have the shopping mall construction running smoothly, do you think you and Tracy would like to take a trip with Joan and I. We love the beach at Tel Aviv, and maybe the four of us can go over there if you would like to, or if you'd rather go somewhere else, we can do that too."

"To show you what a homebody I am, I didn't even know Tel Aviv had a beach. Heck yeah, we'd love to go sometime. Maybe in three or four months we'll have things smoothed out enough to go. Boy, Monty, this has been a great day. Thank you."

"It has been good, hasn't it. I appreciate you showing me your projects, and I appreciate hearing your story. I'm anxious for the FCA athletes to hear it. I'll call you when I get home and find out the dates. Well, it looks like their wanting to crank up the engines, so we had better say so long. Thanks again, Jerry, and I'll tell Bob what a good time we had."

Jerry stood at the door and watched Monty take off and was still in awe of what he had just seen. He decided that since he had lost practically the whole day he should get back to his office and try to salvage what was left of it. He wished he didn't have to go to Barbara and Tammy's, but he told Barbara he would be there, and he felt like he had to go.

When he walked in the door, Beverly handed him a handful of messages wanting him to call different people. He went into his office and sat down, and the first person he called was Tracy.

"Hi Sweetie. What are you doing?"

"I'm making you some cookies."

"That sounds good. I can't wait to have one. I just got back to the office from taking Monty to the airport, and do you know what, Honey? Monty took me on his airplane and showed me around, and I was totally blown away. I've never seen anything quite as luxurious, and do you know what?"

"What?"

"He asked me if you and I would like to go to Tel Aviv with him and his wife when things sort of smooth out here, and I told him we would. Would you like to?"

"Yeah, I've never been to Tel Aviv. That would be a nice trip. I hear the beach is fantastic."

"So you know they have a beach?"

"I thought everybody knew that."

"Not me, but I'm just an unsophisticated Georgia cracker, so how can you expect me to know something like that?"

She laughed and said, "Well, if you will hang with me and Monty, maybe we can teach you about the world."

"I'll try to remember that. Look, I've got to go. I've got a lot of calls to return. I'll probably be eight or eight-thirty getting home. See you then, Love you."

He began sorting through the little 'return call' papers that Beverly gave him, and there were six of them. He put them in the order in which he would call them and didn't care whether he called the bottom two or not, but as it wound up, when he got to them he still had plenty of time, so he gave them a call. Beverly came to his door at five o'clock and asked if he wanted her to stay for anything, and he told her no and thanked her for offering. Then he said, "Tomorrow, if we can find the time, we need to talk about hiring another girl for the office."

"Okay, I may have an idea for one."

Barbara said to come anytime, so he thought he would leave the office at six-thirty and get there early so he could get home before it got late. As he walked up the sidewalk, he was hoping upon hope that Tammy was there so he wouldn't have to have another experience with Barbara the way he did before.

When he reached the door, he rang the bell and Tammy opened the door. He felt a huge sigh of relief. She said, "Hi, come on in. Mama will be in here in a minute. She's in her bedroom on the phone."

In just a few minutes Barbara came in, and when she saw Jerry she smiled and said, "Hi Jerry."

"Hi Barbara. How're ya doing?"

"Good. Listen, the reason I asked you to come over, is to let you know where Tammy and I are on Tammy's situation. I think I told you earlier that she has decided to go to the Kindred Home for unwed mothers. Well, I called them and then Tammy and I went over there and talked to them, and it's real nice. I was pleasantly surprised about the costs because I didn't figure I could afford it, but the way they do is charge by whatever they think you can afford. Since I'm a single mother and mine is the only income, they said our cost wouldn't be very much.

"Also, Tammy has decided to put the baby up for adoption when it's born. Don't you think that's the right thing to do?"

"Yeah, I do. Tammy, I think you're making very wise and mature decisions. I'm proud of you."

When he paid her the compliment, she blushed a little and said, "Well, if I'm old enough to be a mother, I guess I'm old enough to make my own decisions, besides, I saw a girl over there that I know, and she said she likes it a lot, and they take care of everything for you."

She excused herself and went to the bathroom, and while she was gone, Jerry told Barbara, "You know, you could have told me this over the phone. Is there any special reason why I had to come over here?"

"Well, I couldn't see you over the phone, and it looks like we're getting close to not seeing each other anymore, so I just thought I'd like to see you one more time."

"Oh, I see. You're something else; did you know that?"

When Tammy got back into the room, Jerry said, "Well gals, I guess I had better go." He looked at Barbara and said, "I'll be in trouble if I don't get home in time for dinner."

Barbara said, "Tammy, give Jerry a hug and thank him for everything he has done for you," and Tammy went over and gave him a big hug and said, "Thank you."

He hugged her back and said, "You're welcome, but I'll still be around if you need me, okay?"

"Okay; thank you."

Then it was Barbara's turn. She put her arms around him and

gave him a real bear hug. She said, "I don't know how we would have gotten along without you. She held her head back and smiling said, "I wish I could show you how much I appreciate it."

Jerry replied, "You don't need to do anything. I was glad to do it. Promise me you'll call me if you need anything, will you?"

"I promise."

When she got through hugging him, she put both hands on his shoulders and gave him a kiss on the cheek. "Thank you again."

He headed for home and was thankful that he hadn't had a problem with Barbara. He was a little afraid when she hugged him because he didn't know just how free she was with her actions around Tammy, but it all worked out okay. He thought he would stay in touch with them, but he wouldn't have to be as involved as he had been for the last year or so.

Chapter Eighteen

The next morning, Wednesday, Tracy was up at the crack of dawn getting ready to go on a flight to a place where she hadn't been before; Brussels.

Jerry had several appointments and two meetings that day, so they were two busy people. Tracy left first after kissing him goodbye and said she would see him Saturday. She told him that her flight was direct going over, but coming back, they had to stop at JFK in New York, and they would have to lay over there for four hours and ten minutes, making her flight home almost sixteen hours.

As soon as he got to his office, Melissa called. "Hi Melissa; what's up?"

"Are you going to the apartment complex today?"

"I'm going sometime, but I'm meeting several subcontractors, and I have two meetings this afternoon. Why, what do you need?"

"I need to talk to you about these people doing the sheetrock. They're pushing for money before the invoice is due, and I need to talk to you about it. When can I see you?"

"Why don't you come by here and we'll talk in between appointments. It won't take long, will it?"

"No, it shouldn't. I'll come in about an hour or so."

"Okay, I'll see you."

He had told four different subcontractors to come talk to him about doing work at the mall, and as soon as the second one left, Melissa came in. She stuck her head in the door and asked him, "Is now a bad time to see you about this?"

He looked at her and said, "No, come on in."

She went into his office and showed him what she was questioning, and it didn't take but a second for him to tell her to go ahead and pay the contractor. He asked her, "Couldn't you have asked me this over the phone? It would have saved you a trip and a lot of time."

"I guess I could have, but then I wouldn't have been able to see you."

Jerry just shook his head and thought, *that's the same thing*

Barbara said last night. Maybe the two of them got together.

"Is your wife out of town?"

'Yeah, she left this morning."

"Where is she going?"

"To Brussels, Belgium."

"Wow! Okay, if you get lonesome, you know where to find me."

"I know, now get out of here. I'm busy."

The second meeting broke up a little after two-thirty, and he left to go to the apartment complex site, and he told Beverly that he wouldn't be back that afternoon.

Buildings one and two were really looking good, and he didn't think it would be too much longer before they would be in their final stages, and that reminded him that he would soon have to get the people out there to pave the parking lot.

The next four; buildings three, four, five, and six were almost ready for sheetrock. By the time they sheet rocked three and four, five and six would be ready for it. Seven and eight were starting to take shape, and it wouldn't be long until they would be ready.

Jerry was pleased with what he saw, and a little after five he left, reaching home a few minutes before six. Before he went into the house, he went down to check on the horses and spent thirty to forty-five minutes with them. He didn't go into the house until around six-thirty, and when he went in, he fixed himself a Margarita and then went out on the porch to enjoy the rest of the beautiful day.

When he was about half through with his Margarita, the phone rang inside. He went in to answer it, and it was Tom, Wendy's husband. Before he could exchange pleasantries with him, Tom asked, "Are you watching the news?"

"No, I just got home."

"Well turn it on. Terrorists bombed the Brussel's airport today."

"What?"

"Yeah, they're talking about it now on Fox."

"I wonder if the girls are all right."

"I don't know; I sure hope so."

"What do we do, Tom? Do you think anybody at the airline knows what's going on?"

"I don't know. I guess we should sit tight for a while, and surely somebody will call us.

"Maybe you're right, but I'm not going to sit here very long without trying to find out something. If you hear anything, call me, and if I hear anything, I'll call you."

"You know, Jer, I'm trying to be positive about this, and being positive, I feel that if any of our people are hurt that we would already have been notified. What do you think?"

"I think you're probably right. Has the news said what happened?"

"Fox said bombers destroyed the airport's departure hall and killed sixteen people there, and another bomb blew up a metro train, also in Brussels, killing more than thirty people and injuring two hundred and seventy others. They said the airport is closed, so there's no telling when our girls will be back home. I don't care if Wendy has to be gone a few extra days if I just know she's all right."

"That's the way I feel," Jerry said. "Let's get off of here and watch the news and see if we can figure out what's going on."

"Okay, Buddy. Stay in touch, okay?"

"I will. Talk to ya later."

All the channels were talking about the Brussels' bombings, and Jerry went from one to another; from Fox to CNN, from CBS to NBC and back again. At one point, NBC reported a story connected to the bombings, but it was about a man involved, and they called him the 'Man in the Hat' and said he spilled the terror gang's secrets.

The story began by saying after the Brussels airport bombing that killed sixteen people, a man in a black hat was seen walking calmly from the scene. Closed circuit cameras caught the same man prior to the blasts, in hat and glasses and tan coat, pushing a loaded luggage cart alongside the two suicide bombers who would soon detonate their devices. A manhunt began for the mysterious Man in the Hat.

What he told officials about his work for ISIS after his capture, revealed in the just completed trial of another jihadi in the U.K., shows how the terror group runs its operations and hands out its deadly missions.

The Man in the Hat was a prolific burglar, a Manchester United fan with a gambling habit, and a neighborhood friend of several of the plotters in the Paris and Brussels terror attacks who traveled to Syria and Britain as a courier for ISIS.

Mohamed Abrini, 31, a Belgian of Moroccan descent, was picked up, and his confession allowed authorities to identify and charge two men from Birmingham, England as accomplices in the attacks.

Jerry watched as much as he wanted, because all the channels were starting to repeat themselves to fill in time, and no new news was being given.

He called the airline and when someone answered, he said, "This is Jerry Martin; Tracy Martin's husband. Tracy left on that flight to Brussels this morning, and I'm wondering if you all know anything yet. Is anyone there that can give me some information?"

"We don't know too much yet, Mr. Martin, but we do know that everyone on Flight 328 is okay. Our people in Brussels are working with our Embassy over there, and Tracy should be calling you a little later."

"Do you know when that will be?"

"No sir. The number of phone lines is limited, and there are a lot of people that need to call home, so it might take quite a while, but as I said, your wife is safe. In the meantime, if we get anymore pertinent information, we'll call you."

"Okay, thank you very much," and he hung up and immediately dialed Tom.

"Hey Tom, have you heard anything from anybody?"

"Not a word. I'm still watching the news on TV. Have you?"

"I called the airline a few minutes ago, and they told me that everyone on Flight 328 is safe. The guy said the girls will be calling home at some point, but the number of phone lines is limited so it might take a while."

Tom said, "It will probably take a long time because I feel sure the passengers will get first crack at the phones, and there are probably at least three hundred of them. We may not hear from our girls until the wee hours of the morning or later."

"You're probably right, but at least we know they're all right."

As soon as he hung up from Tom, he called Jack to see if he had heard about the bombings, and Jack said he had seen it on the news.

"Jack, the reason I'm calling is to tell you that Tracy flew to Brussels this morning. I called the airline a few minutes ago, and they told me that everyone is safe. I didn't know if you knew that she was in Brussels or not, and I just didn't want you to worry."

"You say she's okay?"

"According to the airline she is. I'll let you know when I hear something else."

"Okay, Jer. Thank you for calling me."

Next, he called Carol, Tracy's sister. "Carol, Hi. This is Jerry. How're you doing?"

"I'm good Jerry. How are you?"

"I'm fine. Listen, the reason I called is to tell you that Tracy is in Brussels on a flight, and I didn't know if you had seen the news or not."

"Actually I haven't. We've been to prayer meeting. What are you saying?"

"Carol, she flew to Brussels this morning and some terrorists bombed the airport over there and killed a bunch of people, but Tracy's okay. I called the airline."

"Thank goodness. Boy, that gal leads an exciting life, doesn't she? I think you might need to lock her up."

"She sure does lead an exciting life and locking her up might not be a bad idea. She needs to write a book sometime. Well, I won't keep you; I just wanted to tell you this."

"Okay. Thank you, Jerry. We love you guys."

"Love you, too. Bye."

He remembered that he hadn't eaten yet, so he went into the kitchen and got some stuff out of the fridge to make a sandwich. While he was fixing it, the phone rang, and he hurriedly answered it, hoping it was Tracy, but instead it was Melissa.

"Hi Melissa. What's up?"

"I've been watching TV, and I remembered you telling me that Tracy left this morning for Brussels. Have you heard from her?"

"No, but I talked to the airline, and they said everyone is safe. I'm hoping she'll call before long."

"I know what you've told me about you and me, but I'll be more than glad to come out there and be with you as a friend; not someone who wants your body. Would you like some company?"

"Melissa, I'm surprised. Thank you so much for the offer, but I'm okay now that I know Tracy's safe.

"Answer me this, will you?"

"What?"

"If you didn't know that Tracy is safe and you were really

worried about her, would you have let me come out there?"

"I don't know, Melissa; maybe."

They talked for a couple of minutes more, and then Jerry said he needed to hang up in case Tracy called. He was too keyed up to sleep, so he sat in his den and watched TV and the bombing story over and over and over.

Finally, he got sleepy and felt like he needed to go to bed because he had a lot to do the next day, so about eleven o'clock he turned in.

It seemed to him like he had just gotten to sleep when the phone rang. It was actually three forty-five in the morning. When he answered, it was Tracy.

"Jerry, Darling, I sure am glad to hear your voice. I hate to wake you up at this ridiculous hour, but I wanted to tell you that I'm okay."

"I'm glad you called. How are things over there?"

"Pure chaos. There are soldiers and policemen everywhere, and they won't let us leave the hotel. They brought us here from the airport in a bus that was completely surrounded by soldiers carrying guns. Part of the airport is blown to bits. It was scary at first, but now that we're safe here at the hotel, we feel pretty relaxed knowing that all the soldiers and police are here to protect us."

"Have they told you when you can leave to come back home?"

"No, the airport is closed, and nobody knows when it will reopen, so I guess we're stuck here for a while."

"Has Wendy called Tom yet?"

"She's on the phone with him now. Honey, I'm going to have to hang up now. There are still several people waiting to call their loved ones. I'll try to call you back whenever I can. I love you."

"I love you, too. Take care."

Even though he had already been told she was all right, her call reaffirmed it, and although his mind was dulled by sleep, he felt a great sense of relief. He looked at his watch, and it was five 'til four, so he went back to bed. He overslept and didn't wake up until seven o'clock. When he saw what time it was, he jumped out of bed and hurriedly got ready for work. He knew Beverly would have coffee at his office, so he didn't make any before he left.

As soon as he got to his office, Tom called, and like Jerry, his fear was relieved when Wendy called. Jerry asked him, "Are you at work?"

"Yeah, I'm here, but I'm like a zombie. I bet I didn't sleep two hours."

"I feel the same way. Let me know if you hear anything else."

"Okay, I will. Have a great day old Buddy."

When he hung up from Tom, he got up and poured a cup of coffee, and stood at Beverly's desk and talked to her while he drank it. Before he finished with it, Melissa came in. Right in front of Beverly, she walked over to him, put her arms around his neck and said, "I've been so worried about you. Are you all right?"

They were standing with Melissa's back to Beverly and him facing her, and while she was still hugging him, he looked at Beverly and raised his eyebrows and smiled. He told her, "I'm fine, Melissa, but thank you for your concern. I spoke with Tracy early this morning, and she's fine, too."

Beverly just smiled and shook her head.

Melissa asked, "When is she coming home?"

"Nobody knows. The airport in Brussels is closed for an indefinite time."

Ten Days Later

Every day since the terrorist attack, Melissa made it a point to see Jerry; sometimes in his office and sometimes at one of the job sites, always with the theme of just wanting to be a friend and nothing else. At every encounter, she would always manage to touch him some way; maybe with her hand on his, putting her face next to his when they were reading something, or maybe just simply brushing up against him. Jerry was no dummy; he knew exactly what she was up to.

Tracy called him once more last Thursday and said everything was still the same. Nobody knew when the airport would reopen, but they were hoping it wouldn't be much longer.

On Sunday morning, Jerry got up to go to church, and stopped at the 129 Café for breakfast before he went. On his way into the café he stopped at the newspaper box and bought a paper. When he got to his booth, he ordered his breakfast, and then unfolded the paper. He was shocked at the headlines. They read "BRUSSELS AIRPORT REOPENS FOR FIRST FLIGHTS SINCE TERROR ATTACKS."

Reading the article carefully and hoping to see something that would tell him that Tracy's flight was on the way, he found that he would still have to wait just a little longer. The article read, "Brussels airport reopened with an 'emotional' flight on Sunday, 12 days after suicide bombers destroyed its departure hall and killed 16 people there."

He did some quick calculations in his head about the time. Brussels was six hours ahead of Atlanta, and the article said a flight took off Sunday, so that meant the paper had to get the news when the plane took off in order to print it in the paper by early morning in Atlanta. He marveled at how fast the news traveled. He continued with the story.

Belgium's main airport had not handled passenger flights since the twin bombings and a separate blast on a metro train in the capital killed more than30 people and injured 270 others.

The first of three scheduled flights departed for Faro in Portugal just after 6:40 a.m. local time, with only about 60-70 passengers. Planes were also scheduled to go to Turin and Athens.

Airport spokeswoman Florence Muls said Sunday's flights were a "symbolic" relaunch after "12 days of difficult moments and horror."

"The people working at the airport were very, very emotional about the situation," she said. "Restarting was our first priority, but always thinking about the victims and the colleagues who were there during the incident."

The first passengers for nearly two weeks fed into a vast temporary marquee housing security controls and check-in facilities. Arnaud Feist, the airport's chief executive, described the partial reopening as a sign of hope.

"In the days that followed, I have also seen much courage, pride for Brussels airport and persistence is being shown by everybody," Feist said in a statement. "That makes me very hopeful for the future of our airport and convinces me that we will emerge stronger than ever from this crisis."

On Monday, the airport will serve a far wider range of destinations, including one plane also due out to New York and two more to cities in Cameroon, Gambia and Senegal.

Jerry was beginning to wonder if the paper was going to say anything about when service to the United States would resume, and when he finally got to the last paragraph saying that one flight was scheduled for New York on Monday, he crossed his fingers and prayed that that was going to be Tracy's flight.

He went on to church and was warmly greeted by everyone who knew that Tracy was on the Brussels flight. His mind was on Tracy and not on the sermon as he wished the hour would hurry and end. While the service was going on, he thought that he would call the airline when he got home to see if they knew anything about the flight he read about.

When he called the airline, he was disappointed to hear that they didn't have any word yet on when Flight 328 would be leaving Brussels, but they promised to call him the minute they heard something. He killed the rest of the afternoon by sleeping and watching a football game on TV, and couldn't wait for the day to end, so he could go to work and get his mind on that instead of Tracy.

Getting to his office at seven o'clock Monday morning, he immersed himself in his work, and a little after eight the phone rang. Beverly hadn't come in yet, so he answered it. On the other end was a familiar voice; Dee Phillips with the airline.

"Jerry, this is Dee Phillips, and I've got some great news; Tracy's flight took off from Brussels at five a.m. Atlanta time this morning and is scheduled to arrive here at eight o'clock tonight. I know you're anxious to see her as we all are, and I wanted to be the one to tell you the good news."

Jerry responded with "Hallelujah; Thank you Lord. Dee, I sure appreciate the call. I'll be there tonight to meet the plane."

Dee asked, "Isn't her car out here?"

"Yeah, but I don't want to wait on her to get home. I want to see her as soon as she lands."

"Okay. I may stay and meet the plane myself. Bye Jerry."

Just as he was hanging up, Beverly came in, and before she could even sit down, Jerry said, "Tracy's on her way home, and he went over and hugged her. And then, while he was hugging Beverly, Melissa walked in and asked, "Well, what's going on with you two?"

Beverly turned Jerry loose and said. "Tracy's on her way home."

"Great," and then she went over and gave him a big hug.

He pulled loose and said jokingly, "It looks like I need to get

Tracy to leave more often if I get hugs like this," and Melissa replied not as jokingly, "Maybe you should."

Jerry and Beverly looked at each other and Beverly just shook her head.

He got to the airport a little after seven thirty and went to one of the airline's counters and identified himself in hopes that he could get into where the crew disembarked. The guy at the counter was very nice and led him to the door to the outside. There were four or five other family members already out there, and they all visited with each other until the plane arrived. Tom never did come, and that surprised him.

Finally, the plane was spotted making its approach, and the excitement grew. It landed and taxied almost to where they were standing, and before the crew could get off, the passengers had to be let off. At last, he saw Wendy, and Tracy was right behind her. He ran out to the staircase and was there when she got to the ground and grabbed her and gave her a big bear-hug. After he hugged her he grabbed Wendy and gave her a big hug, since Tom wasn't there. They talked for a few minutes and due to the circumstances of their experience for the last nearly two weeks, the crew was released to go home rather than do their normal post-flight chores.

Wendy and Tracy hugged each other bye, and Tracy went with Jerry to his car. "Do you mean for me to leave my car out here?" she asked.

"Yeah, we'll come get it tomorrow or the next day. I just want you with me tonight."

All the way home, Tracy told about how things were for the last several days, and when she talked about the terrorists and how most of the European governments were on high alert, Jerry was very thankful to have her home.

When they got to their house, Jerry unloaded the car and went in the house and put his arms around Tracy and said, "Sugar, I'm so glad you're back home," and he smothered her with hugs and kisses.

She pulled away from him after a couple of minutes and said, "Honey, I know what you would like to do, but would you mind if we don't do anything tonight? I'm exhausted and would like to just go to bed and go to sleep. Do you mind?"

"Of course not. You can sleep 'til noon tomorrow if you want to. I'll go on in to work and you can call me when you get up."

While she was getting ready for bed, he still had questions about some of the things in Brussels, and when he asked a question, she would answer, but he could tell she wasn't in the mood for *twenty questions*, so he soon stopped asking. When she was ready, she went over to him, kissed him, and said, "Good night. I love you, and I'll see you tomorrow."

"Okay, Love. Sleep tight. I love you, too."

He got up the next morning, got dressed and went to the office. He drank a couple of cups of coffee there and left to go the apartment site. He told Beverly to tell Tracy, when she called, to call his cell, and about ten thirty she called.

"Good morning," he said.

"Good morning to you. Did you sleep well?"

"Like a log. All I needed was for you to be there beside me. What are your plans for today?"

"I don't have any. I'm just going to rest most of the day."

"Would you like to meet me for lunch?"

"Yeah, if you'd like for me to."

"How about the Cracker Barrel?"

"That sounds good. Which one?"

"The one on Douglasville Highway at say, twelve thirty."

"Sounds like a plan. I'll see you then."

She was waiting when he got to the restaurant, and when they went inside, they had to wait for about ten minutes to get a table. They were soon seated and after looking at the menu, they ordered their lunch.

While they were waiting, Tracy told Jerry, "Honey, I did a lot of thinking while I was stranded last week."

"What did you think about?"

"A lot of things, but mainly you and me."

"I don't know if I like the sound of that. What did you think about you and me?"

"Jerry, I want a baby, and I think I might be ready to quit flying."

"I want one too, and we're trying as hard as we can, but what about this quit flying?"

"We mentioned it before one time after I had been to the doctor, but we never did get serious. What would you think about adopting one?"

"I don't know. Is that something you'd like to do?"

"Well, based on what the doctor said, we've probably got less than a fifty/fifty chance to have one, and if we look into adopting one, we'll have a one hundred percent chance to get one."

"Yeah, but it won't be our flesh and blood. Does that not matter to you?"

"It does, but I know people who have adopted children, and they love them just as if they were their own flesh and blood. I think I'd like for us to consider it."

"Well, let's think about it. I'm not real sure I could love a baby that's not mine."

"Okay, we'll think about it, but you have so much love to give, I know you could love one. I know I could."

They talked about adoption for a while and then they left. Jerry told her not to cook dinner; they would go out somewhere and get something.

The next day Barbara Lawrence, Tracy's supervisor from the airline called and told Tracy that the airline was going to give the crew of Flight 328 an appreciation reception. Husbands, wives, boyfriends and other loved ones were invited as well, and they had rented a room in a nice restaurant. She said it was going to be Wednesday night at six thirty, and she hoped she and Jerry would be there.

Tracy told her they would be there and was pleasantly surprised by the reception because that was not like something the airline would normally do. Barbara told her the crew wasn't going to have to go out for at least another week, and secretly, Tracy thought, *this is great. I'm going to take that time to call or go see some adoption agencies. I won't tell Jerry until I see what they say.*

The reception was a lot of fun. The entire crew of Flight 328 was there, and most of them brought someone with them. Tracy was really happy to see everyone because she was not only best friends with Wendy, she had become close to most of the other girls, and she was glad to meet their significant others. The pilot and co-pilot were there with their wives, and it was just a lovely evening.

Tracy and Wendy gravitated to each other as they usually did, and while they were standing pretty much to themselves Tracy said, "While we were in Brussels, you mentioned that I seemed distant and asked me if there was anything wrong, and I told you no. Do you remember that?"

"Yeah, I remember. You never did tell me what was wrong. Are you going to tell me now?"

"I was wrestling with a decision, and I think I've made it now."

"Well, for goodness sakes, tell me what it is."

"I'm not one hundred percent sure, but I'm probably ninety percent sure, and before

I tell you, promise me that you won't say anything to Jerry and not even to Tom. I'll tell Jerry and you can tell Tom when I get ready, okay?"

"Tracy, this is Wendy; tell me what this is about"

"Like I said, I'm not fully sure yet, but I'm almost positive that I'm going to quit flying and try to adopt a baby."

"Get outa here. You're not serious."

"I'm totally serious."

"What brought this on?"

"Well, Jerry and I have been trying to get pregnant for a long time and haven't been able to, and two or three weeks ago I went to the doctor, and he told me that I had less than a fifty percent chance to conceive, and Wendy, I really do want a baby. This is what I was wrestling with in Brussels. Now be sure you don't say anything to Tom."

"I promise. What am I going to do without you when I have a flight somewhere to the end of the world?"

"You won't have any problem. You and Sue are good buddies. Maybe you all can start rooming together if I leave."

"Darn, Tracy. This sucks."

"I know, but you know, Wendy, as much as I want a baby, Jerry wants one just as bad; maybe even more; I just don't know yet what his true feelings are about adopting one."

"Well, if you quit I probably will, too."

Tracy started to respond to what Wendy just said, but in the midst of their conversation, Barbara came over to them and began talking, and they talked with her for a little while, and then went to their husbands.

The evening had begun at six-thirty with drinks, and dinner was scheduled for seven thirty, but everyone was having such a good time, the cocktail hour ran over until almost eight o'clock. Finally, Barbara took a spoon and tapped loudly on a glass and told everyone she hated to bring a halt to the bubbly, but it was time to take a seat and get ready to eat.

Tom and Wendy sat with Tracy and Jerry with Wendy and Tracy sitting next to each and Tom and Jerry on either end.

The airline outdid itself for the event. Not only was the cocktail hour a lot of fun, but the dinner consisted of either Filet Mignon or Prime Rib; whichever each person preferred. Toward the end of the dinner, Jules Blackstone, the Atlanta Executive for the airline stood and addressed the crowd.

He said how thankful he was that everyone made it home safely, and he praised each person for their bravery and professionalism. He told them that the airline was going to give them two weeks off, and they would be paid for two flights just as if they had made them. That brought a huge round of applause. When he finished with his remarks, the party pretty much broke up. A few couples stood around and talked for a while before they left, but it wasn't too long before the room was totally empty.

On the way home, Jerry said, "I saw you and Wendy engaged in what looked like some deep conversation; what were you gals talking about?"

His question scared her because she wasn't ready to tell him what she was planning, but she managed to say, "Oh nothing, really; just girl talk."

Nothing more was said about it, and they talked about other things. When they got home, they were tired and put on their pjs and went to bed.

The next morning they got up, had breakfast and Jerry left for work. Tracy could hardly wait until it got eight o'clock so she could start calling adoption agencies.

The first one she called Georgia Agape, and the lady she talked to acted as though she was thrilled she called until she told the lady that she wanted an infant. The lady asked her if the baby's race mattered, and Tracy told her she wanted a white one. The lady said the only infants that they had available were either black or Hispanic, and the only white children they had were older; from six-years-old and older. Tracy thanked her and proceeded to go to the next one on the list.

It was a place named The Open Door Adoption Center, and when Tracy told them what she wanted, their reply was almost exactly like the first place she called; no white infants, but older white children were available.

The only other agencies listed in the phone book were agencies that specialized in international adoptions, and she didn't want to do that, but when thinking about it, she thought that maybe if they could get a German or Russian infant, they might consider it. She wasn't sure enough about it to call one of those agencies, so she quit after the two she spoke to.

She was very disappointed, and decided that she would go ahead and tell Jerry what she was doing and she also wanted to get his feedback on maybe trying for a foreign baby. She was afraid that he wouldn't want to adopt, period, and that he would definitely not want to get an international child.

Jerry called around four o'clock and asked her what she wanted to do for dinner, and she told him she was cooking, and it would be ready close to six o'clock.

When he got home, he made the usual Margaritas, and Tracy's timing was right on. Dinner was ready at almost exactly six o'clock. When they were eating, she asked, "How was your day, Honey?"

"Good. I spent time at both projects, and they're both coming along real well, especially the apartments. I'll be glad to get them finished so I can devote full time to the mall. What did you do today?"

"Well, you may not believe this, but I spent some time this morning contacting adoption agencies."

He didn't say anything at first; he just looked at her, and then he asked, "Why did you do that?"

"Darling, I want a baby so bad, and it doesn't look as if I'm going to be able to have one, so I thought I would just check and see what is involved in adopting one."

"What did you find out?"

"I found out that the only white children available are six years old and older. There are no white infants right now. I asked about filling out an application to get one later; when one is available, but they told me that there is a long waiting list, and it would more than likely be well over a year and maybe over two years before we could even think about getting one. They had some black and Hispanic infants, but I figured you wouldn't want one of them."

"You're right about that. I have nothing against black or

Hispanic babies; I just don't want to adopt one. Are you sure you want to adopt a baby?"

"If that's the only way we can have one, yes, I want to adopt one. Let me ask you this; There are some international adoption agencies listed, and I didn't want to call one until I talked to you, but would you consider adopting maybe a German or Russian or Italian baby? Those are white."

"I don't know. Let me think about it. In the meantime, maybe we need to try a little harder to get you pregnant."

"That's fine; we can do that, but I keep thinking about what the doctor said, and it's awfully hard for me to think positive about that."

They talked for a while longer, and then Jerry helped with the dishes. They went to the den and watched TV for a little while and snuggled until they both got worked up, and then they went to bed and tried really hard to make a baby.

After Jerry left for work the next morning, Tracy did a few household chores and then called Wendy. When she answered, Tracy asked, "Wendy, do you know anybody that's ever adopted a baby?"

"No. I don't. Sorry. Have you called any of the agencies yet?"

"Yeah, I called some yesterday, but they don't have any infants. All they have is older children."

"Did you say anything to Jerry?"

"Yeah, I told him. I wasn't going to until I found a baby and was ready to get it, but their not having any changed the whole dynamic."

"What did he say?"

"Well, he didn't say no, and that's a good thing. I asked him about maybe trying for a Russian or Italian or some other European white child, and he said he would have to think about it."

"Tracy, I take that back; I do know someone who adopted a baby, but they don't live here anymore. They moved to Nashville, I think."

"Do you know their name?"

"I can't think of it right now, but I'm pretty sure Tom knows."

"Will you see and let me know? I'll try to find them and give them a call."

"I'll ask him when he gets home tonight."

"Thanks, Babe."

"You were saying that you asked Jerry about a foreign child and he said he would have to think about it. Do you think he'll give in on it?"

"I don't know, but Wendy, there has got to be a way other than through an agency. I wonder if a lawyer could help."

"I just had a thought. You know, there are homes for unwed mothers, and I'll bet there are some here in Atlanta. Surely, all those babies don't go to adoption agencies. There have got to be some that are adopted directly from their mothers. Why don't you call some of them?"

"That's a good idea. I may just do that."

"Good for you. Trace, Listen, I'm glad you called. I was going to call you to see if you would like to go to the mall and maybe have lunch."

"Today?"

"Yeah, what about it?"

"I guess I can. Where and what time?"

"How about I meet you at Belk's in the shoe department at eleven o'clock?"

"I don't know if I can get there by eleven or not, but I'll try."

"If you don't I'll wait on you. Now hang up and go get ready."

"Okay. I'll see you."

The subject of adoption didn't come up while they were shopping, but it did when they stopped for lunch. "You know, Wendy, the more I think about getting a baby, the more excited I get. I'm going to really get down to business on this."

Wendy said, "Well, you're getting me excited, too, and I'm not even thinking about having a baby."

Tracy looked at her with a big smile and joked, "I just had a good idea."

Wendy asked, "What is it?"

"You can get pregnant and I'll adopt your baby."

She laughed and said, "Yeah, right. I wish I could get pregnant."

With that comment, Tracy got serious. "Girlfriend, we've never talked about that. Are you not able to have children?"

"No, I'm afraid not."

"Gosh, I'm sorry, and I'm sorry for what I said."

"It's perfectly all right. I've known it for years, and Tom and I

204

just decided we would make the best of it and be contented with each other."

"I'm still sorry for what I said."

"Don't be silly. Ten years ago it would have bothered me, but now I guess I'm calloused to the thought, and it doesn't bother me in the least."

"Let me ask you another question. I've been thinking about this ever since the reception last night."

"What is it?"

"Were you serious about leaving the airline if I adopt a baby and leave?"

"I was very serious. Traveling the world just wouldn't be the same without you. I've thought about quitting a couple of times, but wasn't too serious because you and I have so much fun together on our trips."

"I hate for you to quit because of me."

"I would only do it because I wanted to."

Trying to change the subject, Tracy asked, "Have you ever bought any jewelry from Imposters?"

"No, I don't even know what that is."

"It's a jewelry store that has beautiful jewelry, but everything is synthetic. The stones all look real, but they're not. You know that pretty emerald ring of mine that you like so much? Well, it's not real."

"You're kidding."

"Nope. Let's go down there and see what they've got."

Wendy had a ball at the jewelry store, buying earrings, two bracelets and a pendant. Tracy was conservative and only bought one pair of earrings. As they left Wendy said, "I'm going to come back to this place. Tom's probably going to kill me now when I show him all the stuff I bought, so I'll have to wait 'til later to get anything else."

At three thirty Tracy said, "Wendy, I need to go home and start dinner. Jerry has been working so hard, he's exhausted when he gets home, and I want to have a nice dinner for him. I keep thinking he bit off more than he can chew with those two big projects, but he doesn't seem to think so."

"That's a typical man for you. You can't tell them anything; they think they know it all."

"I know, but I couldn't do without my big Jer."

On the way home, she tried to think of someway she and Jerry could adopt a baby without going through an agency, and for some reason she thought, *I'll bet a lawyer could help us. I'm going to try to find one.*

As soon as she walked in the door she got out the phone book and turned to the yellow pages under Attorneys. She didn't know any of them, and it looked to her like there must have been a thousand. She began turning the pages, and it looked as if there were more personal injury lawyers than any other kind, but after looking at many pages, she came to a section that said "Family Law," and in the description of their practices, some of them had the word "Adoption" listed. She got a piece of paper and a pen and wrote down the numbers of all that she found that had adoption listed.

Chicken Parmesan was one of Jerry's favorites, and since she was hoping he would be in a good mood when he got home, that's what she fixed. She had made it earlier and put it in the freezer, so all she had to do was take it out and put it in the oven at three-fifty until it got hot. Chianti went well with it, and she had bought two bottles earlier and still had one, so she felt like she was all set.

Just as she had hoped, Jerry was in a great mood when he came in. He got his costs figures that afternoon, and it seemed that the apartments up to that day had come in under budget, and of course, if that continued all the way to completion, the savings would be his. He made their usual Margaritas and then, when he saw what Tracy had fixed him for dinner, he was really pleased.

After he had told her about his day, he asked her, "What did you do today; anything exciting?"

"Yeah, I had an exciting day. I met Wendy and we had lunch and did a little shopping. I told her about talking to the adoption agencies, and we talked some about adopting a baby. Honey, did you know that she and Tom can't have children?"

"Yeah, Tom told me several years ago."

"Well, I didn't know it until today. As close as Wendy and I are, you'd think I would know something like that about my best friend."

"You'd think."

She kinda held her breath and asked, "Honey, have you thought anymore about our trying to adopt?"

"Yeah, a little."

"Well, what have you decided?"

"Trace, I'm not sure. I have mixed emotions about it, but I love you so much that I'm willing to do anything that will make you happy, and if adopting a baby will do that, then let's do it."

She went over to him, took the Margarita out of his hand, and put her arms around him and kissed him. She said, "Thank you, my Darling. I truly believe that if we can find a little boy or girl that our lives will be complete. Let me ask you something."

"What?"

"You are such a good man and so sweet, how did you manage to stay single until you were thirty-five-years-old?"

"He smiled and said, "I guess I was waiting on you."

With that remark, she kissed him again, and then asked, "Are you through with your Margarita?"

"Yeah, I'm through."

"Okay then, sit down, and I'll bring your dinner to you."

While they were eating, she asked, "Honey, do you think it would be wise to try to find a lawyer to help us find a baby?"

"I don't know. Do lawyers do that?"

"I'm not sure, but I was looking in the yellow pages and several of them were listed under what they called 'Family Law', and then under the Family Law description it had 'Adoptions' listed, so I'm just assuming they do. Would you mind if I called one or two?"

"No; I don't care. Knock yourself out."

Tracy got up and went to the phone table where she had listed the Family Law Attorneys and brought the list back to him. She said, "Here is a list of those attorneys. Do you happen to know any of them?"

He looked at the list and said, "Yeah, I know Rosemarie Newkirk. We went to school together."

"Good. I'll call her first."

And then Jerry asked Tracy, "Now look; just because we're going to try and adopt a baby doesn't mean we're going to stop trying to have one of our own, does it?"

"Absolutely not. We may even try harder if that's possible."

"I just wanted to be sure."

True to her word, she tried as hard as she could when they went to bed that night.

Chapter Nineteen

Jerry was still in a good mood when he got up the next morning. He didn't get Tracy up before he left for work; he just leaned over and kissed her goodbye as he left. He stopped at Hardees on the way to the office and had his food with a cup of coffee after he got to the office.

Things had been going so smoothly on both job sites, he wasn't prepared for what was about to happen. A few minutes after he sat down at his desk, Bill Case called.

"Good morning, boss."

"Good morning Bill. How's it going?"

"It was going good until a few minutes ago, and now, we have what might be a major problem."

"What in the world are you talking about? I thought everything was running really smooth."

"It was until a bulldozer uncovered a graveyard over in section four, and we had to stop. The dozer operator said he had uncovered graves before, and you have to contact somebody with the federal government in order to continue working."

"Did he say who you have to contact?"

"No sir; he just said somebody with the federal government."

"Okay. Sit tight, Bill. I'll call Frank Thomas. He'll probably know what to do. After I talk to him. I'll call you back."

He dialed the bank and asked to speak to Frank. The operator rang Frank's phone, and Melissa answered. "Frank Thomas's office."

Jerry asked, "Melissa? Why are you answering Frank's phone?"

"Hi, good looking. Frank had to step down the hall for something, but he'll be back in just a minute. Is there anything I can help you with?"

"Not this time. I need to talk to Frank. It's really important. Can you go get him for me?"

"I guess. I normally wouldn't do that, but let me see what I can do."

"Okay. Thanks."

It was only a minute or two until Frank answered. "Good morning Jerry. What's up?"

"Good morning, Frank. Bill Case just called and said a bulldozer just uncovered some graves over in section four and stopped work. The operator told Bill he had done that before somewhere else and they had to get in touch with the federal government about it. Do you know who has to be contacted?"

"Oh man! No, I have no idea. Let me call Clark Randle or Steven Carroll; they'll probably know. I'll call you back."

"Okay. Thanks. Do you think I ought to have Bill send the men home?"

"I would say so. This sounds like a serious deal."

Frank called back in about twenty minutes and said, "Jerry, I talked to Steven Carroll, and he said your bulldozer likely uncovered a Creek Indian burial site, and there are federal agencies that look after those things. He said The National Park Service is who we have to talk to first, but the guy I called was out and will have to call me back in about an hour. I hope he's wrong, but Steven said we might have to be shut down for quite a while, depending on the number of graves and the information they can come up with. I know you don't want to hear this, and neither do I, but it looks as if our hands are tied. I'm sorry."

"So am I, but my Dad taught me that something good comes out of every situation, and the good that immediately comes to my mind is that I can concentrate on your apartments during this time off. You know, it won't be long before you can rent the first sixteen units."

"I like your attitude; you're not a quitter."

"Frank, when you hear from the guy at the Park Service, call me on my cell phone. I'm going out to the mall site and see for myself what's going on."

"Okay, Buddy, I'll call you."

When he got to the site, he drove down to section four, and there was a small crowd gathered around one spot. He spotted Bill Case and parked his pickup. The bulldozer operator was there, and he had called the owner of the excavation company to come. Other workmen from other subcontractors made up the rest of the group.

Jerry went over to where the bodies were and sure enough there were bones and other artifacts that had apparently been buried with them. His cell phone rang and he answered, "This is Jerry."

"Jer, Frank. The National Park Service guy just called and said he wants to come out and look at the burial site and wants me to come with him. Can you wait out there until we get there? And oh yeah, he said we couldn't work anymore until the situation is resolved, so you'd better send everybody home that you have working."

"Okay. Will do, and yes, I can wait for you. Are you coming now?"

"Yeah, I'm going to meet the Parks man out there, so we'll both be there around the same time. If he gets there before I do, his name is Revel Oldham.

Frank got there a little before Revel did, and when Revel arrived, Frank introduced him to Jerry. They walked over and looked at the remains, and Frank asked him, "What do you think?"

"I think they're definitely Indian based on the items uncovered with them."

And then Frank asked, "What's the next step? We can't afford to be shut down for any length of time."

Revel replied as if he had memorized a script, "Native American human remains, graves, and ritual objects located on tribal land are encouraged to be protected *in situ,* and that means protected in its original place. In cases where in place preservation is not possible, or if archaeological excavation is necessary for planning or research, or if the remains are inadvertently discovered, then consultation is necessary prior to excavation under an Archaeological Resources Protection Act permit. If remains covered by the law are discovered, the project will be stopped for thirty days while the review and consultation process proceeds."

Frank asked, "Does that mean we will have to stop work for thirty days?"

"It's possible. I'll have to report this to the Archaeological Resources Protection people, and they will be the ones to make that decision."

Frank then asked him, "What do we do with these remains?"

"You'll have to leave them where they are until the ARP people come out and decide what is to be done. In the meantime, you'll have to provide protection for them to keep someone from coming in and destroying the site."

"What kind of protection are you talking about?"

"Whatever it takes to protect the site. You might have to hire an armed guard until the ARP decides what to do with everything."

"When will the ARP people be out here?"

"I don't know. I'll contact them when I get back to my office. I'd say it will more than likely be tomorrow or the next day."

Frank said, "Can you call them on your cell phone?"

"No sir. I'll have to wait until I get back to my office."

"Well, do what you can. This project is costing millions of dollars and you don't realize how much it costs to have to shut down. What if we uncovered the rest of the remains, if there are any, and moved them to a place that is out of the way."

"I'm afraid you can't do that, Mr. Thomas."

"Okay, but try to rush those people, will you?"

During a lull in the conversation, Dan Rogers, the owner of the excavating company asked Jerry, "Jerry, can I see you for a minute when we finish here?" Jerry nodded yes, and they continued.

As they were winding up their meeting, Bill Case asked Revel Oldham, "Mr. Oldham, what would happen if we had just continued on with the grading and didn't stop to report the find? Would anybody know the difference?"

"Probably not, but you would know it, and being a human being, somewhere down the road, you would tell someone about this, and they would tell someone. Before long it would get back to the government, and you would possibly have to close down a large part of the mall in order for equipment to get in and dig up a large section, including some of the businesses.

"I don't know what your plans are for this part of the mall, but let's say Dillard's or Macy's or some other big tenant is going to be In this very spot; would you want to have that store close? They would have to empty their store and can you imagine the labor involved in that. All that doesn't even include the law suits that are sure to follow, so it's good that you stopped when you did and called us."

Bill acknowledged that he was glad he didn't let the bulldozer continue on, and Jerry gave him an *atta boy* for it as did Frank.

Before they left the site, Jerry told Bill, "Bill, get in touch with some security company and have them send a guard to watch over the burial site, and to have them guard it around the clock until further notice and have them send someone immediately."

"Okay, but where will the guard stay?"

"I don't know. I guess he or she can sit in their car as long as they keep an eye on this area. You might tell them to send a man in case he has to use the bathroom."

Frank told Jerry, "Jerry, can you come by my office when you leave her? I think we need to talk about all this and decide what to do next."

"Yes sir. Bill can look after this, and I can come just as soon as I talk to Dan, the owner of the excavating company. It won't take but a minute."

Jerry motioned for Dan Rogers, and when Dan got to where he was, he asked, "What do you need, Dan?"

"Jerry, I heard that guy say you might be shut down for thirty days, and I just need for you to know that I can't afford to wait thirty days to start back on this job. I have to keep my equipment moving. I hope to come back when you're ready, but I just want you to know."

"I understand completely, Dan. Your equipment can't bring in anything sitting idle. When we get ready to start up again, I'll call you, and if you can come, great, but if you can't, we'll still be friends, okay?"

"You're a good man, Jerry Martin. I appreciate you."

He looked at Frank and asked, "Are you ready?"

Frank said, "It's almost lunchtime and will be by the time we get back. Want to grab a bite before we go to my office?"

"Yeah, that sounds good."

"Okay, do you like Ruby Tuesdays? You can get soup and the salad bar, and that makes a good lunch. I think I'll call Melissa to join us because you two will be working together pretty closely until this situation gets resolved."

"Ruby Tuesdays is fine with me."

When they got into the restaurant and ordered their lunch, Jerry began the conversation. "Frank, I don't want to sound like a *skin flint*, but who's going to pay for those guards; your company or mine?"

Laughing, Frank answered, "Okay, Mr. *Skin Flint*, we'll pay for them."

Jerry had a big smile on his face, and he said, "Thank you very much."

Lunchtime was devoted mostly to eating, and not much business was discussed, although a little was sprinkled here and there. At one point Jerry said, "Frank, a while back we said that you and Marilyn and Tracy and I were going to get together and go to dinner, but we never did do it. We need to do that. Why don't you talk to Marilyn, and I'll check Tracy's schedule, and let's do it within the next week or two?"

"It's a deal. I'll talk to Marilyn tonight. Melissa, remind me to do that."

"She didn't have a very pleasant look on her face when she said, "Okay."

Frank picked up the check, and after he finished settling up the three of them went to his office. All three went to the rest room before sitting down to talk.

Frank began. "Jerry, what's this shutdown going to do to you?"

"I don't know yet. One thing I'm pretty sure about is that it's going to affect some of my subcontractors. I have made a concentrated effort to find the highest quality contractors that I could find, and even though we're only talking about a thirty-day delay, that's enough to really hurt most of them. I figure most them will have to take on other projects if we're down for the full thirty days. And of course, when you're dealing with the government, thirty days can turn in to forty-five or even sixty days.

"My position as General Contractor doesn't give me any kind of edge on getting things moving, but you and your group are made up of very influential businessmen, and you may be able to see that this consultation that Revel talked about moves quickly. I'm not sitting where you are and thirty days either way may or may not make any difference to the completion date, but it does make a difference to the subcontractors and even to the common laborers."

"That's one reason I'm so thankful to have you. You can explain things to me from your point of view that I probably wouldn't even think of without your comments. Thank you, Jerry."

Jerry went on. "I think I told you earlier that this is going to allow us to double up on the work on your apartments. I've thought a lot about this since I told you that, and I'm going to take every man that I can get out there and knock those things out in a hurry. The first sixteen units are practically finished, and we're going to get the other forty-eight not too far behind. A few of the subcontractors we are planning to use on the mall can be used on the apartments, and that will help them to survive the thirty day shutdown."

Frank asked, "Won't that cut some of the apartment's subs down some?"

"Yeah, it will, actually, but my Dad told me one time that fifty percent of something is worth a lot more than a hundred percent of nothing, and that's what some of those people are going to have to contend with. When we get started back on the mall, I'll take care of them, and they know I will, so don't worry about it. Everything's going to be fine."

Frank looked at Melissa and said, "That's one of the things I like about this guy. He's not only smart, but he also cares about people and wants to take care of them."

She said, "Yeah, I can see that. I like him, too."

Jerry was surprised that she would say something like that to Frank, and he said, jokingly, "Aw, you all are just saying that because it's true." They all laughed and Jerry said, "Frank, do you have anything else that you need me for? If you don't, I need to get back to my office and start calling some of the subs and tell them about the shutdown."

"I think we're through here. Can Melissa help you make some of your calls?"

Melissa was shocked when he said, "Yeah, that would be a big help. Thank you."

She said, "I'll get my stuff together and meet you at your office. Frank, I might not be back this afternoon."

"That's all right. Just do what you need to do to help our friend here."

When they got to Jerry's office, Jerry asked Beverly for a list of the subcontractors that he had scheduled to work at the mall, and when he sat down and looked at them, there were around thirty listed. In Beverly's usual efficient way, she had grouped them into categories by the type of contractor and then in alphabetical order, making everything easier to find.

While he looked over the list, Melissa stood behind his right shoulder and leaned over him with her long, black hair cascading down, brushing his face. Instead of his being as *standoffish* as he normally was, all he could think of at that particular time was how good she smelled, and when he couldn't justifiably linger any longer over the list, he separated some of the names and gave them to her.

She stood there for a minute and read over the list and intentionally rubbed her face up against his, and as she moved away, she kissed him on his ear. He moved away from her and turned his head and looked up at her. She was looking down at him, and she smiled when he looked at her. He gave her what could be called a half-smile, and that satisfied her for the moment.

He told her what to tell the ones she called, and the list went down slowly. Whenever either of them would tell about a burial ground being uncovered at the mall site, whoever they were talking to had several questions, and Jerry would never be rude to any of them by cutting them off and not answering their questions. He instructed Melissa to be polite and accommodating to everybody she called as well.

Melissa actually called more than Jerry did because Jerry received several calls in between the calls he was making. Five o'clock came, and they still had twelve to call. Beverly stuck her head in the door and said bye and left. When she left, Melissa came back into Jerry's office from the little office that she had been using and as soon as she got in there, his phone rang. It was Tracy.

"Hi Sweetie. How are you?"

"I'm fine. How are you?"

"I'm good. It's been a trying day."

"What's happened?"

"I'll tell you when I get home. Did you call a lawyer?"

"Yeah, I called two lawyers."

"What did they say? Can they help us?"

"Maybe. I'll talk to you about it when you get home. The reason I called was to see if you would like to eat out."

"That's fine with me. I'm going to be leaving here in just a few minutes."

When he hung up, Melissa said, "Darn, I was hoping you would have time to go have a drink, but I heard you say you will be leaving in a few minutes. What is she calling a lawyer for?"

"Didn't I tell you?"

"Okay, smart ass. You've told me that before. I'm just interested."

A thousand thoughts ran through his mind in a matter of about two seconds, and he thought that if he told her they were trying to adopt, it might cool her off some, so he said, "Tracy wants to adopt a baby."

"Adopt a baby? Can't she have one?"

"No."

Being very crude, she asked, "Is something wrong with her?"

He was beginning to get a little steamed and he answered, "No, she's all woman, but I'm going to tell you something you probably don't know. A year or so ago, her car slid off a wet road and went down a forty-foot embankment. She hung upside down by her seatbelt for an entire week before someone found her, and as a result of the internal injuries she suffered, she might not be able to have a child."

"Oh, bummer. I'm sorry, Jerry. I was out of line."

"It's okay. I just want you to know that Tracy is a real woman. Let's go home."

He started cleaning off his desk and she went over and put her arms around him and said, "I'm sorry. Will you forgive me?"

"Yeah, you're forgiven," and with that she pulled his head around and kissed him flush on the lips.

At the very first contact, he didn't resist, it was so enjoyable, but after just a few seconds, he pulled away and said, "Melissa, you know I can't do this, no matter how tempting it is. Turn me loose; I've got to go home."

She released him and kissed him on the cheek at the same time. They looked at each other, and they both smiled. Jerry said, "You're evil. Did you know that? Now get out of here."

"I'll be back in the morning to help you finish calling those people," and then, smiling, she said, "and anything else you might need my help with. Good night."

On the way home, Jerry called Tracy and asked her if she had decided where they were going to eat, and she said she would like to go to Darryl's, so when he got home, he pulled in the driveway, and she came out, got in the pickup, and off they went.

While they waited on their food, Tracy said, "You told me when I talked to you that today has been a trying day. Did something go wrong?"

"You could say that. This morning a bulldozer that was grading the mall site ran over and uncovered an Indian burial site, and the government shut us down for at least thirty days until they find out who the remains are, how many there are, and what to do with them. They are assuming the bodies are Indians. Creek Indians used to live in that area. It has caused a real problem in terms of scheduling subcontractors and several other things. We spent the better part of the afternoon calling subs and canceling their schedules."

"Who's we?"

"Frank sent Melissa over to help me."

With a certain amount of contempt in her voice she said, "I see. Was little Melissa a lot of help to you?"

"You might not want to believe it, but she really was. She was a big help, and I'll have to call Frank tomorrow and thank him. Speaking of Frank; I told him I would check with you and your schedule, and he's going to check with Marilyn about the four of us going to dinner one night in the next week or so. I should let him know something tomorrow. Do you have your schedule for the next month or two?"

"Jerry, you know I don't. The airline is giving us two weeks off, and they haven't set up a schedule yet. I can go anytime this week or next, but after that we'll have to see."

"Okay. Maybe we can set it up for this coming weekend. Is that all right with you?"

"Yeah. Just let me know when."

"Now, tell me about your conversations with the lawyers."

"There's really nothing to tell. Both of them help with adoptions, but right now they don't have any clients trying to adopt out any infants. They did say that they usually have one or two they are trying to find homes for, and they both said they will probably have one or more within the next couple or three weeks. They said it costs a lot of money, and the figures they gave me made me decide that maybe we can't do it right now."

"How much are they talking about?"

"They said the money is spread out. A large part of it goes to the mother, and then there are all sorts of legal fees, and of course they get a sizeable cut, so by the time it's all said and done, it costs around fifty-thousand dollars. I told them that was ridiculous, and we couldn't afford to do that. We'll just have to find another way."

"That is ridiculous. Don't worry, Sweetie; we'll find a way."

Calling Frank the next morning was a priority for Jerry. When

217

Frank answered, Jerry said, "Good morning, Frank. Did you sleep well last night?"

Frank kinda laughed and said, "Yeah, except I dreamed about Indians all night. Did you?"

"Better than I thought I would. Listen, I talked to Tracy last night about going to dinner with you and Marilyn, and she said this weekend or next weekend will be fine. We can go either time."

"Why don't we make it this Saturday. We are going down to Destin next weekend. I've got a golf game scheduled. Is that okay with you?"

"That's fine. Just let me know when and where, and we'll see you there."

"Have you ever been to the Atlanta Athletic Club?"

"No, that's out of my league, Frank."

"It's not really. I happen to be a member, and you'd be surprised at some of the people who belong. Is seven-thirty all right with you and Tracy?"

"That's perfect. We'll see you then. Thanks, Frank."

He hadn't much more than got off the phone when Melissa came in. Trying to be cute she said, "Good morning, Boss."

He looked at her and replied, "Good morning."

She asked, "Are we ready to start making calls?"

Jerry, acting like a smart-aleck replied, "Yeah, I think we're ready. Tell you what, Melissa; I'm going to let you start with the subs, and I have several people I have to talk with concerning the apartments. If I get through before you finish, I'll help you with the subs. We only have about a dozen or so, don't we?"

"Yeah, there aren't many."

It took until lunchtime for Melissa to finish calling the rest of the subs, and when she finished she went into Jerry's office where he was at his desk looking at some brochures of things that were possibly going into the apartments. She walked over to where he was and stood behind him and put her hands on his shoulders and massaged the tops of both shoulders. It felt so good, he just sat there for a minute with his eyes closed, enjoying the treatment before he realized what was happening.

And then, he reached up and pushed both of her hands away and said, "You can't do that. I almost told you that I'd just give you thirty minutes to stop until I realized what you were doing."

"Why? I was just being kind to a friend. Do you want some lunch?"

"I don't think so. I'm going to put a big push on the apartments, and I have got a lot to do."

"You've got to eat."

"I'm really not very hungry. I may go somewhere after a while and get something, but right now I don't want anything. My mind is too absorbed with the apartments. You go on and get you something, and I guess there's nothing else for you to do here today, so you might as well go on back to your office, and I'll see you later."

She looked him in the eye and said, "Boy, you're a romantic devil."

Taken aback by that remark, he looked back into her eyes and said, "Melissa, it's not my job to be romantic to you. I have someone at home that I try to be romantic with, and even if she were here, I wouldn't be romantic because this is a construction company where we build things; not play hanky-panky. Can you understand that?"

"Yes, boss, I understand."

She kept standing there, and in a minute, Jerry said, "Bye, Melissa."

She took the hint that time and left, but not before going over and kissing him on the cheek. As she was leaving she said, "Bye, Mr. Unromantic."

He just smiled and said nothing.

Beverly overheard the exchange and asked, "What was that all about?"

"Oh nothing. Beverly, if you look up the definition of *flirty* in the dictionary, you'll probably see her picture.

Saturday rolled around and Tracy and Jerry both wanted to be sure they were ready for the Atlanta Athletic Club, one of the most exclusive places in the whole southeastern United States. Jerry was Mr. Cool, as always, and Tracy was normally Ms. Cool, but this date brought out the nerves in her. She started fixing her hair in mid-afternoon, and then couldn't decide on what to wear, and she took so much time, they were rushed when it came time to leave.

Frank and Marilyn were already there when they arrived and they immediately went inside. Frank had made reservations for seven-thirty, and their table was ready for them.

The waiters all wore white jackets and the tables were set with white fabric tablecloths. Jerry wasn't sure, but the silverware looked to be sterling. He chuckled inside when he thought, *boy this is not the 129 Café.*

Frank asked, "Would you like a cocktail to start?"

Tracy and Jerry both ordered Margaritas, their favorite, and Marilyn and Frank each got a Vodka Martini.

Making general conversation, Marilyn asked Tracy, "Where are you going on your next flight, Tracy?"

"I don't know yet. They haven't made the schedule. They gave us two weeks off, and we'll probably find out where we go sometime next week."

Frank asked, "If you don't mind me asking, why did they give you two weeks off? I thought you folks really kept on the move."

"Normally we do keep on the move, but after our experience the last couple of weeks, they thought we needed a break."

He asked, "What happened in the last couple of weeks?"

"I thought Jerry would have told you. Did you see on the news where terrorists bombed the Brussels airport?"

"Yeah, I saw that."

"Well my flight was on the way to Brussels when that happened and when we landed, everything was a real mess. Part of the airport was destroyed and there were wall to wall soldiers and policemen everywhere. They closed the airport for twelve days and we were stranded until it reopened."

"I had no idea. Why didn't you tell me, Jerry?"

"Well, Melissa knew it, and I just figured she told you."

Marilyn asked Tracy, "Are you all right, Tracy?"

"Oh yeah. None of us were hurt, but it was real scary at first. Then after we saw all the soldiers and policemen at our hotel, we sort of relaxed. When we got back, the airline decided we needed a break, so they gave us two weeks off."

"Did they catch the terrorists?"

"I think they caught one or two, but it's my understanding that there are some more that are still at large."

"I think I'd die if I had to go through something like that," Marilyn said.

"No, you wouldn't. You would handle it just fine. You've got to remember that there are about twenty-five people that make up our crew, and everybody backs up everybody else. It's like the old saying; there is strength in numbers."

"Well, I'm glad you're home, and I'm thankful that you're all right."

Jerry said, "Honey, tell Marilyn what we're trying to do."

Tracy said, "Are you sure?"

Jerry said, "Yeah. These are our friends, and friends share with each other."

"Okay. What Jerry's talking about is we're going to try and adopt a baby."

"Wonderful," Frank said. "How far along are you in the process?"

Jerry said, "Actually, we're just in the talking stage. Tracy visited a couple of agencies, but they didn't have any infants, and she called a couple of lawyers, and the money they talked about was astronomical, so we're trying to figure out how to find one.

The waiter came and Frank interrupted and asked, "Are you all ready for another one?"

Everybody said they were, so the waiter left to get their seconds.

Marilyn asked Tracy, "Tracy, it's none of my business, but are you trying to adopt because you can't conceive, or do you just prefer to adopt?"

"The doctors are not one hundred percent sure that I can't conceive, but due to some severe injuries I suffered in a car accident a year or so ago, they are almost sure that I can't, and there are some other things keeping me from it as well."

"I am so sorry."

"Thank you, but do you know something, Marilyn? I have got such a good man that even if I can't have his baby or find one to adopt, I'll be happy to just be his wife. At any rate, even if we don't adopt, I think I'm going to stop flying and stay home with him."

When she said that, Frank said, "Wow! Jerry, where did you find such a woman? I've never heard anything anymore loving that what I just heard. You're a lucky man."

That brought them to a good stopping place. Their waiter came to get their orders. Frank had talked about how good their filet mignon was. So, that's what each one ordered. The ladies ordered the eight ounce and Frank and Jerry the twelve ounce.

Jerry looked over at Frank in between bites and said, "Frank, you weren't kidding when you said the filet mignons were good here. I don't think I have ever had one as good. As a matter of fact; everything is excellent."

"I'm glad you're enjoying it."

They took their time eating and enjoyed each other's company. When they finished their meal, they ordered coffee and had a lemon tart to top off an outstanding meal.

Marilyn was intrigued with Tracy's experience in Brussels and asked several questions which Tracy was happy to answer.

Their reservations were at seven thirty, and when Jerry looked at his watch it was ten after ten. They had been there for almost three hours, and if Frank and Marilyn enjoyed it as much as Jerry and Tracy, the evening was a huge success.

Soon, the waiter brought Frank the check. He looked it over, wrote something on it, which Jerry assumed was the tip, and signed it. He asked if everyone was ready, and they got up and left. Tracy and Marilyn promised that they would get together and have lunch one day and maybe do a little shopping. Frank and Jerry said they would see each other Monday.

Chapter Twenty

Five Months Later

Forty-eight apartments were complete and had been rented. They were so beautiful and of such high quality that when they were offered for rent, they were grabbed up in just a few days. The last two buildings containing sixteen more units were in their finishing stages and would be put up for rent within a very short while.

Frank was already talking about building some more; maybe sixteen buildings next time. That would translate into one hundred and twenty-eight units, and of course, he wanted Jerry's company to build them.

Jerry was trying hard to hold him down until the mall was finished which would more than likely be another seven to eight months. They lost forty days when a bulldozer dug up some Indian graves, and that threw them behind.

Since the apartments were virtually finished and the mall was more than half built, he was hoping that he could finally get started on his White Rock Estates project. That was going to be a major undertaking with forty-five high-dollar homes in the three-quarter of a million to a million-dollar price range.

Things have gone so well for him and he was so thankful that he eagerly looked forward to going with Monty Shepherd to speak at the various youth meetings so he could tell them how good God is and explain how a series of coincidences brought so many things together for him, and how he gives God the credit for all of them. One of the few things that he and Tracy have been praying for without an answer is the prayer for a baby.

They have both pretty much dismissed the hope for a child of their own, but in its stead, they would like to be able to adopt one. Sometimes prayers don't get answered just when people want the answers. Instead, prayers are answered when God wants to answer them, and He's always on time. They have both been praying hard for an infant and feel sure that at the right time, one will become available to them.

Tracy left the airline as did Wendy, and they are spending a lot

223

of time together having a ball. Tennis is one of their main past times, and they have even started playing golf. Shopping is still one of their most important duties; buying something one day and taking it back the next. Jerry and Tom don't care as long as large department store bills don't come in.

Melissa is still under foot, and most of her time with Jerry has become legitimate after so long a time. Frank gave her the job of recruiting tenants for the mall and it's necessary for her to be in close touch with Jerry to come up with target dates.

One day, while she was in Jerry's office, Barbara Mills called. "Hi Barbara," Jerry said. "I haven't talked to you in a while. How are you?"

"I'm fine. How are you?"

"Doing great. How's Tammy?"

"She's getting big and she's very uncomfortable. She's due in just about four weeks."

"Man, time flies, doesn't it?"

"What can I do for you today?"

"I need to see you, Jerry. When can we get together?"

"Most anytime. Tell me where and when."

"Can you come to my place tonight?"

"To your place. Will I be safe?"

"Yeah, you'll be safe. I'll try to control myself."

"What if I come when I leave here? Will that be too early?"

"No, that will be fine. I'll get home around five-thirty."

"All right. I'll see you a little after five-thirty."

"Thank you, Jerry."

"Your welcome."

When he hung up, Melissa said, "Who was that?"

"Didn't I tell you?"

"No, smart ass, you didn't."

"It was my girlfriend."

"Barbara?"

"Yep, Barbara."

She said, "I'd just like to know who this Barbara is. One day I'm going to find out."

"Good luck."

He left the office at five-twenty and arrived at Barbara's at five forty-five.

She must have been standing by the door because the minute he touched the doorbell, she opened the door. "Hi Jerry. Come in."

They sat down; Jerry on the sofa and Barbara in a chair. He asked, "What's cooking?"

"Jerry, Tammy has a problem. I think we told you a while back that when she has the baby, she's going to put it up for adoption. Did I tell you that?"

"Yeah, as she was getting ready to go to the unwed mothers home."

"Well, there was a couple who wanted the baby and we agreed to let them have it, and we thought everything was all set, then over the weekend, I got a call saying they are splitting up and won't be adopting Tammy's baby. We had planned to move to Jacksonville when the baby was adopted, and now we don't know what to do. You have always come up with the right answers to things, and that's why I called you. Do you have any suggestions?"

"Let me get this straight. You're telling me that the people who were going to adopt Tammy's baby have backed out, and you don't know what to do with the baby. Is that right?"

"That's right. We need your wise counsel."

Jerry didn't say anything for a good minute. He just bowed his head and said a prayer, thanking God for His answer to their prayers.

Barbara didn't know what to make of his behavior, and then he raised his head and said, "Barbara, I don't know how to tell you this so you will understand, but I'm certain God caused this to happen. Tracy and I have been trying to find an infant for the last five or six months, Tracy and I have been praying that God would deliver a baby to us for adoption, and now you tell me this. Could Tracy and I adopt Tammy's baby?"

She burst into tears, and got up and hugged him. She said, "Jerry, once again you're the answer to prayer. Of course, you and Tracy can adopt the baby. I'm sure Tammy will be thrilled when we tell her."

He asked, "By the way, what is it; a boy or girl?"

"It's a little boy. Excuse me Jerry. I want to call Tammy."

"I want to call Tracy, too."

When Tracy answered the phone, he said, "Guess what."

"What?"

"I found us a baby."

She screamed and asked, "Where?"

He said, "Do you remember Tammy?"

"Yeah, I remember her. Is it her baby?"

"Yeah, and it's a little boy. It will be born in about four weeks. Do you want it?"

"Of course, I want it. Jerry, I'm so happy. When can we see Tammy?"

"I don't know anything yet. I'm at Barbara's right now, and I've got to ask her some more questions. It might be too late to see her this evening, but I feel sure we can in the morning. I'm going to hang up now and get some more information, and I'll call you on my way home. And oh yeah, Tracy. Be sure you thank God for this blessing."

When he hung up from Tracy, Barbara was still on the phone with Tammy, and when she hung up, she told Jerry that Tammy was just beside herself. She was absolutely thrilled to death and wants to see you guys. I told her that I'd see if you all could come over there in the morning.

Jerry said, "We definitely can. Now tell me a little more about this. What do we do first? Do we have to get a lawyer? Do they handle this at the home? We know nothing about adopting a baby, so you're going to have to lead us."

"There's not much to do. The other couple has already done most of the stuff. The main thing that will have to be done is change their names to yours and Tracy's on the paperwork. The home's lawyer will probably have to make a new contract saying that the baby is yours and that Tammy has no legal right to him after he's adopted. I don't know what all will have to be done, but I do know that there is very little.

"Okay, Barbara. I guess that will do it for today. Tracy and I will go over to the home in the morning and see Tammy and talk to the folks over there to see if there's anything we need to do."

Barbara asked, "Jerry, can I hug you? This will be a thank you hug and not one of the other kind."

"I'd love for you to hug me, Barbara," and they hugged for several seconds. When they finished, Jerry said, "Barbara, I've got a confession to make."

"What is it?"

"Do you remember the last time I was over here when Tammy was gone? Well, on the way home, I almost turned around and came back."

"I wish you had," and then she reached up and gave him a little peck on the lips.

"I've got to run, Barbara. Thank you. You and Tammy have made my day."

"You and Tracy have made ours, so thank you, too."

As he was leaving, he turned around and said, "Barbara, would you mind calling over to the Kindred home and telling them what's going on, and that Tracy and I will be over there in the morning?"

"I'll be happy to. Good night."

On the way home, he called Tracy. "Sweetheart, it looks as if it's a done deal. You and I are going to go over to the home in the morning and find out just what we have to do. Barbara didn't seem to think there would be too much for us to have to do because the couple that was originally going to adopt the baby had already done most of the detail work."

"Did she say how much it costs?"

"She doesn't know that. We'll have to ask that question in the morning, but I feel sure it won't be nearly as much as those lawyers wanted."

Tracy met him at the door when he got home and they just stood there hugging. Tracy said, "You can't possibly know how happy I am right now. I can't wait 'til in the morning. If we leave the home knowing for sure that we're going to get the baby, I'm going to call Wendy, and we're going to start planning the nursery. In fact; I'm going to call her right now. I need to tell somebody about this."

While she talked to Wendy, Jerry made the Margaritas. He handed hers to her, and she kept talking while she sipped on it. She talked and talked and before long her glass was empty, so he got up and fixed her another one and gave it to her. She was about two thirds through that one when she and Wendy hung up. She started over to sit down next to him, and then she thought, "Oh, I need to call Daddy and Carol," so she called her daddy first and then Carol, and didn't talk nearly as long as she did to Wendy.

After a very restless night, they both got up a little after five; bleary-eyed but excited. Jerry thought they probably shouldn't get to the home before nine-thirty or ten o'clock and the time just dragged on until time to leave.

When they arrived, they were both a little nervous. Tracy held Jerry's hand as they walked from the parking lot to the front door, and once inside Jerry introduced himself and Tracy and told the lady why they were there. Her name was Mary, and she said Barbara had called and Tammy was about to worry her to death, wondering when they were going to get there.

She asked them to step into an office off the reception area. "We need to get some information, and if you don't mind, I'm going to call Tammy to come and sit in with us. Do you mind?"

"Absolutely not; call her."

It seemed like Tammy was there before Mary put the phone down. Unlike the whole time Jerry had known her, she was totally different. As soon as she entered the room, she went over and hugged him with a big bear hug. She talked freely, which was a big change, and everything about her seemed to have improved.

Mary went over everything and when she was finished, she told Tracy and Jerry, "Well, Mr. and Mrs. Martin, you are now the parents of a little boy as soon as Tammy gives birth to him. Then, Tracy asked her a question. "Mary, will it be possible for me to be with Tammy when she gives birth?"

"That's up to Tammy. What do you say, Tammy?"

"That will be fine, but I want my mother in with me, too. Is that all right?"

"It is, and that will be very meaningful to this little boy when he's told about it in later years." She said, "Well folks, that's all I have unless you have something."

"I don't," Jerry said. "Tracy, do you?"

"No. I'm sure I'll think of something after we leave, but I'll ask it later."

Jerry told Tammy, "Tammy, we're going to get something to eat. Can we buy your lunch?"

"I'd like that. Thank you."

"Anywhere special that you'd like to go?"

"Do you like the Pizza Hut?"

"We both love the Pizza Hut. Is that where you want to go?"

"Yeah."

"Okay, let's do it."

When they got to Jerry's pickup, he noticed Tammy just looking at how high the cabin was. "Do you think you're going to be able to get up there, Tammy?"

"I think so; I'm gonna try."

"Here, let me help you. You can sit up front, and I think that will be easier to get in. Grab hold of my arm."

She did and the two of them were able to get her up to the seat. They all laughed about it when they were all in the truck.

It was a fun lunch. Tracy and Tammy talked non-stop about the baby, and Tracy talked about fixing up one of the spare bedrooms at their house into a nursery.

Jerry took her back to the home when they were through and helped her down out of the truck. They said their goodbyes after Tracy promised to stay in close touch until the baby is born.

They left the Kindred home and before Jerry took Tracy home, he went by his office to pick up something he would need when he went to the apartments later that afternoon. Tracy wanted to say hello to Beverly, so she got out and went into the office with him. When she got inside, not only was Beverly there but Melissa was too. She gave Beverly a hug and enthusiastically told her that they had found a baby. When she saw Melissa, she politely spoke and turned her attention back to Beverly.

Jerry found what he went to get and came back through the front and asked, "Ready to go?"

She said, "Yep. See you later, Beverly. Nice to see you again, Melissa," and they left.

On the way home, Tracy said, "Honey, if we're going to change that small bedroom into a nursery, we'd better get started, don't you think?"

"You're right about that. What are you trying to say?"

"If I go to Sherwin Williams and pick out some paint, do you have any painters that could come and paint it before the baby is born? I'm going to go buy a baby bed and other furniture tomorrow, but I won't have it delivered until the painting's done. Does that make sense?"

"You're a pretty smart broad, did you know that?"

Being cute she said, "I know."

"Tell you what; you go get the paint this afternoon, and I'll have someone out tomorrow to paint it for you. Is that soon enough?"

Still being cute she said, "Well if that's the best you can do, I guess it'll have to be."

He dropped her off at home and went straight back to his office. He wanted to call Bob and also Monty Shepherd before he went to the apartments.

Bob was very pleased when Jerry told him about the baby and told him to give Tracy a kiss for him. He called Monty next, mainly to tell him how God worked out the adoption, more than just the adoption itself, and Monty said, "Jerry, your story about how God worked things out between you and your financial people is wonderful, but what you're telling me now is even more fantastic. I hope you'll tell it at your next speaking engagement. When did you say it will be born?"

"He's due in four weeks. I'll let you know when he gets here."

"Great. I'll be anxious to hear from you. Jerry, the two stories you have told me are what I once heard a minister call a Godincidence. In case you don't know what a Godincidence is, it's when something good or special happens, and it feels like God caused it to happen just for that person. I think in this case that person is you and Tracy. Congratulations, my friend."

Monty always made him feel good, and when he finished talking to him he got up to leave for the job site, and it dawned on him that he hadn't told Frank about the baby, so he went back to his desk and called him.

"Frank, hi. Remember us telling you and Marilyn how we've been trying to adopt a baby, but were having a hard time finding one? Well, we found one, and the story is amazing. I know you're busy and I won't take the time to tell it to you right now, but I'm anxious to tell you, and I'd like for Marilyn to hear it too."

"That's wonderful. When are you going to get it?"

"It hasn't been born yet. He's scheduled to arrive in about four weeks."

"You said 'he'. It must be a little boy."

"It is, and I can't wait for him to get here."

"Jerry, I appreciate you calling. This is wonderful, and I'm very happy for you and Tracy. I'm in a meeting, so I have to go, but I'll see you when I get back in town next week."

When he finally got off the phone, he went to the apartments job site and from there he went home for the day.

For the next three weeks, activities were normal, but then things started to get crazy the fourth week; not so much for Jerry, but for Tracy. Tammy was due in another four or five days and Tracy was a nervous wreck. Jerry was hoping to take a few days off when the baby arrived, but there was so much going on, he didn't know if he'd be able to.

Chapter Twenty-One

Finally, at five thirty Friday morning, the Kindred home called and told Tracy that Tammy was going into labor, and they were taking her to the hospital. They told her where they were taking her, and said she could come and be with Tammy if she wanted to. She told them of course, she wanted to be there with Tammy, and she got out of bed and hurriedly showered and dressed and left, and left Jerry in bed.

As soon as she got out of the shower, he got up and got ready, but took time to drink a cup of coffee before he left because he didn't think the baby would come for a good while.

While he was sitting in the waiting room, Tracy came in one time and told him Tammy was at eight centimeters, and it looked as if she would give birth before too much longer. She was doing fine and there were no problems so far. She went back in, and Jerry poured a cup of coffee from the coffeemaker in the waiting room.

At eight o'clock he called his office and told Beverly he wouldn't be in and explained what was happening. He told her he would call after the baby was born and give her an update. He also told her he was going to come into the office Saturday to try and plan out the next week for everybody and then try to take off two or three days.

She asked him if they had decided on a name yet, and he told her they weren't sure; they were toying around with some, but hadn't made up their mind. He told her they were thinking about trying to come up with something that would have Tracy's Dad and his Dad in it. Jack's real name was John and Bob's name was Robert, and they thought John Robert might be good. He didn't want to call it Bobby because Jack might feel slighted, and if they called him Jackie, then Bob might feel slighted, so they didn't know what they were going to do yet. "Being a Georgia Cracker, I thought Bobby-Jack might be good, but Tracy quickly put the quietus on that."

"I can see why. And then she said, "I really like John Robert. Jerry, why don't you name him that and call him B J or J B?"

231

"Bev, that's a great idea. I'll run it by Tracy. Thanks."

While he was sitting there, waiting, he wondered if Tracy had called Wendy. He doubted she had because she left home so early, and a sign said no cell phones beyond that point, so he called Tom. He figured it wouldn't hurt if they got two calls.

About an hour later, he looked up, and Wendy and Tom walked in to keep him company and to see the baby when it was born. It had been a long time since Tracy came out to see him, and as luck would have it, she came out shortly after Wendy and Tom got there. She hugged them both and said, "It shouldn't be much longer. Tammy is almost at ten centimeters, and the doctor said that when she gets to ten, the baby should come." She smiled and said, "You all hang in here and my baby will be here shortly, and then you can see him."

Wendy said, "I can't wait."

Tracy thanked them for coming and thanked them for being their friends, and left and went back to be with Tammy. It was only about fifteen minutes later when Jerry's phone rang.

"Honey, we've got a beautiful little boy. He has all ten fingers and toes and is picture perfect. They're cleaning him up now and will be bringing him and Tammy to her room in just a few minutes. If you all want to see him, come down the hall where you are until you come to another hall on your right. When you get there, turn right and you'll see double doors on your left. We'll be coming out those doors, so just wait right there."

Just a few minutes after they got to where Tracy told Jerry to come, the door opened and they came out with Tammy in a wheelchair, holding the baby. They stopped for everybody to see them, and in a minute, Tammy did a touching thing. With tears running down her face, she held the baby up and said, "Here, Tracy; here's your little boy."

When she did that, the whole group cried, including Tom. Even the doctor's eyes were watering. It was a very touching moment. Tracy took him and held him as if she would never turn him loose.

Wendy and Tom left a few minutes after they saw the baby, and Jerry stayed for little while, and then he left. He didn't want to wear Tammy out because she was tired and needed to rest. Barbara and Tracy were planning to stay for a while, and Tracy had to find out when she could take the baby home. Surprisingly, they told her she could take him after they finished checking him out, physically, which would probably only be a couple of hours.

When she found that out, she called Jerry. "Honey, you're going to have to come back; they said we can bring the baby home in two or three hours. You'll have to bring the car seat, and we'll have to leave one of our cars here, because I think I need help this first time.

As soon as she got off the phone, a nurse came and asked her if she was Mrs. Martin, and when she said she was, she asked her to follow her down to a desk just outside the nursery. She had a paper full of questions for her. One of the questions asked for the baby's name, and Tracy told her she would have to call it to her because they hadn't decided on one yet. There were other questions she would have to get back to them with as well, and when she finished with the paperwork, the nurse told her some of the things to expect with the newborn. She gave her formula and feeding instructions, and a follow-up appointment with the doctor. Tracy had really been looking forward to that moment, but now that it was there, she was a nervous wreck. She could hardly wait until Jerry got back, because he was always her rock, and she felt sure he would take it all in stride.

When he got back, he went to Tammy's room to get Tracy and tell Tammy and Barbara good bye. Tammy was asleep and Tracy had gone back to the nurse's station to ask some questions. Barbara was there, and he thought she looked awfully sad.

"Barbara, I'm glad you're still here because I want to talk to you."

"What about?" she asked.

"Are you still planning to move to Jacksonville?"

"Yeah, the company I work for is going to let me transfer down there. I'll be doing the same thing, but Tammy will be in new surroundings, and hopefully she has opened her eyes and will restart her life from scratch. Jerry, we both owe you an awful lot. If it hadn't been for you that night she and those two boys broke into you house, she would have gone to jail, and you and I both know that's not good.

"This baby is not her fault, but she had to suffer the consequences just the same, and you and Tracy bailed her out once again. In Florida she won't have you, so I hope the last nine months have been a learning experience, and she will turn into a fine young woman. I'm sorry, Jerry; you wanted to talk to me and I've done all the talking. I'll hush so you can tell me what you wanted."

"The main thing I wanted was to find out how you stand financially. Are you okay?"

"Yeah, we're making it. There's nothing left each month, but we're managing."

"Are you going to get a raise when you move?"

"I haven't heard of any; I doubt it."

"Are you going to buy a house or rent when you get down there?"

"We'll probably just rent an apartment."

"Well, how about your moving expenses; do you have them taken care of?"

"No, and they scare me. I hear it's really expensive to move long distance."

"It is. Now here is what I'm offering to do for you and Tammy to try and help you out some. Barbara, when you find a place to live in Jacksonville, I'm going to pay for your moving expenses, and to help you get started down there, I'm going to give you ten thousand dollars to do with what you want. You have my numbers and address, and I want you to call me if you ever need anything for something you can't handle."

She got up and hugged him and kissed him on the cheek. She thanked him again and told him goodbye. He told her to tell Tammy goodbye for him, and she said she would.

Tracy came back about that time and she went through the thanks and goodbyes as well, and then she and Jerry left to take their baby home.

On the way, they talked about naming the baby, and they couldn't agree on any of the names, and then Jerry told her that he had talked to Beverly. "Did she have any good ideas?"

Jerry said, "Yeah, I thought she had a good one. I told her we were wanting to come up with a name that would honor both our Dads, but if we called him Jackie, it might hurt Dad's feelings, and if we called him Bobby, it might hurt Jack's feelings. She said she would like to see us name him John Robert, like we had thought; after both our Dads and call him B J or J B. What do you think about that?"

"I love that. Let's do it, you want to?"

Jerry said, "Let's call our Dads when we get home; want to?"

"Great idea. I love you, New Daddy."

"I love you back, New Mama."

"And we both love you, B J."

When they got home, Tracy busied herself with getting little B J settled in and asked Jerry if he would call her Daddy and her sister, Carol, and tell them they were home with the baby.

He only had to tell them once. They both came almost immediately. Then he called Bob, and he said he would be down tomorrow.

With all the love that that family had to share, little B J Martin was going to grow to be a very happy little boy.

Two weeks later, Monty Shepherd called. "How're you doing, Monty?"

"I'm doing great. Listen, I called for two reasons. First, I'm assuming you guys have your new baby. Am I right?"

"You're right. We've had him now for about two weeks, and Monty, he's already a star. I'm anxious for you to see him."

"I'm anxious to see him. Maybe it won't be too long. Jerry, the other reason I called is to run something by you. On Wednesday of next week, the University of Kentucky is having a combined meeting of several of the student Christian organizations, and they have asked me to speak. I got to thinking about you and your stories, and I was wondering if you would be willing to share them with those students."

"Did you say it's on Wednesday?"

"Yeah, Wednesday night at seven-twenty-five."

"Monty, I don't know. I would have to lose two days' work to go that far, and I just don't see how I can do that."

"Oh, you won't have to drive; We'll pick you up in my plane on Wednesday afternoon and bring you back after the meeting on Wednesday night. Does that help?"

"Yeah; when you put it that way. Yeah, Monty, I'll be glad to tell them my story."

"Great. Can you leave around three o'clock Wednesday afternoon?"

"Yeah, I can do that."

"Okay. You know where the private planes are at the Atlanta airport. If you can, we'll meet you at three o'clock. We'll be in a

Gulfstream G650 with Shepherd Apparel painted on the sides."

"I'll look forward to seeing you then. I'm not very good at speaking in public, but I'm anxious to tell people how God has worked in my life."

Once again, Jerry was blown away by the luxurious Shepherd Apparel plane. The flight only took an hour and fifteen minutes, and it took him nearly that long to explore and marvel at the plane's interior.

The meeting was held in the Student Center, and while they didn't count, there appeared to be well over a hundred students present. Several minor things were covered first, and then the program was turned over to Monty and he gave a very, very inspirational talk, and Jerry could understand why he was in such demand as a speaker. Monty only spoke for about fifteen minutes because he wanted to give time to Jerry, and when he finished his talk, he jokingly introduced him as a reformed Georgia Bulldog.

Due to the strong competition between Southeastern Conference schools of which both the Kentucky Wildcats and Georgia Bulldogs belonged, Jerry was welcomed with much applause and a smattering of boos mixed with a few cat-calls. When he walked to the mike, the first thing he said was "How about them Wildcats," and the place exploded with applause.

The boos he heard when Monty introduced him made him a little nervous, but the roaring response to his question about the wildcats set him much more at ease. He gave them a few seconds to quieten down, and then he said, "When you start through life, if you're a believer, you're going to find that God truly works in mysterious ways, and I want to tell you two stories tonight that illustrate that in my life. Actually, there are three, but tonight we'll only talk about two of them."

He began by telling them what he did for a living and how the kids breaking into one of his houses led to the events in both stories. He elaborated on both and the time flew by. He didn't intend to talk so long, and his talk lasted for about thirty minutes, but no one seemed ready to leave.

He ended his talk by saying, "I've been trying to find a word that best describes the happenings in our lives, and I think I have found it. The word is DESTINY. The dictionary says that destiny is the predetermined course of events, and I'm convinced that

236

everything that has happened to my wife and I was predetermined. If you're a believer and have faith, you might not have the same kinds of things happen in your life, but God will definitely look after you. Thank you."

He received a thunderous applause when he finished, and it was funny when he heard several calls of Bulldogs, Bulldogs.

On their way back to Atlanta, Jerry and Monty were talking about the gathering, and Jerry said, "Monty, I really enjoyed that. I got a kick at the end when some of them yelled Bulldogs. I was afraid I would be scared, but for some reason, I wasn't."

"That's because you were talking about what God can do. You did a great job, and I think everybody there enjoyed what you had to say." Then joking, he said, "If you ever get tired of the construction business, I think I can get you a job on the speaking circuit."

www.ingramcontent.com/pod-product-compliance
Lightning Source LLC
Chambersburg PA
CBHW060426180626
46817CB00007B/2690